HASTEN
TO THEIR
END

HASTEN
TO THEIR
END

PENNY RICHARDS

First published by Level Best Books/Historia 2021

Copyright © 2021 by Penny Richards

This novel is entirely a work of fiction. The names, characters and incidents portrayed in it are the work of the author's imagination. Any resemblance to actual persons, living or dead, events or localities is entirely coincidental.

Penny Richards asserts the moral right to be identified as the author of this work.

Library of Congress Control Number: 2021942233

First edition

ISBN: 978-1-953789-37-2

Cover art by Level Best Designs

This book was professionally typeset on Reedsy.
Find out more at reedsy.com

This book is dedicated to the real Virginia (Ginny) Evans... friend, sounding board, critic, librarian extraordinaire, most innovative book signing event person EVER, "nag"ravator, and most loyal fan. Thanks for everything you've done to help my book sales, dear friend.

Praise for HASTEN TO THEIR END

Author Penny Richards has written a murder mystery that has captured the stressful world of pedestrianism from the competitive nature of sport to the struggles of the training for such a multi-day contest. On top of that, the protagonist must not only perform as a professional athlete, but during a competition, be on the lookout for clues to identify a killer. – Harry Hall, author of the award-winning *The Pedestriennes, America's Forgotten Superstars*.

Penny Richards vividly evokes the bygone era of competitive walking matches—and weaves in a page-turning mystery. Hasten to Their End brilliantly captures the sights and sounds of a six-day walking match, the color and excitement, recalling a time when watching people walk in circles for days was not just a form of entertainment, but a source of mystery and intrigue as well. Congratulations! – Matthew Algeo, www.malgeo.net

Chapter One

September 1881

89 Dearborn, Chicago

Pinkerton Offices

L illy Long pushed through the street entrance of the Pinkerton offices and headed toward the stairs. Uncertainty dogged her every step. When she and McShane left Ft. Worth two months earlier, she had been harboring serious doubts about her new profession and was more than tentative about returning for another assignment. While she loved the idea of delivering justice for victimized women, she had begun to question her ability to deal with the brutalities that accompanied those deliverances.

She had planned on pondering her quandary while spending some time with Pierce and Rose, but she soon learned that William Pinkerton had other ideas. William-like, he had signed her up to train with famous fencing master Colonel Thomas Hoyer Monstery, arguably the best teacher of various forms of self-defense to ever draw breath. William claimed that honing her skills would better equip her to deal with the many things that might crop up in her new calling. She strongly suspected that McShane had told their boss about her low spirits.

After fighting so hard to get hired by the agency and maintaining her desire to go to battle for society's ill-treated women, it maddened her to realize that she lacked the nerve to tell him 'no,' so she had done as he wanted.

Monstery believed that properly proficient women could be as forceful and prepared for unexpected, dangerous circumstances as men, without compromising one iota of womanliness. Lilly liked that about him, even though he made few concessions to her gender. Male or female, he demanded and got the best a student had to give, and she possessed the bruises and aching muscles to prove it. And here she was. About to embark on yet another assignment that would expose her to only God knew what.

She opened the door to the outer office. A quick glance assured her that nothing had changed since her last visit. Harris, William Pinkerton's secretary, who was pounding on his Remington typewriter with purposeful vengeance, peeked up at her over the wire rims of his glasses, a twinkle in his pale blue eyes.

"Good morning, Harris. I trust the world is treating you well."

Harris returned her bright smile, revealing an impressive set of false teeth. "Indeed, it is, Miss Long. And you?"

"I'm glorious, thank you."

The words gave lie to the fact that every muscle in her body ached, and she felt more than twice her twenty-three years.

"Is that a new frock?" Harris asked, gesturing toward the fawn-colored walking dress with its brown and green plaid collar and cuffs.

"It is." She had splurged for the meeting and purchased fabric for a new fall dress, which she'd sewn herself. Pierce Wainwright, the man who had raised her from the age of eleven, was not just the only father she had ever known, but as dramaturge of the Pierced Rose Theater Troupe, he was as skilled with a needle as he was with putting on a quality stage play, a trait he had passed on to Lilly.

"Quite nice."

"Thank you, Harris. Are we expecting Agent McShane?"

"We are."

The words were just spoken when the door opened and her reluctant partner, Andrew Cadence McShane, stepped inside, doffing his bowler as he entered. Had she not known better, she might think he'd consulted with her, so perfectly did his attire complement hers. His brown sack suit echoed the darker brown in the plaid of her dress.

Their gazes met. Though she despised feeling anything for the man who had been foisted on her when she was first accepted into the agency, there was no denying that her heart never failed to miss a beat whenever she saw him. Her chin rose a fraction and her fingers tightened on her reticule. Dratted man! And drat her mother's wayward blood that flowed through her veins! With his boxer's physique, black hair, and dark-blue eyes, he was a fine specimen of a man, despite the scar etched onto the left side of his face.

He stood in the doorway, giving her the once-over, as well. If his scowl was any indication, he was not the least happy to see her. Fine. Good. He and Harris said their 'hellos' and Harris left his desk to announce their arrival. Only when he left the room did McShane speak.

"Miss Long." The words were accompanied by a slight incline of his head.

"Agent McShane." Proudly, her voice and eyes matched his for coolness.

Since they had been forced to work together, they'd vacillated between a reasonably comfortable working relationship and an awkwardness worthy of green striplings. McShane's manner had been fine at his sister's wedding to Simon Linedecker the previous month, and now this! She sometimes thought her partner's feelings were more unpredictable than any woman's; however, she could not fault his professionalism in the field, which, after all, was the most important thing.

"I trust you've benefitted from your time off," he said, maintaining an air of politeness.

She lifted her shoulders in what she hoped was a casual shrug. "I've been training with Colonel Monstery."

A trace of familiar deviltry gleamed in his eyes. *Finally!*

"And how are you enjoying it?"

She cocked an eyebrow at him. "Enjoyment and training with Monstery are words that should never be used in the same sentence."

Before he could comment, Harris announced that William would see them.

Lilly rose and McShane made a sweeping gesture for her to precede him into their boss's office.

The elder Pinkerton son approached them with an outstretched hand. "Miss Long. Agent McShane. I hope your time off was agreeable."

Lilly took one of the leather wingback chairs facing his desk and gave him a humorless smile. "It was…quite an experience."

Laughing, William went back to his chair, and Cade took the seat next to her. "If it is any consolation, and though Monstery is stingy with his praise, he told me it was evident that you'd had previous instruction in fencing and shooting. He was well-pleased with your progress in those areas."

"How kind of him to say so. I labored hard enough for it. I never again want to feel as inadequate as I did in Ft. Worth." She stifled a small sigh. Had she just committed herself to another assignment?

William's reply was another smile. "And what of you, McShane? Are you ready to return to work?"

"I am, sir."

"Excellent!" William peered at them over the steepled tips of his fingers. "Tell me, what do the two of you know about pedestrianism? Specifically, women's endurance walking."

How could any female striving to change the way the world viewed the fairer sex *not* have heard how a few daring ladies were challenging the status quo of a sport once dominated by men?

Pedestrianism was the undertaking of walking a prescribed number of miles in a certain length of time with little rest or sleep. It had become a popular spectator sport and source of entertainment to the thousands of Americans who, thanks to the Industrial Revolution, had more ready cash and time on their hands than ever before. Thousands filled the race venues to see which man—or woman—would defy the odds and win the competition and the money. It sounded quite boring to Lilly, who failed to see why anyone would want to watch exhausted, sleep-deprived people walking 'round and 'round a track for hours on end.

"I've heard of it, though I can't say I know much about it," she said at last. "However, I do applaud any woman who strives to leave the world a more equitable place for women everywhere."

Another smile toyed with the corner of William's mouth. "Knowing that you are an ardent advocate for your gender, I expected as much, Miss Long."

"I've heard of it, as well," McShane offered, "but I'd never seen a competition until recently. A friend and I went to watch one for a few hours after my sister's wedding." He shrugged. "I can't say I was impressed."

"Oh?"

"It seemed to me as if the winning lineup was a foregone conclusion, and the contestants made certain those expectations materialized. It felt contrived...phony, even."

"Very astute, McShane. And therein lies part of the problem."

Lilly looked from one man to the other. "Problem?"

William pinned her with his direct, intelligent gaze. "Endurance walking has been around Europe for a good while, and the first notable account of it in the states was back in 1861. A man called Edward Weston and a friend made a wager about whether or not Lincoln would win the election. The loser agreed to walk the four-hundred-seventy-eight miles from Boston to Washington in ten days, with the goal of arriving in time for the inauguration. Weston made it in just four hours over that time." William chuckled. "He might have succeeded had he not been bedeviled by dogs and bill collectors along the way."

Lilly blinked in astonishment. *Four-hundred-seventy-eight miles in ten days?*

"It boggles the mind, does it not?" William said. "There are those who endeavor to walk five-hundred miles in six days."

"I cannot believe that, sir!"

"It's true, Miss Long. Anyway, in due course, several women came along, trying to prove that they were as hardy as the men, and for a few years, pedestriennes have been quite the rage. Ladies—many from other countries—have made names for themselves as well as considerable amounts of money, while proving they were able to hold their own in the sport. Unfortunately, the races have been plagued with problems from the beginning, and many maintain that the last race of any significance was in San Francisco this past May."

"What happened?" McShane asked.

"In a nutshell, pedestrianism has become a casualty of its own success, especially the women's races. Despite challengers stepping up from every walk of life, only a handful of women have dominated the competitions, and they are true athletes—disciplined, well trained, and with every quality needed to ensure proper care of themselves."

"I'm not sure I follow you, sir," Lilly said.

"The successful walkers, like Ada Anderson, Bertha Von Hillern, and May Marshall have actual trainers who help build their endurance, fashion them a healthy diet to aid in energy and fortitude and advise them on strategy."

"Strategy? What kind of strategy can there be in walking and resting?" Lilly asked.

"Ah!" William said, holding up a finger. "But when is the opportune time to take that rest? At regular times each hour? When you're ahead? One approach has been to walk a mile at the end of one hour and another immediately following. This tactic gives the walker a longer resting period, while still satisfying the rules, that usually require that the miles be walked in 'consecutive hours.'" He shook his head.

"It's a bit risky, and some critics even feel ungentlemanly, but it is allowed, nevertheless. Make no mistake, Miss Long, this is a serious undertaking, and the women who are successful possess the ability to plan how they will maneuver the course and exploit their strengths. It takes an excessive amount of focus and a single-minded nature to be successful."

Traits that all women who made a difference must possess, Lilly thought. Still, she did not understand why a woman, or a man for that matter, would want to subject himself to such an undertaking. The money must be significant.

"New walkers come from all over the country and even Europe," William continued. "They are often in desperate financial straits and see these competitions as an opportunity to make amounts of money they could not earn in any other way, even though they come ill-prepared and have no idea what's in store."

"What is considered serious money?"

"Two-hundred dollars to a thousand or more per race, depending on the venue, the manager, and if they contract to get a portion of the gate receipts."

"*Two hundred to a thousand dollars?*"

"A staggering notion is it not?" William said with a dry smile. "May Marshall, who is arguably the most productive walker to date, has earned more than thirty-thousand dollars during her career, but she's getting a bit old for a pedestrienne."

Lilly felt her chin drop. *Thirty-thousand dollars!*

Even Cade looked flabbergasted.

"And that's why there are so many women willing to give it a try. Most have little if any training, and they are not prepared physically or mentally for the realities of the races, but they see it as a rare chance to get ahead."

"What do you mean, mentally unprepared?" Lilly asked.

"Make no mistake, Miss Long, mental hardiness is as crucial as physical aptitude. Perhaps more so."

She was still mulling over the money involved when McShane asked, "If the purses are so generous and there are so many women willing to give it a try, why is the sport in trouble?"

William drummed his fingers on the desktop. "First, these untrained women provide little challenge to the established athletes, which speaks to your earlier comment about the winners seeming a foregone conclusion.

"Of late, other controversies have arisen. More and more ministers are condemning walking on Sundays, possibly because their congregants are skipping services to watch. In fact, several churches have made it their mission to stop the races once and for all."

Lilly listened in awe. How had she missed hearing more about this unusual sport? Probably because she was busy solving crimes in other places.

"There are the usual allegations of organizers not living up to their contracts, and grousing men who resent women making inroads into what they consider a male sport. And then there are the physicians who have reevaluated their original opinions that the walking would be healthy, and now insist the physical sufferings are simply much too hard on any woman's constitution."

Lilly gave a slight *humpf* of disgust. "Colonel Monstery believes that with proper training women can be just as efficient as men, an opinion I endorse as well."

"Knowing you as I've come to do, I would expect nothing else from you, Miss Long," William said with a slight smile. He cleared his throat. "There is also the usual crop of prima donnas who demand all sorts of special treatment, though the good Lord knows they already get plenty of that."

She was wondering what that 'special treatment' might consist of when he added, "Oh! And let's not forget to throw in marital infidelities and accusations of fraud."

"Fraud?"

"Oh, yes. Many spectators are convinced that the women must have a twin to step in now and then, since it seems impossible for one person to maintain the punishing pace for such prolonged periods of time, which brings to mind the allegations of drug use for stimulation and to mask symptoms."

"Good Lord!"

"The problems bear a remarkable resemblance to those that plague male competitions," McShane noted with a degree of sarcasm. "Am I wrong in assuming that much of the disapproval is based on the fact that we are talking about women?"

"No, McShane. You're exactly right. Many men do not take kindly to a woman besting them at anything, which several pedestriennes have done. Siding with the men, the newspapers that once championed the sport now call it a brutal form of entertainment. The fans are still supportive for the most part, but the storm of criticism from those in opposition is gaining ground."

Lilly felt her irritation rise. "Brutal is a strong word, Mr. Pinkerton," she said, unable to see how a walking footrace could be as debilitating as he implied.

He gave a sardonic lift of his bushy eyebrows. "Still unconvinced, Miss Long? Did I mention that even though the contestants change shoes often, their feet become blistered and bleed, muscles cramp, and they often suffer hallucinations from sleep deprivation, risking sanity and total collapse? And there is the small reality that some of the races last up to six weeks."

"What?" McShane's incredulity matched Lilly's.

"Oh, yes. Some are mere hours, some last a week, and others are true tests of endurance. As I mentioned, more and more physicians are asserting the competitions are too strenuous for the fairer sex, calling them 'cruel tramps' and 'walking torture.'"

Walk for more than a month? With little sleep or rest, blistered feet and collapse? Dear, sweet heaven! It certainly sounded cruel and torturous. Brutal. Despite her belief that women were as capable as men, she did not see how any human, female *or* male, could take that kind of...well, *abuse*.

"How can the human body bear that sort of ill-treatment?"

William shook his head. "I'm not sure anyone understands it, but there are some walkers who don't appear to suffer unduly. More grit? No one knows. I've heard it said that the human body can withstand almost anything if the mind is strong. It is truly a medical mystery."

"Dear Lord," McShane murmured, glancing at Lilly in disbelief. "It sounds like walking death."

"I'd say that's a reasonable comparison," William said with a slow nod.

"This is all interesting, sir, but I'm curious as to how and why the agency is involved."

"Yes, of course," William said, "I'm afraid my personal interest in the sport carried me away."

"I understand. Without doubt, it's a fascinating topic."

"Yes. Well, a while back, when the sport was floundering on the east coast, J.D. Ames, a former boxing promoter who loved the sport moved it west, hoping that a new location with a new promoter and fresh ideas would reestablish endurance walking as a major event."

"I gather it didn't work," Lilly said.

William shook his head. "Unfortunately, the walkers took their personalities with them. Keeping the clashes from leaking to the press proved to be a full-time job for Ames. The race that took place in San Francisco this past May was disastrous."

McShane leaned forward. "How so?"

"Ames was found dead the morning of the race."

Lilly drew in a sharp breath.

William looked from her to her partner. "The authorities called it a suicide, but his wife, Dora, refuses to let them close the case. She's convinced he was murdered, which is where we come in."

"Why does she doubt the police?" Lilly asked.

"A few months before his death, Ames was a victim of embezzlement. The guilty party fled before charges could be filed. Then, six weeks or so before his death, he and Dora were attacked in his office. Dora was roughed up somewhat, and J.D. was beaten so badly they feared he might suffer paralysis. He recovered, but the thieves made off with all the cash in his office as well as a championship belt valued at fifteen-hundred dollars."

"*Fifteen-hundred dollars?* What was it made of?" Lilly quipped. "Gold?"

"As a matter of fact, Miss Long, it was. The belt contained twelve ounces of gold and twice that of silver. I believe there were some diamonds as well."

McShane swore and quickly apologized. "I had no idea the sport was so lucrative."

"Neither did I," William said. "When Ames regained consciousness, he claimed that his assailant was Tad Connelly, none other than the accountant they caught embezzling. Dora concurred. He seems to have vanished once again."

Lilly's mind raced. This was beginning to sound like the most curious case she had worked on to date.

"In an interesting turn of events, Ames had a visitor the day before he was found dead, one Leonardo Bertolini."

McShane made a slight sound.

"Have you heard of him?" William asked.

"I have," McShane said. "His wife, Rosalie, was walking the day I went to watch with my friend."

"Rosalie Bertolini, better known as La Bella Rosa, is a top walker from Italy who is proving to be an excellent competitor."

"And Leo," McShane added for Lilly's benefit, "is her philandering husband, who cheats on her wherever and whenever the mood hits. They say she once stopped in the middle of a race to drag him away from a woman in the audience."

"Very true," William said. "After the melee, the officials refused to let her return to the track, so in effect, his behavior cost her first place. They separated."

"My friend didn't mention that," McShane mused. "How are they connected to the murder?"

"For reasons unknown to anyone but the two of them, they reconciled and headed west. Since Leo is an excellent promoter, I'm going on the assumption that he was able to get his wife top billing as well as top dollar for participating in the first race." William gave a lift of his shoulders. "I suspect their reconciliation is mutually financially beneficial for the moment."

"So, La Bella Rosa and Leo were in San Francisco when Ames died," McShane said.

William nodded. "Yes. Mrs. Ames—Dora—says Bertolini met with her husband the day before his death and told J.D. that he knew that between medical bills and the theft he'd suffered, he was broke. She claims Bertolini did his best to strongarm J.D. into relinquishing control of the enterprise for a sum that would pay off his debts with a paltry amount left over."

"Why would Bertolini want control if it was failing?" Lilly asked.

"He hoped that by moving the races to the Midwest, he might resurrect them yet again. According to Mrs. Ames, J.D. considered accepting the deal, but then changed his mind. His body was found in a park near their home the following morning with a single gunshot wound to the chest.

"They found a note in his handwriting in his vest pocket, stating that because of his inability to pay the walkers, he couldn't live with the shame of failure for defaulting on his debts."

McShane's frown deepened. "Yet Mrs. Ames still believes it was foul play?"

"Yes."

"I understand her point of view," Lilly said. "It's hard to imagine ending your life over a few debts."

"Men think differently than women, Miss Long," McShane said in a tense tone. "A man's self-worth is directly tied to his ability to provide, and honor plays no small part of a man's self-esteem."

Though the words were not said unkindly, Lilly felt as if she had been chastised. A vagrant, unwelcome memory of her wretched, pseudo-husband, Timothy, slipped into her mind. Tim telling her how he hated asking her for money, how demeaning it was...

She gave a slight shrug. "I understand. It seems to me that suicide makes even more sense, so I still fail to understand why Mrs. Ames is so certain it was foul play."

"The authorities found a gun near Ames's body that he'd purchased after the attack in the office. Mrs. Ames insists he never shot the weapon, yet two of the six bullets had been discharged."

"Well, that puts a different perspective on things," McShane conceded. "There's no way he could have shot a second round after shooting himself, unless he flinched and missed the first time."

"Exactly Mrs. Ames's point," William said. "The police showed little interest in delving into it, just as they had in trying to find Tad Connelly after he robbed and beat them."

"To be clear," Lilly said, "even with her concerns about Bertolini, Mrs. Ames still believes Tad Connelly is responsible for her husband's death."

"Let's just say he is her principal suspect, but she postulates that it could be any of several individuals. Bertolini might have killed Ames in retaliation for turning down his offer to buy, perhaps believing that being a woman with little understanding of the business, Mrs. Ames might settle for less than he'd offered."

Lilly bristled at the remark but remained silent.

"To add to the confusion, there have been a few walkers who made comments about getting even with Ames after he didn't pay them what they'd contracted for. One particularly vicious threat was made by Elsa Dengler, a pedestrienne from Germany."

Lilly's head was spinning. "It sounds quite a mess."

"'Many mickles make a muckle,' Miss Long." William quoted the old Scots saw with a wry smile, and a glimpse of his rare, dry humor. "It *is* quite a mess. In short, Mrs. Ames demands answers, and the two of you are to get them for her." He picked up two small journals from his desk and offered them to McShane, who handed one to Lilly.

From previous assignments, she knew that the pages contained an overview of the facts they'd just heard, details of the mission, a list and description of people involved, and the general plan the agents were to execute to determine the truth.

"What, exactly, are our roles?" McShane asked.

"Dora Ames is sponsoring a race right here in Chicago at the Palmer Roller Rink in ten days' time. You, Miss Long, will go as a Leila McShane, a new pedestrienne recently arrived from Ireland. You have been successful in walking distances in a prescribed amount of time, just as Weston did when he first started out.

"Even though you have done few track walks, you've come over for a chance of making a name for yourself in hopes of sending for your family. You have done a bit of theater in Dublin, so you will be able to give the spectators a taste of what Ada Anderson did before she retired last year. McShane, who has an extensive background working with Thoroughbred racehorses, will go as your brother and trainer."

At first glance, the plan was certainly plausible. One of the agency's best tactics was to send operatives undercover to infiltrate the lives of those in question. She and McShane had posed as married domestics for a wealthy family in New Orleans and a former lady of the evening and her bodyguard in Ft. Worth. He had already pretended to be her husband, so acting as brother and sister would pose no problem. Over the past months, she had learned that his acting skills were not inconsiderable. Still, Lilly was more than a little troubled by the memory of William saying that some of the competitions lasted more than a month.

Blistered feet.

Hallucinations.

After spending almost eight weeks training with Monstery, she was as fit as she had ever been, and playing the role of an Irish woman would be no challenge; she'd done that in Louisiana.

"But sir! I'm not trained," she reasoned, even though she knew it was a dispute she would not win. "If it were boxing or fencing, I might make a bit of a showing, but as an endurance walker I'll only make a laughingstock of myself."

"Calm yourself, Miss Long," William said, holding both hands out, palms down. "Instead of walking a certain distance in a certain time, the pedestrienne who walks the farthest in six days will be the winner."

Her heart sank. "B...But that's almost a week!"

William's smile could only be described as unrepentant. "Yes. From midnight Saturday until midnight the following Friday. Don't worry, my dear. The main thing is that you and McShane will be in a position to evaluate the situation and either confirm or eliminate Mrs. Ames's suspects one by one."

Lilly bowed to the inevitable. "If I'm forced to drop out early—which I'm bound to be—what happens?"

"It's of little consequence, Miss Long," he assured her. "There are always new and untrained women, and most of them drop out when things get tough. No one will think a thing of it, and if you and McShane stay until the race ends, it's believable that you would like to see how things unfold, is it not?"

Lilly sighed.

"Mrs. Ames assures me that all the main players will be there in one capacity or another, so needless to say, I expect you to sort things out and find the responsible party."

"She's still in control of the business, then?" Lilly asked.

"Yes. As I said, Ames turned down Bertolini's offer."

Though Lilly had dozens more questions, she sensed that the meeting was over.

"We'll do our best, sir," McShane assured their boss.

"I know you will, McShane. I know you will."

Chapter Two

Two days later

"Holy mother of pearl!"

McShane's oft-used expression was Lilly's response at seeing the array of clothing hanging on a makeshift wooden rack in the Pinkerton storeroom. "Surely you don't expect me to use all this?" she said, looking from the rack of clothing to Harris, who cleared his throat and rocked up and down on his toes.

"Well, certainly only what you think you will require, Miss Long. Mr. Pinkerton was adamant that you have everything you might need to make the proper impression on the spectators."

His forehead pleated in a frown of worry. "Surely, he mentioned that as a former actress, you can mimic Ada Anderson by doing some costume changes and singing or playing the pianoforte now and again?"

Lilly sighed. So that's what William meant. From McShane's belief that the bonus entertainment was more interesting than the race itself, and what she had heard some of the walkers had done to entertain, she was beginning to wonder if the whole thing might be nothing more than an extravagant burlesque show.

Wringing his hands, Harris rose on his toes again. "I rented some things from a local shop that provides costumes for masquerade parties. Do you think it's too much?"

Poor Harris. Like the rest of them, he was doing his best. Lilly went through the rack of clothing and pulled out a pair of breeches, or tights, or whatever one might call them. She drew in a sharp breath. How on earth could she possibly get into them? And if she did manage it, every curve of her legs and other portions of her anatomy that no one besides a husband should see would be revealed to all!

An image sprang to mind from her time with Monstery, a photograph of Ella Hattan that hung on his wall. The woman, one of the most celebrated swordswomen of the time, wore ankle-length breeches that were so tight they looked like a second layer of skin. Those were topped with a pair of short pantaloons that barely covered her *derrière*. No, no, and no! Lilly was prepared to portray whatever character was necessary to catch criminals, but she could not expose her body in such a shameful way. She raised her troubled gaze to Harris.

"What am I supposed to do with these?"

"Um...I believe you are to wear a frock of some sort over them. One moment." He held up a finger and rushed toward the door, only to return in a moment with a small stack of broadsides, which he shoved toward Lilly.

Each was an image of the most popular pedestriennes. Lilly gave a sigh of relief. In every instance, the dresses they wore over the tight trousers were knee-length or mid-thigh. That was much better. And then she saw a poster of a walker that showed a scandalous portiont of bare legs between the tops of their socks and the hem of her dress. She sighed.

"Oh, I forgot! Agent McShane just arrived with your shoes."

"I have shoes."

As if on cue, McShane entered the cluttered room, brown paper-wrapped packages swinging at his sides. "I'm sure you do, Miss Long," he said, gesturing for her to take a seat on a nearby chair. "I'll wager that none of them are designed for walking several hours a day."

Indeed, they were not, she thought, automatically doing his bidding. *And by the way, a good morning to you, too!*

McShane gave Harris a quick smile. "I have this, if there is something needing your attention, Harris."

"Oh," Harris said, "there is always plenty to do around here." With a toothy smile in return, he left the room.

"I got you three pairs of shoes," McShane informed her, dropping to one knee. It looked, she thought, as if he might be preparing to propose, though his tone was anything but romantic. He slipped a hand around her ankle and loosened a small button on the taupe shoe she wore.

"Three pair! Why so many?" she asked, tossing the proposal image aside in the same way he tossed her footwear to the floor. He slid an ugly boot onto her narrow foot.

"Were you so taken with the amount of money at stake that you missed the part about blisters and bleeding feet?" he asked, glancing at her as he tightened and tied the leather laces.

She had not seen much of him of late, but it seemed he was back to his usual no-nonsense self. Wondering if she would ever understand the blasted Irishman, she sat back in the chair and clutched the arms. "Believe me, I heard. What in blazes am I getting into, McShane?"

He looked up from her other foot and offered her a grim smile. "The good Lord only knows," he said with a shake of his head "It certainly ought to be interesting, though, don't ya think? Walk around a bit and see how those feel."

Lilly stood and looked down at the horrendous leather boots. At least Hattan's shoes made some small concession to style. Lilly walked a few feet and said, "They are far too large. I'll have blisters in no time."

"Of course, you will. That's a given. We'll have you wear two pair of my woolen socks."

She stopped walking back and forth, turned, and planted her hands on her hips. "Why not just get me a pair that fit?" she asked, frowning.

"There needs to be room for swelling."

"Ah, yes. Swelling," she said with a thoughtful nod. "Thank you for the reminder. I had managed to block that from my mind along with the blisters and bleeding."

He disregarded her blatant sarcasm. "Just so ya know, I have been tryin' to find out all I can about how to treat ya when things go wrong, which, I fear they are bound to do. I've been in touch with a local doctor who is quite a fan of the treks, and he tells me that one of the favorite things to do is pour whiskey into the boots. It helps the pain or swelling or some such. And those thick soles will protect your feet should anyone put tacks or glass on the track."

She stopped midstride. "Surely you don't believe all those things that William said about sabotage?"

He shrugged. "It has been known to happen, so we ought to be mindful, don't ya think?"

"Of course. Again, thank you so much for the reminder, but what I think, *brother dear*, is that you make a superb Job's comforter."

She half expected him to laugh. He did not.

"You knew it wasn't going to be a picnic, lass. And believe me, I'm not having an easy time of it learning everything I need to know to pass myself off as yer trainer. Just because I'm supposed to know how to train and treat racing horses, doesn't necessarily mean that I know how to train and treat humans, now does it?"

She gave a disgusted snort.

He grew serious. "This is no joke, Lilly. We leave Tuesday and the race begins at midnight Saturday. We'll have four days to get ready, and I have to at least know fundamental training protocol."

She went back to the chair and sat down so that they were eye to eye. "Such as?"

"Well, for starters, it seems everyone establishes a daily routine designed for each individual walker. Early nights, up at the crack o' dawn for a long mornin' walk, a bit o' breakfast, then another walk. It varies from walker to walker and trainer to trainer. I'm prepared to be flexible."

He seemed to remember something and fumbled in his vest pocket. "I bought you one of those new pedometer doodads, so we'll have an idea of how far you've walked."

"How kind," she said with only the slightest hint of mockery.

"Then you'll have another walk or maybe some other physical activities later in the day, so's you'll be fit on starting day."

Or so worn out she wouldn't make it the first twenty-four hours.

He began to untie the boots. "I've been trying to find the medicines I'll need to doctor your feet, as well."

"You do know Pierce was taking medical training before he left England. He might know something that would help. I wonder if he could get free and come," she mused, as her partner slipped a canvas shoe onto her right foot.

"I thought of that," he said, "and I've already contacted him. He says there is no way he can get free just now. Sorry. But he did give me a few pointers.."

"As am I."

"Try these," he said, giving her knee a brotherly pat.

The canvas shoe fit much better. They weren't nearly so cumbersome and heavy, and they had a certain amount of give that might help when the swelling started. She gave a sigh of resignation and sat down to try the third pair. "I may as well hear the rest of it. What else can I expect?"

McShane pulled up a three-legged stool and sat with his elbows resting on his knees, his hands dangling between. "We'll all be sleeping on a cot in a tent in the middle of the rink."

"Rink? A *skating* rink?"

"The Palmer Roller Rink to be exact. With all her financial difficulties, it appears Dora can't afford anything like The Exposition Center. But Edward Weston has been using roller rinks for a while now with great success."

Lilly was about to ask who Edward Weston was when McShane said, "P'raps Dora feels if they're a good enough venue for the likes of an Astley Belt winner, they'll be good enough for her competition."

"I am assuming the Astley Belt is a pedestrian contest of some sort."

"You would be assuming correctly. The Astley Belt winner is declared Long Distance Champion of the World. It's the most coveted prize in the pedestrian world."

Lilly rolled her eyes heavenward.

"And Palmers is no small place, ya ken. Fortunately for Dora, it's near the edge of the city, so there's a vacant patch of land behind, where she plans to hold some boxing matches and have some other vendors and events. It's good planning to have extra things available, and because of J.D.'s involvement with boxing, she knows a bit about it."

"Will you be competing?"

He was careful to avoid her gaze. "No. I'll be too busy taking care of you. That's my job. I don't intend to let ya down the way I did at the Acre."

"You didn't let me down."

He did look at her then. Distress filled his eyes.

"Didn't I? That was a wretched state of affairs all around. Certainly, more than any of us expected when we set out to find out what happened to your friend, Nora."

"It was."

His grip tightened on her foot. "You were lyin' on the floor with that beast on top of you, and for a moment I thought you were dead."

Lilly was a little taken aback by the intensity radiating from him.

"Lass...are you all right with this?" he asked, finally looking her in the eye.

"All right with what?"

"Going back into the fray, so to speak."

She wondered what he saw when he looked at her that would cause him to question her readiness and willingness to go back to work. She thought she had been hiding her uncertainty reasonably well. Clearly, she had not.

A montage of memories—few of them pleasant—from her time in Hell's Half Acre flashed through her mind. Even though she had used the maneuvers McShane had taught her about protecting herself in a close skirmish, she'd barely escaped being overpowered by Eli Wilkins. That frightened her more than she wanted to admit to him, or even herself.

Was she ready to face God knows what again? Probably not. Despite honing her skills with Monstery, as well as learning new ones, she realized that no amount of training could prepare any operative for potential threats, because no one could predict what form it might take.

"What makes you think I'm not ready?" she asked, her voice quivering the slightest bit.

"I saw the way you were when we left Ft. Worth. It was as if someone had jerked the heart and soul right out of ya."

"That's how I felt." She forced herself to meet his steady gaze. "Did you say something to William?"

"What makes ya think I did?" As she had, he answered her question with one of his own.

"Well, I thought I was going to visit Pierce and Rose for a while, and the next thing I know, William has me signed up with Monstery. He had to have known something of what I was feeling, and how could he unless you said something to him?"

Instead of owning up to discussing things with William, McShane once again answered her question with one of his own, something she had come to expect from the Irish.

"Why didn't ya tell William 'no?'"

She gave a slight lift of her shoulders. "I intended to."

"Monstery *was* my suggestion," he said after a lengthy pause. "I told William that I thought you needed to practice up on your swordplay and pistol and that I felt strongly that you should learn a bit of boxing."

"It would have been easier just to let me quit and go back to the stage."

"Quitting is always easier, but if you'd quit, all those women out there waiting for you to come help them would have had no hope."

At that, she burst out laughing. The sound was tinged with bitterness. "That's going a bit too far, McShane, even for you. I'll be believin' you kissed the Blarney Stone." The last was said with an Irish accent.

He offered her a crooked smile. "I'll not be denyin' that," he said. "But it troubled me, the way you were. I don't want you ever feelin' that helpless again. It was a bad thing that happened there, Lilly. For you and for Erin..."

At the mention of his sister, his voice cracked.

Without thinking, she leaned toward him and gripped his forearms. "Try not to think about it. Don't let the likes of Wilkins and his ilk rob you of any more than they already have. And stop blaming yourself. Things happen we have no control over."

"That's what Erin told me before she married Simon. She said that life hadn't been good to her in the past, but that she couldn't let those things ruin her future. That she wouldn't let them."

"Your sister is a remarkable woman," Lilly told him, meaning every word.

"And Simon is a good man who loves her very much."

"He does that." He shook his head. "He's just not the type I thought she'd fall for."

"Nor I. But perhaps he is the kind of man she needs. Because of his own sister's circumstances, he understands better than most what Erin has been through, and he loves her despite it."

"Maybe he loves her because of it."

"I don't understand."

"Maybe he sees in her what we do, that she's still a wonderful, caring person who hasn't let her past embitter her or drag her down."

"Perhaps, he does," Lilly agreed, removing her hands from his forearms. "And perhaps, because she knows he understands, he's exactly the kind of man she would love."

McShane gave a slight shrug and started untying a shoe.

"I want to be like Erin."

His head jerked up and he regarded her with a frown. "What?"

"My greatest fear is that the longer I do this the less it will bother me. I don't want to become immune to the ugliness and suffering we deal with," she confessed, meeting his questioning gaze with directness. "I don't want to lose my compassion, because the caring is what keeps me going."

He looked stunned by her outburst. "You won't."

"How can you be sure?"

"Because that's what makes you you, and I can't see anything changing that."

Despite McShane's belief in her and her abilities, at day's end, she was feeling overwhelmed and melancholier than ever. How had she let William talk her into such a bizarre assignment? How had she let him talk her into any assignment at all when it had been her intention to quit the agency and go back to the theater?

You're fooling yourself, Lilly. As terrible as things were in Ft. Worth, as terrified as you were and as hopeless as it all seems when you know there are more victimized women out there every day, you know that you will never give it up. Scared, insecure, lacking the skills you need, fearful that you will see so much cruelty and pain that you will become unsensitized to it...none of it makes a difference in the long run.

She knew that because of Kate and the man who had killed her, because of Timothy, because there'd been someone to pick her up and help her when she had no one, she would keep doing whatever the agency asked.

Chapter Three

I t was mid-afternoon by the time Cade rustled up a depot wagon to haul them and their supplies to the Palmer Roller Rink. William had stressed that it must appear that they had traveled to Chicago from somewhere else.

The drive to the rink was approximately thirty minutes. Protected from the September sunshine by the standing top that extended over the driver, Lilly was content to take in the sights along the way.

The day was glorious, with random trees dropping leaves along the boulevard like flower girls dropping rose petals down a church aisle. The breeze blowing off the lake gave a definite chill to the air, giving rise to shoppers and business owners donning warmer clothing, mostly woolen skirts and cloaks.

Arriving at the rink, McShane paid the driver and swung Lilly down from the carriage. Together they went inside to let Mrs. Ames know they had arrived, while the driver unloaded their luggage and provisions.

A square oak table sat near the door, most likely where Mrs. Ames acknowledged the arrival of the pedestriennes and gave them their instructions. No one was around, so McShane rang a bell, much like those used in hotel lobbies.

While they waited, Lilly examined the place that would be their home for the foreseeable future. The large, oval-shaped structure was supported by huge arched beams that ran from floor to ceiling.

A two-foot-high by approximately ten-foot-wide dais for spectators surrounded the entire rink, and a waist-high railing prevented onlookers interfering with the skaters—in their case walkers—as they passed, yet still allowed maximum visibility.

A place for a band, complete with a piano, had been set up at one end. Walkers had been known to play a ditty or two during the competitions, and some even sang now and again. With a disposition that favored order and organization, Lilly could not comprehend all the ins and outs, the rules, or the general feeling of pandemonium that apparently accompanied the upcoming event.

A tanbark track, eight to ten feet wide, had been laid around the entire floor; red, white, and blue bunting draped the rails of the platform. Notices on the walls advertised everything from the new Tiffany pedometer to a remarkable new walking shoe with built-in springs designed by a cobbler, John Welsher. Several department stores and other establishments actively sought walkers fortheir own inner-city leagues.

A handful of tents had been set up around the edge of the arena infield. So far, there was one at each end of the oval, and only one near the center. These would be the living quarters for the competitors for the duration of the race.

Lilly had learned a lot about the sport the past two weeks, including that larger races sometimes allowed furniture dealers to supply each contestant furnishings in exchange for the privilege of hanging an advertising placard on the exterior of his or her tent.

There had been nothing in her contract to make her think they would receive anything nearly so fine. Besides, she knew McShane had shipped or brought everything they would need. They would be sharing sleeping quarters once again, but since she would be sleeping in short snatches of time whenever he thought it was opportune, and he would be sleeping the same way, she supposed it would not present a problem. Besides, they had shared a room in New Orleans without incident, so there was no reason for any uncomfortable feelings on her part.

"How big do you think it is?" she asked, her gaze moving from the interior space to her companion. He stood with his legs spread slightly apart and his arms crossed over his chest, regarding the area thoughtfully.

He shrugged. "Just guessin', o' course, but somewhere between an acre and an acre and a half."

"How many turns around the track do you think we have to make to equal a mile?"

"Seven, according to the information Mrs. Ames sent."

"Seven times around the track." Lilly sighed and glanced up at him. Biting back a grin, she asked, "Why didn't you get me shoes with springs?"

For a moment, he looked bewildered. "Springs?"

She gestured toward the advertisement.

He glanced at it and turned back to her. Seeing the glint of humor in her eyes, he responded with a familiar observation. "Ever the grateful one. Didn't I buy ya three pair of walking shoes?"

She laughed then. "Indeed, you did."

"Besides the ones with springs were eight dollars a pair," he added.

"Hello there!"

They turned to see a woman approaching, a smile on her face. Short, blonde, plump, and pretty, she had blue eyes that twinkled, a smile that put dimples in her cheeks and a melodious voice that would have served her well had she chosen the stage as a career instead of athletic promotions.

"I'm Dora Ames," she said, extending her hand to Lilly. "I'm sorry you had to wait."

"Leila McShane," Lilly provided. "Everyone calls me Lil." They had chosen to stay as close to the truth as possible, which made their lies easier to remember. In fact, she and McShane had even decided Leila McShane had been married to a scoundrel who had run away with another woman. A common enough tale to be believable and close enough to what Tim had done to evoke the right kind of emotion should the topic arise.

"My new walker from Ireland!" Dora said, clapping her hands with glee. "Wonderful!" She turned to Cade. "And you are Mr. McShane?"

"I am, but I'm her brother and trainer, not her husband, thank the good

Lord." The information was paired with his most charming smile. He extended his hand. "Andrew McShane."

"Good, good!"

What was good? Lilly wondered, fixing her smile in place and stifling the urge to groan. That McShane was her trainer/brother or that he was not her husband? She suspected it was the latter. All the man had to do was smile, and every woman within eyesight was smitten. She watched as Dora tucked her hand into the crook of his arm and guided him to the railing.

"When did you arrive in the states?"

"Three weeks ago. I felt Lil might need some time to rest before the race after such a long voyage." He laughed. "It's a fine line, knowing how much of either is too much or too little."

Dora smiled. "It certainly is, and I'm not sure anyone has figured out the perfect formula to date." She glanced at Lilly and spoke to Cade. "I understand this is the first of this type of race your sister has competed in."

Tired of the woman ignoring her, Lilly stepped nearer. "It is," she said before Cade could answer. "I'm accustomed to walking against my own times."

"This will be quite a departure, then," Dora said. The expression in her blue eyes was indecipherable, but Lilly thought she might be reassessing her opinion of her newest walker.

Dora gestured toward the center of the rink. "Feel free to put up your tent anywhere in the available space," she told them. "I assume you brought everything you'll need...medicines, food, that sort of thing."

"I believe so, thank you. The instructions you sent were most helpful, but perhaps I can pay someone to run out and purchase any items I may need throughout the race. I don't like the notion of leaving my sister for any length of time once we get started."

"I'm sure we can find someone," Dora assured him.

"When will we meet the others?" Lilly asked. She was eager to meet her competitors so that she could begin forming some idea of their personalities and gauging if any of those who had raced in California were capable of murder.

"It's hard to say since they all have different training schedules," Dora told her. Movement from across the rink near one of the corner tents caught her eye. "Oh! There's Leo with Jocelyn now."

Leo? Bertolini? Eyes wide with disbelief, Lilly glanced at her partner. What on earth was Bertolini doing here? McShane looked as baffled as she felt. Glancing across the way, Lilly saw a tall, dark-haired man making gestures that could only be interpreted as angry.

The person on the receiving end of his tirade was a henna-haired woman about Lilly's size who stood with her hands on her hips, listening. There was no mistaking the fury on her face, and though they couldn't hear what she was saying, her actions spoke volumes. As they watched, the woman stamped her foot, whirled around, and stormed into her tent.

Clearly exasperated, Leo Bertolini threw his hands into the air and strode across the infield toward them. McShane looked at Lilly with raised eyebrows.

Dora's disgust was apparent. "That woman! If she didn't have so much public appeal, I'd not waste a minute's time on her. She's always been difficult, but since her husband's death while we were in California, she's become even more so."

"Who is she?" McShane asked.

"Lady Jocelyn Baldwin."

The English actress turned pedestrienne?

Lilly's mind whirled. The now-ageing woman had once been an actress of some renown in Europe, best known for her portrayal of Shakespeare's Venetian beauty, Desdemona. She, like the fictional Desdemona, was a true beauty. Or had been. Now in her late thirties or early forties, she was getting old for the sport...and the stage.

"Is she really from the aristocracy?" Lilly asked.

Dora gave a tight smile. "Hardly. The truth lies closer to the rumor that she is the illegitimate daughter of a licentious baron, who refused to acknowledge her. Her detractors gave her the name Lady Jocelyn because of her uppity ways, and because it makes a mockery to her claim to be a part of the upper class. She despises it, but it's stuck."

28

"She's beautiful," Lilly acknowledged.

"You should have seen her ten years ago," Dora said. "As often happens with beautiful women in the public eye, she had the misfortune to grow older. Consequently, several years ago, she was replaced on stage by some young actress. According to Jocelyn and the rumor mongers, the newcomer secured the honor by sharing a bed with the troupe's manager."

A common enough occurrence. If Lilly had learned anything since becoming part of the Pinkerton agency, it was that there was no lack of infidelity in any sector of life.

Regardless of Jocelyn's difficult personality, Lilly wondered at the possibility of forging an alliance with the former actress. No one else had managed to do so but coming from the same background might give her an advantage.

"She is difficult, to say the least," Dora added as the tall man came bounding up the steps.

His hair, as dark as McShane's and tamed with brilliantine, was brushed straight back from his face, throwing his unusual features to advantage. His cheekbones were high and pronounced, but not unattractive, his chin and jawline square and angular, and he had what could only be deemed a "Roman" nose. A mustache, with slight waxed curls at the end, draped a sensuously shaped mouth.

Unconcerned about baring his problems in front of strangers, he blurted, "She refuses to walk on the track at the same time as Elsa."

Dora gave a slight shrug. "Well, after the San Francisco debacle, we knew to expect something of this sort. We can discuss what to do about it later."

Smiling for the benefit of Lilly and Cade, she gestured toward them. "Leo, I'd like you to meet Lil McShane and her brother, Andrew. She's recently come over from Ireland to join the others trying to make their mark as a pedestrienne." Placing her hand on the Italian's upper arm, she said, "Leo Bertolini, my manager and promoter."

Both Lilly and Cade smiled politely and shook hands with the man who had offered to buy the entire enterprise from Dora's husband just hours before he was found dead. Leo's handshake was slack, weak. Just like the man, was Lilly's suspicion. He held her hand a bit longer and tighter than was acceptable before she pulled free.

"Delighted to make your acquaintance, Miss McShane," he said, with a smile calculated to let the recipient know that he was interested.

"Leo is married to La Bella Rosa."

Leo's smile vanished, and Lilly wondered if Dora said it as an explanation, or a not-so-subtle reminder to the Lothario who stood before them.

"I've read about her," Lilly said, lying to them all but figuring her comment was vague enough to withstand any close scrutiny. "She's remarkable. I only hope to be half as talented as she is one day."

"Thank you, Miss McShane," Bertolini said with a slight bow. "I'll make sure she hears of your admiration."

"I'm sure the McShanes would like to get settled, Leo," Dora said. Pointing toward a closed door with a makeshift sign bearing her name, she added, "That's my office. If you need anything and you don't see Leo around, I'll do my best to help you. In the meantime, feel free to set up your tent wherever you like."

After McShane shook hands with them both again, they disappeared behind the closed door, their heads close, their whispers indecipherable, Bertolini's arm around Dora's waist.

"Be careful of that one, little sister," her partner warned. "I think he intends to add you to his list of conquests."

Lilly glared at him. "Really, McShane! You give me too little credit. I may have made one mistake, but I have learned a thing or two since then. And I know a weasel when I see one."

"Do ya now?"

"Oh, just go away and leave me alone."

"No chance, lass," he said, getting serious suddenly. "I know you must be as tired as I am, and putting up a tent is the last thing you want to do, but if you'll help me set up the tentI'll treat you to supper."

"You or the agency?" she asked with a lift of her eyebrows.

"Does it matter? Either way, you don't have to pay."

* * *

30

Lilly was exhausted by the time they finished setting up the tent. She barely had the energy to freshen up before she and McShane strolled down the street to a restaurant where they dined on roast chicken, potatoes, and creamed English peas. He looked as weary as she felt; after all, it was he who had borne the brunt of assembling the tent and unpacking and arranging their supplies to the best advantage.

The canvas covering, which would be home, refuge, and haven for the duration of the race, was approximately a twelve-by-twelve square. He'd set up their cots on opposite sides, and together they'd made up the temporary beds with the unbleached muslin sheets they'd brought. Their cots were separated by a plain rectangular table he had found in the back of a storeroom at the Pinkerton offices. Two bentwood chairs completed their dining/sitting area.

There was a small gas stove for cooking, and another, smaller table that held a bucket of water and a dishpan. Wooden boxes held a variety of pots and kitchen utensils, others held non-perishable foodstuffs, plus coffee, tea, herbs and various alcoholic beverages they might need.

A washstand with a plain ceramic bowl, pitcher, and chamber pot were hidden from view behind a screen should anyone pass by while the flap was open. He'd hung a small bell outside the tent's opening for visitors to alert them of their presence.

By ten o'clock, the electric lights had been turned off and the noise from the other pedestriennes and their assistants was dying down. She and McShane were in their cots, trying to relax and listening to the unfamiliar sounds of their new environment.

"Neither Dora nor Leo had much to say about his wife," McShane said, speaking into the darkness. They had been so busy since arriving they'd had no time or privacy to discuss their impressions and observations. "How do ya think Rosalie Bertolini feels about her husband's *business* arrangement with Mrs. Ames?"

Thinking of the flirtatious Dora Ames brought out Lilly's cynicism. "Pray, Andrew, do not tell me that you are suggesting that there is more between those two than boss and promoter," she stated in her best scandalized tone.

She heard him chuckle in the dark. "Well, they looked very chummy to me."

"More than chummy, I'd say." Lilly had zero sympathy for any man who would be unfaithful to his wife, or vice versa. "What kind of woman partners up with the man who, by her own admission, might be involved in her husband's death?" She asked, verbalizing the thought that had been troubling her ever since they'd met Dora's assistant, or partner, or whatever he was.

"Dear, dear, Miss McShane! I do believe you lost the last of your naïveté in Ft. Worth."

She made a scoffing sound. "Perhaps not all of it, but I'm getting wiser by the minute."

"Indeed, you are. As for your question, I can't begin to understand the workings of Mrs. Ames's mind, but even William told us that Leo is an excellent manager and promoter. He's exactly what Dora needs if she hopes to make this newest debut work."

"What about poor Rosalie?" Lilly asked.

McShane sighed in the darkness. "That's harder to pinpoint since we haven't seen any interaction between her and Dora or her and Leo for that matter. Who knows the true state of their marriage? If their reconciliation is genuine, I'd say she's most likely livid, but if it's only an arrangement to make the most of her racing opportunities, perhaps she doesn't give a fig."

"He's a worm."

She heard another short burst of laughter. "You give him far too much credit, sister dear."

"Maybe I do." After a few moments, she asked, "What do you make of Lady Baldwin's refusal to walk at the same time as Elsa? I wonder what's going on between them?"

"Jealousy would be my guess."

"Yes, but why? And it seems so extreme for just a race."

"Like Dora said, Lady Jocelyn is getting older, and her popularity is showing signs of waning a bit. I don't know anything about Mrs. Dengler except what William told us, but Dora says they're both able to pack the house. Even when you compare them to the most successful walkers, those two are still a couple of the biggest toads in the puddle, and I'll wager Leo and Dora will soon figure out a way to make things work."

"You know, I admire her."

"Lady Jocelyn?"

"No, Dora."

"I thought you agreed with me that her relationship with Leo is disgraceful."

"It is, and I do, but on the other hand, I find it admirable that just a few months after her husband dies, she's committed to fulfilling their dream. That takes vision and boldness and backbone. She could have just given up."

"Don't get so caught up in your admiration of her that you lose your objectivity." McShane's voice echoed in the dark. "Need I remind you of Prudence Purcell's actions?"

Prudence was the preacher's wife who had left her grandson and daughter to die to cover her husband's sin. She had completely fooled Lilly.

"You're right. What are your feelings about Ames's death? Do you think Dora is right in suspecting Elsa?"

She heard him chuckle in the darkness. "From what William said, Dora suspects everyone, and as far as I'm concerned, everyone connected to that race in California is suspect until we prove otherwise. But I'm keeping an open mind. If I've learned one thing since I've been in this business it's that any time money is involved, you never know what a person will do."

They were silent a moment, and then Lilly said, "One more thought." Again, she heard him sigh. "I wonder why Elsa signed on for this race after she walked out on J.D. in California, and more importantly, why would Dora let her if she suspects that Elsa is complicit in her husband's murder?"

Her only answer was a soft snore.

Chapter Four

Wednesday

C ade roused Lilly from a restless sleep at daybreak. Groaning, she lifted heavy eyelids and saw his big hands wrapped around a mug of coffee. She rolled to her side and dragged the pillow over her head. "Go away, McShane."

"Rise and shine, lass. Time to start yer trainin'." He leaned down and whispered in her ear. "And don't be forgettin' we have a murder to solve."

His breath tickled, and she stifled the shiver that ran through her. She loved the way he rolled his Rs and hated that she loved anything about him. Glaring and flouncing to her back, she found him sitting on the edge of her cot.

"That's the spirit!" he told her, giving her thigh a pat. "I'll just leave the coffee on the table while I go find the necessary. Be dressed by the time I get back, or I'll drag you out of there and dress ya m'self."

Lilly was pretty sure he was teasing, but there was a look in his eyes that might or might not have been a dare. She was fully dressed and sitting at the table sipping her coffee when he got back. She had chosen a navy and white striped pair of the too-small-looking trousers, topped with a long-sleeve, loose-fitting navy-blue shirt that came to mid-thigh.

As she feared, the snug pants showed every curve of her legs, but at least her *derrière* was covered. She was embarrassed to be seen in them, but she would die before she let on. Thank goodness Rose wasn't here. She would have a conniption.

"D'ya have your pedometer?" he asked.

"I do."

"Then finish your coffee and let's get started."

* * *

After a day and a half of training, Lilly had decided that McShane was not the ogre she had imagined him to be. So far, it had gone better than she anticipated. He hadn't forced her to a fast pace, as she'd expected. The race wasn't a sprint, he reminded her. This was all about distance. Endurance was what counted. Just stay on your feet and keep walking.

It sounded easy enough, but the tales she'd heard were never far from her mind, constant reminders that it would be stupidity to ignore the facts. Still, it was not as unpleasant as she'd expected, and even though the day had started out cool, she was perspiring freely by the time they returned for their lunch break. They were just outside the entrance of the rink when a carriage pulled to a stop, and the driver helped a woman down.

She was short, with ash-blonde hair, and wore a dated, rust-hued walking dress that did nothing for her stocky figure. Her delivery to the front door of Palmers meant one thing. She was a competitor. She spoke to the driver, who was unloading her cases. Her German accent was unmistakable. The new arrival was the famous Elsa Dengler.

Spying Lilly and Cade, she pointed a gloved finger at him. "You, there! Do you mind lending this man a hand?" Her tone was authoritative, sharp, but she *had* asked, not demanded.

Ever polite, McShane assured her he would be glad to help, taking the cases the driver handed down and setting them to the ground. When they had finished, she paid the fare, and without being asked, Cade picked up two of the bags and carried them inside the building, while Lilly held open the door.

This time Dora was waiting at her station. With thoughts of what happened in California uppermost in her mind, Lilly was anxious to see

Dora's reaction to the newcomer, but all she did was note their presence and turn to Cade.

"Mr. McShane, if you'll help bring in the rest of Mrs. Dengler's luggage, I'll see to it that some of the workers get it wherever she wants."

"Of course, Mrs. Ames."

Only then did the two women deign to look each other over. Their expressions could only be described as 'wary' or 'cautious.' Dora spoke first.

"Elsa."

"Dora."

"I trust you had a good trip."

"Goot enough."

Dora pretended to be looking for something among the short stack of papers on her makeshift desk. "I was somewhat surprised when you signed on for the walk since you refused to participate in California."

The subtlest of taunts. Either Dora was not one to mince words, or she was fishing for a reason Elsa had swallowed her pride and come to Chicago. Acutely aware of everything about the new arrival, Lilly already had Elsa's motivation figured out. She had been unable to collect the money she claimed she was owed by J.D., and she needed cash. Lilly was certain of it.

"No more surprised than I when you agreed to allow me to compete."

They had forgotten Lilly was standing nearby. Watching their conversation was like observing a carefully choreographed dance. Each word was chosen with exquisite care. Civilized. Yet somehow Lilly grasped that the unspoken undercurrents were treacherous.

Dora's smile was strained but served well enough. "Well, your quarrel was with J.D., not me. You will find that I'm a businesswoman, and as such, it would be foolish of me to deny the public a chance to see one of their favorite pedestriennes."

Which translated to what Dora had said in an earlier conversation. As troublesome and problematic as both Elsa and Lady Jocelyn might be, they had hundreds of devoted supporters. Their participation in this latest attempt to revitalize women's endurance walking would guarantee greater audience attendance throughout the six-day event. To ensure her success, Dora needed big crowds, and competitors like Jocelyn Baldwin, Elsa Dengler, and La Bella Rosa would guarantee she got them.

Their motivation was much easier to recognize. Fame and fortune. They were putting themselves through the grueling undertaking for a chance at momentary fame and the possibility of a sizable payday, one of the few ways a woman could get either. The problem was, there were so many personal jealousies among them that the whole thing could blow up at any moment, ending everyone's hope for success.

"Your husband and I had our differences," Elsa acknowledged with a nod, "but I was truly sorry to hear of his death. I have lost a husband, and I understand how difficult it is to hold things together alone."

"Yes, it can be stressful," Dora agreed with another of those taut smiles. "Thank goodness for Mr. Bertolini's helpful experience. I don't know what I'd have done without his help."

"Leo?"

Elsa's surprise, like Lilly and Cade's, was unmistakable.

"Yes, Leo. You may have heard that he and my husband were in negotiations before his death. Leo and I have entered into a partnership. He's my new manager and promoter. He's been invaluable in getting things up and running here."

Lilly detected a hint of triumph in Dora's smile.

The German walker's face was a study in reflection. She, too, must surely be wondering why Dora had aligned herself with the man who had tried to take advantage of her husband's misfortune.

Before Elsa could reply, Dora said, "I've been wondering about your lack of a trainer since Jerome…left the business."

Lilly tensed in anticipation. This was something she and McShane had not heard. Not only had William neglected to tell them that Elsa's trainer was missing, but they also hadn't been informed that she had one.

"That is certainly putting it nicely," Elsa said, with a grimace. "He deserted me in more vays than one."

"I'd heard as much."

Troubled by their false politeness, Lilly turned away from the women back toward the rink. Was Dora implying that there'd been something more between Elsa and her trainer than pedestrianism? She turned back to the two women just as McShane entered with the remaining bags.

"Here's Mr. McShane with the last of your things. I see the two of you have already met."

Elsa turned a polite smile his way. "Actually, we haven't. I only asked him to help get my things inside." She extended a slight smile and a gloved hand to Cade. "Elsa Dengler. Please allow me to compensate you for your trouble."

"I wouldn't dream of it, Mrs. Dengler. It was my pleasure. I'm Andrew McShane." He gestured toward Lilly. "This is my sister, Leila." He favored the ladies with one of his most charming smiles. "Everyone calls her Lil."

Elsa and Lilly exchanged smiles of greeting and polite nods. The difference in Elsa's manner talking to McShane was marked.

"You are her promoter? Manager? What?"

"I do a bit o' everything," McShane said, "but mostly I train her."

"I see."

The exterior door burst open, and the sounds of a disturbance of some sort interrupted the conversation. Like the others, Lilly struggled to see who or what was causing the commotion, but the glare coming through the stained-glass transom robbed her of everything but the fact that the newcomer was a tall woman carrying a portmanteau in each hand.

"May I be of assistance?" Dora asked.

The stranger focused on the sound of the voice as she drew nearer. "If you're in charge, I'm supposing you can. I'm looking for Miss McShane." The woman shielded her eyes with one hand, straining to see as her eyes adjusted to the inside light.

It was a voice Lilly hadn't heard in far too long. She pressed her lips together and blinked fast to keep from bursting into tears. *Rose!* What on earth was Rose doing there?

Before she could say anything, McShane extended his hand. "Mrs.

Wainwright!" he said in a hearty voice. "We weren't expecting you just yet."

As usual, he was quick to pick up on the unexpected event, and even faster interjecting himself into the conversation.

Rose took his hand. "So good to see you, Mr. McShane."

"And what capacity are you here in, Mrs. Wainwright?" Dora asked.

Rose released McShane's hand and turned to Dora. "My husband was unable to come, so he sent me as a medical associate in his stead. I have worked with him extensively through the years and am quite familiar with his treatment methods."

She offered Dora a bright smile. "He was quite resolute in his insistence that Miss McShane have proper medical care during the competition."

Well done, Rose! The last thing Lilly expected was Rose coming in Pierce's stead. When the necessity arose, as it did from time to time, she was quite self-reliant in the world outside that of the theater, but she made no secret of the fact that she preferred staying close to her husband.

As Lilly listened to the exchange, she wondered what McShane was thinking about the addition of this new, unexpected complication into an already challenging situation. As usual, his features revealed nothing of his thoughts.

Dora smiled pleasantly. "Let me finish with Mrs. Dengler and I'll be right with you."

Lilly could hardly wait for Dora to finish dispensing the formalities, rules, and advice. She wanted to get Rose away from all the onlookers and fling her arms around her neck. She wanted to hear about the troupe and how Pierce was doing. She wanted to know everything!

Dora handed Elsa some papers, told her to fill them out and bring them back as soon as possible.

"I'll have them to you first thing in the morning," Elsa assured her.

"Excellent."

Dora called for someone to help Elsa with her bags and, satisfied she was taken care of, she turned to Lilly and McShane.

When Dora was satisfied that the McShanes were taken care of, she said,

"It's been a pleasure meeting you. And thank you again for your help."

McShane assured her that he was more than happy to be of help, and then the three were headed across the rink toward the tent. As soon as the flap fell shut behind them, Lilly flung her arms around the neck of the woman who had taken her into her home and her heart after Kate's death.

A streetwise, no-nonsense kind of woman, Rose allowed Lilly to hold her close for a moment before disengaging herself from the embrace. "Away with you," she said holding Lilly at arm's length. "Let me look at you."

Lilly laughed and let Rose look to her heart's content.

"You're far too thin," she said at last. "Why is your face so red and your hair all a jumble? And what in the name of all that is holy are you wearing? Even prostitutes don't dress so shamefully."

Lilly sighed. As happy as she was to see Rose, she knew it would be a long ten days. Though she had known Rose would disapprove, comparing Lilly's attire to that of a prostitute was not the reaction she'd expected. She glanced at McShane, who stood at the tent opening, his arms crossed over his chest, watching the exchange with a considering expression.

Her gaze begged him to explain.

Instead, he extended his hand. "Hullo, Rose. I'm Cadence McShane. Andrew while we're here. I'm sure Pierce told you about me after his visit to Louisiana."

Rose's shrewd gaze took him in from head to toe. "He did," she acknowledged, lifting her chin and lacing her fingers together at her waist. "He spoke most favorably of you; however, I prefer to form my own judgments."

"I understand," he said. "So why are you here? Surely you didn't come all this way to take my measure."

She looked from him to Lilly and back again. "Young man, you heard me tell that woman out there why I'm here. Or were you not listening?"

"Seriously?" Lilly said. "Pierce sent you to take care of me during the race?"

"Of course, silly child." She gave a droll smile. "The fact that I bedeviled him somewhat might have swayed him. In the end, he said he supposed that the more eyes and ears we had on things, the better."

40

"Did he tell you anything about what Lilly will be doing?" McShane asked.

"Not much. He said she'd be walking a lot and would get really tired and that she needed someone to be there to take care of her aches and pains. And cook."

The Pierced Rose Troupe lived on the road and travelled so much that they had no proper home. Cooking was something Lilly had never learned to do. The notion of Rose cooking was hard to imagine.

"You know how to cook?"

Rose frowned at her. "I did have a life before I started following the theater, young lady."

The comment took Lilly aback. She had never thought of that. Somehow, she and Pierce had always been together. Inseparable. With Lilly put into her proper place, Rose gave her attention back to McShane.

"It's a bit more than that," he said, taking her by the shoulders and sitting her down in one of the chairs. "Let me explain." And for the next few minutes, that's what he did. He gave details on how the race worked, what Lilly would be up against, and what everyone's job would be.

Rose crossed her arms over her breasts in a gesture that spoke of her disapproval. "Mr. McShane, I do not care to hear all this. It sounds positively dreadful! How is the poor child going to survive? She'll need to eat good meals and get her rest if she's to walk so long and far."

"Unfortunately, Rose, that is in direct opposition to how the races work. She'll often eat as she walks and sleep in fits and starts. When she's had all she can take, however long that may be, she'll quit."

"It sounds positively wretched." Rose waved a hand toward Lilly. "Please tell me she won't be wearing this...sort of clothing. It's absolutely disgraceful."

Lilly saw McShane's patience turn to exasperation. He managed to control it, just. "Think of this outfit as you would her costume for a play, say if she was actin' as a young gent."

Rose thought about it for a moment and nodded. "I hadn't thought of it that way."

"Well, I don't mean to be harsh, but it's the way things are done, so you

41

might as well get accustomed to it. And you can't be coddlin' her. You must remember that she is nothing to you but a girl you've come to take care of. Other than that, she means nothin' to you? Do you understand?"

Lilly knew that Rose was trying her best to grasp what the next several days would bring. As they all were.

"I do. There is no need to raise your voice."

McShane planted his hands on his hips and drew in a deep, calming breath. Somehow, he managed to hold his tongue. "Good. And if you think she's thin now, you won't know her in a few days."

Rose shook her head and mumbled beneath her breath, "'Like as the waves make towards the pebbled shore, so do our minutes hasten to their end...'"

"Well, that's certainly depressing!" Lilly said. "What on earth was that all about?"

"It's a line from one of the bard's sonnets," Rose said in a thoughtful tone. "Number 60 if I'm not mistaken. With all that mindless walking and the shape Andrew says you'll wind up in, it sounds like a walking death."

"Dearest Rose, I don't think it will be quite that bad," Lilly said with a slight smile of encouragement. "I have no intention of walking myself into the grave. As McShane said, I can quit when things get too bad."

"You don't have any quit in you," Rose scoffed. "Now, I'm exceedingly weary, so I would appreciate it if you could help get my bags to that little hotel down the street."

"You really ought to stay with us," McShane told her.

"Here?" she echoed, looking around the small living quarters.

"Aye. We'll all be sleeping whenever we can spare a minute, but when Lilly comes off the track, we'll both need to be here to do whatever needs doing. I'll have neither the time nor a way to come and fetch ya."

"But where will I sleep?"

"I'll send for another cot. We'll be fine."

Finally, Rose agreed. Lilly wasn't sure if McShane had convinced her that she needed to be on hand at all times, or if Rose thought she should stay to act as a chaperone. She was not inexperienced in the ways of the world. She knew full well what could happen between two young people who were forced into close contact for extended periods of time. Lilly stifled a giggle. If only she knew what a pain in the behind McShane could be.

Once Rose had been convinced to stay, McShane announced that he would make a late breakfast, and then Lilly would have another long walk. As he cooked, he filled Rose in on their assignment, including what they knew about the things that had happened in California that led to Leo and Dora's partnership.

"Lilly and I are here to find out if Ames really did commit suicide, or if something more sinister is going on as Dora believes."

Rose listened in awe. "Murder! And here I was thinking that the theater was a cesspool of impropriety and drama."

McShane's mouth twisted into a wry smile. "I've come to realize that people are people, no matter what they do for a living. Far too many of them will do whatever is necessary to get what they want."

They were just finishing the meal that consisted of boiled eggs, Irish brown bread, and a cold veal cutlet when the bell outside the tent tinkled and Leo poked his head inside.

"In case you're interested, Andrew, the company sponsoring the boxing matches is setting up behind the rink. They should be working out a schedule of bouts by this afternoon."

"Thank you, Leo."

Leo glanced at Rose and smiled at Lilly. "Hello again, Miss McShane."

"Mr. Bertolini," she replied with a polite nod. "This is my medical helper, Mrs. Wainwright."

He and Rose exchanged pleasantries. "Please call me Leo, everyone. There is no need for formality here." He gave his attention back to McShane. "I hope you'll sign up. I believe there's decent money involved." Without another word, he vanished from the aperture.

"You are going to fight, aren't you?" Lilly asked.

"I believe we already had this discussion."

"What can possibly happen to me in the time it will take you to go a few rounds?"

"I've no idea," he said with a shake of his head, "but havin' been with you through three assignments, I'm not doubtin' that you'll manage to get yourself into some kind of grief just when I won't be there to sort things out."

She was torn between giving him the evil eye and sighing because she knew he was right. She took another bite of her bread.

"Don't get your knickers in a twist, either of you," Rose said. "Go sign up for your boxing, Mr. McShane. You forget that I'm here to keep an eye on Lilly while you're busy with other important things, like beating someone bloody."

He regarded the older woman for a moment and then gave a slow nod. "You're right. In fact, it's a blessin' you came. Havin' you around will free me up to do some investigating while Lilly's on the track." He slapped his hands on his knees and stood, grabbing his cap off the trunk next to the doorway as he passed. "I'll be back before ya know it. And then we'll walk."

* * *

Cade saw several men milling around behind the rink, hammering more stakes into the ground, setting up the boxing ring, and unfolding and placing wooden chairs for the spectators who would fill the blue-and-white striped tent in a few days. A smaller tent with a makeshift bar stood off to one side, and a long-haired, bearded man was stacking crates of liquor.

Good for Dora. A place a man could wet his whistle with a beer or enjoy a shot of whiskey while watching the matches was always a nice attraction. From the information she had sent, this was one of two bars that would be serving the spectators. If the number attending the event was as high as predicted, it would be next to impossible for one pub to quench the thirst of the crowd.

Across a narrow alley in another vacant lot, an additional canvas structure had been erected. The banner above the opening proclaimed a Methodist affiliation and announced that there would be services three times daily. Times were given for morning, afternoon, and nighttime services. Cade could only imagine the hellfire and damnation sermons that would mingle and blend with the shouts of men betting on the boxing matches. He wondered if there would be any other blood sports setting up, like dog or cockfighting.

As he made his way through the throng to the registration table, he saw Dora Ames approach the man at the bar. There was a lot to manage, and like Lilly, he had to admit to some admiration for the woman who was responsible for overseeing an event of this magnitude. Even though it was small in comparison to many others, it was still a huge undertaking, requiring hours of planning and execution, not to mention the never-ending problems that were bound to crop up.

Ten minutes later, signed up for two matches throughout the following week, Cade made his way back toward the rink's rear entrance. His gaze automatically moved to the grog shop. Dora was still there, but the conversation appeared to have gone cockeyed.

The man stood with his arms folded across his chest and a look of irritation on his face. Dora's fists were planted firmly on her hips. From what Cade had learned about women in his thirty-plus years, she looked a little wrathy as his Ma used to say. None of his business. He passed the tent and let himself into the roller rink. It was time for Lilly to go a few more miles.

Chapter Five

Friday

"**R**ise and shine, Lil!"

Rose's voice roused Lilly from a deep sleep. Two thoughts vied for her attention. First, she was starving, and second, she would have to feel better to die. Every muscle in her body screamed in pain, and a weariness that far exceeded any she had felt while working with Monstery was a weight pressing down on her entire body.

She wanted to open her eyes, but the task seemed far too difficult until she registered the smell of toasting bread and fresh-brewed coffee. Their mouthwatering promise made the effort almost worth it.

"C'mon, lass! The sun'll warp your ribs if you lay abed much longer." McShane's urging was accompanied by a not-too-gentle shake of her shoulder.

She groaned and opened one eye. He looked disgustingly awake and far too energetic for such an ungodly hour. "The sun's not fully up ."

"Get up, Lil," Rose said. "Your oatmeal is hot. I put lots of butter and molasses in it. Do you want tea or coffee?"

Oatmeal. Lilly heaved a great sigh, though the effort was almost more than she could bear. Oatmeal was the food your mother gave you when you were near death's door. Quite apt, on second thought. Placing her palms on the mattress, she pushed herself into a sitting position and groaned with the effort.

It was at least a start to her day.

She had no more than finished dressing and was plaiting her hair in a long braid when she heard two people talking outside the rear of the tent.

"You will *not* humiliate me the way you did in St. Louis!"

The words were low and filled with fury. Lilly's Italian was a somewhat rusty from non-use, but she had little trouble understanding every word the woman spoke to her companion.

"You will not carry on with any of those vapid cows in the spectator's stands who fawn all over you, and especially not with your new *partner* or that Irish redhead you've taken a fancy to."

Rosalie Bertolini. La Bella Rosa. Considering the topic of conversation, there was little doubt who she was talking to or what the conversation was about. A quiver of anger shot through Lilly. *She* was the new redhead. Somehow, Rosalie had heard of Leo's flirting. How dare they drag her into their sordid relationship! It was all she could do to keep from stomping out there and confronting them.

Refusing to acknowledge her suspicions one way or the other, the man countered, "And don't you forget that you promised not to walk off the track for *any* reason and render yourself disqualified from this blasted race!" Like his wife's, his tone was hushed but furious. "We were in agreement on this."

Lilly now had no doubt the conversation was between Leo and Rosalie. Whatever reasons were behind their unexpected reconciliation, it appeared caveats were attached, limitations that La Bella Rosa felt Leo was not adhering to.

"Perhaps if you try to control your lust and fulfill your part of the bargain, there will be no cause for me to do anything except what I came here to do," Rosalie muttered.

"Control my lust?" Leo laughed, a muted, mocking sound. "If you were a proper wife, there would be no need for me to seek my pleasures elsewhere."

Both Rosalie and Lilly gasped at the blatant callousness of the criticism. She clamped her hand over her mouth, praying neither of them heard.

"So now it is my fault." The slight quaver in Rosalie's voice was evidence of her pain. "I have never denied you access to my bed. Never!"

"There is a huge difference between allowing your wifely duties and being a wife," he accused. "I need a flesh and blood woman who will kiss me back, who acts as if she enjoys it. A woman who will take an active part."

Something that sounded like a sob came from outside the tent walls. "Did it ever occur to you that I might be exhausted when I finish a race?"

Again, Lilly thought she heard a tremor in Rosalie's voice. It must be hard for the popular walker to know her husband thought so little of her and to deal daily with his infidelities.

"There is nothing on me that doesn't hurt when I finish a race, Leo. Every muscle in my body aches or spasms and my mind is still filled with nothing but the simple act of taking another step. Can you not understand how hard it is? Do you care so little for me that you cannot show me the simplest of kindnesses?"

"This is a meaningless conversation," Leo snapped. "You just do what we came here for, and everything will be fine."

"And the same goes for you. Beware, husband. If you are not discreet, you know what I can do to you!"

Bravo! Lilly thought. Rosalie had found a bit of spirit.

"Is that a threat, my dear?"

"Take it however you wish."

There was a lengthy silence followed by a sob and, though she couldn't see, Lilly knew that Leo had left his wife standing outside the tent. Then Lilly heard her walking away.

"Lil!" The sound of McShane's voice brought her attention back to the moment. "Yer oats are gettin' cold."

"Sorry," she said, moving from behind the screen, her fingers working at her hair. She pulled a ribbon from her pocket, wrapped it around the end of the braid, and tied it tight. She was anxious to tell him what she had overheard and see what he made of it.

Oh, how far she'd come in a few short months! There had been a time she wanted to hoard every piece of the puzzle she gathered, partly because she wanted the recognition that came with bringing the guilty person to justice, and partly because she wanted to prove to the agency that she was as capable as any man in their employ.

Working with McShane had shown her how much she had to learn as well as how many things could go wrong. She realized the value of having someone else on her side, someone who might be able to decipher a piece of the puzzle she couldn't. And, when it came to physical actions, there were few who made her feel safer than her reluctant partner.

"Are you all right?" Rose asked, setting a cup of coffee and a bowl of oatmeal in front of Lilly. "You look a bit peaky."

"I'm fine." She stirred the butter, cream, and molasses into the already congealing mass and glanced at McShane, who was working on his own bowl of oatmeal while scanning the morning news. Reaching for the milk pitcher, she said, "I think there is trouble in paradise."

"What?"

"What do you mean?"

McShane and Rose spoke simultaneously. Leaning across the table so that she could speak lower, Lilly said, "While I was getting dressed, I heard Leo and his wife arguing behind the tent."

McShane refolded the newsprint and picked up his coffee. "How do you know that's who it was?"

"I recognized his voice, and they were both speaking Italian. Who else could it be? Besides, they were discussing very personal things." She glanced at Rose and back at Cade. "Husband and wife kinds of things."

McShane frowned at her. "Such as?"

"I don't think we should discuss it in front of Rose."

"Oh, for heaven's sake!" she said, slamming her mug onto the tabletop, "I'm a woman grown, and living in the midst of a theater troupe, I imagine I've heard it all by now. If I haven't then it's high time I did, wouldn't you say?"

"Yes, but—"

"Lil…"

"Fine!"

Lilly took a breath. "Rosalie was laying down the law about Leo not starting any flirtations during the race. Do you recall William saying Rosalie

49

had seen Leo with a woman in St. Louis and left the track to confront him?"

"I do. The officials refused to let her return to the track, so she lost a race she'd probably have won. It was quite a shame."

"What about him telling us how everyone was shocked when they showed up together in San Francisco after separating soon after that?"

"What are you getting at?"

"After overhearing their argument, I'm positive that they reconciled so they can both continue to profit from Rosalie's success. Think about it. It's a perfect symbiotic relationship. She needs him to take care of her and manage where and when she competes. She can trust him to find her the best venues and get the best possible contract in terms of money and treatment. And he needs her because she's the big breadwinner."

McShane shrugged. "It makes sense. What else did they say?"

"He said that she should remember that she isn't supposed to leave the race for any reason. I had the feeling they were reminding each other of promises they had made at some time or another. She also warned him against the 'new Irish redhead', which I assume is me."

"I would think so, yes," McShane said with a fleeting smile. "He seems to have taken a liking to you, which could be good for learnin' things."

"Lovely."

"Anything else?"

Lilly glanced at Rose once again, almost guiltily. "He told her that he might not have such a roving eye if she were more…uh, cooperative in the bedroom. They talked about that a bit." She gave Rose another fleeting look. "You know, about how exhausted she is when she finishes a race."

McShane swore. "The chap is all heart, isn't he?"

"*Hmpf!*" Rose said. "If you ask me, if he were half as good in that area as he seems to think he is, she might be more inclined to be *cooperative*, exhausted or not."

"Rose!"

Rose gave a dismissive wave of her hand. "Stop looking so shocked. I didn't fall off the turnip wagon yesterday."

"Excellent point, Rose," McShane said, not bothering to hide his grin.

"There is such a thing as quality over quantity."

Recalling her brief, disastrous association with Tim, as well as her annoying attraction to her partner, Lilly wondered what a man like McShane would consider *quality*.

"Just my point."

"So, how did they leave things?"

"She threatened him."

"With what?"

"She said something along the lines that he should heed her warning, or he knew what she could do to him. What do you think she meant?"

"I've no idea. Everyone in the pedestrian circuit and half the world of spectators knows he cheats on her every chance he gets. So far, that hasn't seemed to affect his success as a promoter or trainer, so I'm guessing she knows something he's done that might bring him to ruin."

Lilly's forehead furrowed in thought. "Do you think it has anything to do with his deal with J.D. in San Francisco? We know Leo was pressuring Ames because he was in a financial bind, but do you think it's possible there was more? Could Leo have been blackmailing him for some reason?"

"Like what?" McShane pressed.

Lilly shrugged. "Perhaps the whole embezzlement scheme and the robbery were false? Maybe Ames hid the money." She threw her hands into the air in frustration. "I don't know, but there are lots of possibilities."

He regarded her with a thoughtful expression.

"You have a point, Lil," Rose said. "It seems the whole world is trying to cheat someone, or everyone is looking for a shortcut."

"Rose is right. We need to keep doing what we're doing. Keep eyes and ears open. Maybe something will crop up."

"I agree." Sensing the conversation was at its end, Rose said, "Lilly, finish your oatmeal. You're going to need something to stick to your ribs today if McShane works you as hard as he's been saying. And don't forget to take a scarf. It turned off right chilly last night."

Lilly took a bite of oatmeal to keep from saying something she shouldn't.

* * *

By the time Lilly finished her training for the day, she was anything but cold. Try as she might, she could not imagine what the next few days would bring. Her pedometer showed she had walked ten miles. She was feeling rather proud of that when she remembered that Allan Pinkerton often walked twelve miles a day after suffering a debilitating stroke. Then there was McShane. He had taken every step she had and was hardly winded. Drat the man!

To her profound relief, not only did Rose have supper almost ready, she had warm water in the washbowl and more in the kettle. Lilly went through her nightly ablution and donned her gown and robe. She and McShane had long ago passed the it-isn't-decent-for-a-man-to-see-a-woman-in-her-nightclothes-unless-they-are-married stage. If Rose objected, she would just have to put it in her pipe and smoke it, as Pierce would say.

To Lilly's surprise, Rose made no comment. She'd had the day to observe the inner workings of the people and practices involved with pedestrianism. Perhaps she'd made her peace with them.

McShane barely glanced at her as he took her place behind the screen.

"You look worn to a frazzle, Lil," Rose said, stirring something delicious smelling on the stove. "This will be nice and hot in a few minutes."

"Thank you, Rose. I'm famished." Lilly took a seat at the table, picked up a slice of some crusty, dense-looking bread, and began to slather it with butter. "I appreciate your coming to look after us. And don't let this alarm you, but I hear I will look far worse in a day or so."

"So, everyone keeps saying." Rose gave her a troubled look over her shoulder. "I am not looking forward to any of this, let me tell you."

"Nor am I."

By the time McShane emerged from a wash and brush up, Rose was ladling thick beef stew filled with carrots, potatoes, and meat into some bowls. With his wet hair brushed back from his face, clean-shaven, and with his usual spicy scent accompanying him, McShane took his place at the table and rubbed his palms together in anticipation.

"This looks wonderful Rose," he told her with one of his rare smiles. "How'd ya manage the bread?"

Rose blushed with pleasure. "I got it from a little bakery down the street."

Lilly sighed. Was there any woman on the planet he could not win over if he set his mind to it? Most would say that McShane was more ruggedly attractive than traditionally handsome. Even so, his were the kind of looks that challenged women. The dangerous kind that dared them to believe the lie in his eyes that said she was the one he had been looking for. The only one who could complete him...save him. In short, Cadence McShane was the embodiment of the sort of man she had sworn to avoid after Timothy Warner had tricked her into a sham marriage.

Yet, like it or not, Kate Long's blood ran through Lilly's veins, making her as susceptible as the next woman to a charming smile and a polished line. Thanks be to God McShane was usually all business. There were times, though, when a situation warranted that he turned on the charm. His tactics often made her heart beat faster, but she was discerning enough to recognize them for what they were.

Much harder to resist were the scarce moments she caught brief glimpses of what she called the true McShane. Seeing him having a tea party with his nieces, watching him talking earnestly to Robbie, the abandoned lad he had rescued from the streets...those were the moments she guarded against, the truly hazardous moments when she realized that with the slightest effort he could take and break her heart.

She knew he had all the masculine needs Leo Bertolini spoke of, but for the most part, he seemed unaware of her as a woman. She understood. Deep inside he still grieved for his wife, Glenna. Still, they had one thing in common. One thing that bound them. They were both out for justice, and that suited Lilly just fine, especially since she needed to focus on the upcoming race and gathering information about J.D. Ames's death.

"What did you do today?" she asked Rose.

"Oh, the usual things one does when moving into a new area. I went around introducing myself to the neighborhood as it were, and letting people know that if they had no medical person on their team, I would be happy to help however I could. I shared my parsley with one of the others…Virginia Evans from here in Chicago. She's been Lady Jocelyn's cook for more than three years now."

She and McShane took their places at the table. "I wanted to see who was who and get a sense of what kind of people they are. Pierce says I have an uncanny way of seeing into the heart of a person."

"Indeed, you do," Lilly said. She tasted the stew. "Oh, Rose, this is delicious! I apologize for doubting you."

Again, Rose blushed with pleasure.

"Did you discover anything interesting?" McShane asked.

Rose donned a haughty expression and gave a scornful sniff, worthy of the stage anywhere. "Well, it's nothing but a bit of gossip, and not relevant to the case at all, but while I was visiting with Ginny, I met *Lady* Jocelyn in the flesh."

"And?" Lilly prompted.

"I was not impressed in the least. Ginny says she's difficult to work for, always short and spiteful. Being with the theater for many years, I know for a fact that she has no cause to put on airs. They say she's illegitimate, and she was an almost obscure actress in England before coming here." She took a bite of her stew. "But I do recall hearing that she married well."

Lilly frowned. "If that's true, why did she come to America and become an endurance walker?"

"Maybe they live separate lives for some reason or other," McShane ventured.

"That makes sense," Lilly said. "Does Ginny know anything about it?"

"If she does, she didn't say. She did tell me that the husband died shortly after they arrived in California. There seems to be some problem with the will, and Lady J. can't retire until it's settled."

"Another widow with money problems. Interesting," McShane said.

"So, we have no idea why she took up pedestrianism, but it appears that she's trapped in the circuit until she gets her money matters resolved," Lilly speculated. "Not that it excuses her behavior, but that would make most people resentful. Plus, she's getting older and knows her days in the sport are numbered."

"Do you suppose that's why she doesn't like Rosalie?" Rose asked.

"What do you mean?" Lilly dipped a piece of bread into the stew's thick gravy. "I was under the impression that the feud was between Jocelyn and Elsa. What does she have against Rosalie?"

"Well, it's more what Rosalie has against Jocelyn," Rose told them. "Apparently, Jocelyn and Leo were involved while they were in California."

"Good grief! The man must be insatiable!"

"Evidently." Rose gave a dismissive wave of her hand. "As for all the other, Leo has dealt with it."

McShane frowned. "What other?"

"Lady Jocelyn refusing to walk on the track at the same time as Elsa. Leo has worked it all out. Lady Jocelyn has agreed to walk at the same time as the others as long as she's allowed to walk in the opposite direction."

"And Elsa is agreeable?" McShane asked.

"I get the feeling that Lilly is right about Elsa's finances," Rose said. "I don't think she has much choice."

"That'll be a damn hotchpotch."

"Oh, I agree, Mr. McShane," Rose said, "but I don't think Lady Jocelyn really cares as long as she gets her way, and I'm of the opinion that getting her way is something she's quite good at."

"Call me Andrew," he urged, tearing off another bite of bread. "I don't suppose you have any idea how she convinced Leo."

"No, but I did see them talking on the street corner earlier when I went to get the bread."

"Could you hear what they were saying?"

"Not a word. At first, she seemed in a terrible bad humor, and he seemed... almost, well...seductive acting. I got the impression he was trying to soften her up."

McShane smiled his approval. "Well done, Rose. I believe Pierce is spot-on with his assessment of your talents. There is every chance that he was telling Lady Jocelyn whatever she wanted to hear to keep her from pulling out of the race. After all, he's partnering with Dora, and they both have a lot riding on its success."

"Do you think Mrs. Ames and Mr. Bertolini are in some sort of romantic attachment?"

Cade and Lilly exchanged a look. "We have no proof, but Lilly and I believe they are. The gossip is that he threw Jocelyn over for Dora soon after her husband died."

Rose's mouth dropped open in shock.

"You're doing a fantastic job, Rose. Just keep doing what you're doing. You're as likely as we are to stumble across something important."

"There is one more thing."

Lilly and McShane looked at her expectantly.

"That Elsa woman was out and about as well. In fact, she came up and introduced herself to me, which I thought was very nice, considering that most of the walkers are far too wrapped up in their self-importance to speak to the likes of me."

"Was she just being sociable, or did she want anything in particular?" McShane asked.

"She mentioned being worried about this race because she's been without a trainer since San Francisco."

Lilly recalled overhearing Dora ask Elsa about that the day she arrived. "Did she say what happened?"

"Well, it didn't make a lot of sense to me, but Ginny said her trainer, Jerome I think she called him, just up and left the day after Mr. Ames was found dead."

Very interesting. "And Ginny has no idea why?"

"No, but she says the theory floating around is that when Jerome heard that Dora didn't believe her husband killed himself, he was afraid the law might try to pin it on him."

"Why would they?"

"It seems there were hard feelings between him and Mr. Ames because he refused to let Jerome set up his bar during the big race. They argued, and then Mr. Ames turns up dead a few days later, and Jerome flies the coop."

"Leaving Elsa without a trainer."

Rose nodded.

"I'll have a word with her first thing in the morning," Cade said. "Who knows what I might find out?"

Chapter Six

As soon as he finished breakfast, Cade went in search of Elsa Dengler. He was anxious to make her further acquaintance and see if she might divulge something to give him fresh insight about what had happened in California.

"Mr. McShane," she said when he showed up at her tent. "How can I help you?"

"Rose told us about the loss of your trainer, and we all wanted to offer to help however we can."

She smiled, and the simple gesture lifted her plain countenance to one of almost prettiness. "I'm afraid my training has been hit or miss since Jerome walked out on me. I've done the best I could on my own, but I fear I will be sadly lacking."

She forced a slight laugh. "But, it's too late to vorry about it now." She stood aside. "Please come and sit. Vould you like a cup of coffee?"

"No thank you," Cade said, pulling out a chair for her and seating himself on the opposite side of the table.

He smiled. "My sister and I are new to this country, but from what we've heard about your past wins, I expect you will make an excellent showing."

"Thank you for that."

"I agree that it's too late for help with your training, but Rose, our medical associate, and I want you to know that we will be here to offer any advice or assistance, medical or otherwise that you might need, so long as the timing doesn't conflict with Lil's. If that were to happen, I'm certain Mr. Bertolini would be happy to step in and help out."

"Your offer is most kind, Mr. McShane, and I vill take you up on it if necessary, but my son arrived just this afternoon to assist me. He doesn't know much about the valks, but he can be trusted, and that's quite important in this sport."

"That's very true, from what I've heard," Cade said with a lift of his heavy eyebrows.

"As for Mr. Bertolini..." She sighed as if she were trying to gather the courage to speak. "Let me make myself clear, Mr. McShane. Rosalie is a rising star to whom God has given vhatever it takes to be a success at this game. Believe me when I tell you that there is no love lost between us. Ve are fierce competitors in a very demanding sport, and I vill do everything within my power to beat her on any given day. In my opinion, her husband has little to do with her success beyond his ability to get her into some very prestigious competitions. In fact, I feel that she vould be better off vithout him."

Cade managed a shocked expression. "Really? Why?"

"Because he keeps her stirred up all the time with his indiscretions. Just look at him and Mrs. Ames!"

Cade feigned wide-eyed surprise. "You don't think they—"

Elsa raised her fair eyebrows in query. "And you don't?" When he made no immediate answer, she continued, "Besides the fact that I don't like him much, his close affiliation with Dora keeps me from too much interaction with him."

"I don't understand."

"Surely you've heard that before his death, Dora's husband and I had a misunderstanding."

Cade hedged. "As I said, we haven't been here long. What kind of misunderstanding?"

"Jerome had negotiated a deal with J.D. saying that I vould be paid an appearance fee of two-hundred dollars whether or not I competed. Jocelyn Baldwin and I were his spectator draws, and I assume she negotiated the same sort of agreement."

When she said the former actress's name, Elsa looked as if she'd taken a bite of a green persimmon. After hearing her praise of La Bella Rosa and her abilities, the rivalry between Elsa and Jocelyn appeared to be more than just professional jealousy. It was something that needed sorting out.

"At the last minute, Jocelyn demanded she be allowed to change directions on the track vhenever she felt like it. J.D. agreed, as long as she had completed a full mile before doing so. She was the only competitor allowed that flexibility. Several of us felt it was unfair, and we complained to J.D. with no result. I felt as if I had been disrespected and decided I vould not compete."

"That's understandable."

"It wasn't so much that I minded that particular issue. What I minded, and still do, is that Jocelyn Baldwin thinks she can make demands that no one else can. And she does. Make no mistake about it, Mr. McShane, she gets vhat she wants one vay or the other. She always has."

Cade noticed the tightening of Elsa's mouth and wondered what else Lady Jocelyn had demanded and received.

"When I decided not to participate, I asked J.D. for my appearance money. Even though he knew the arrangement he and Jerome had made, he refused to give it to me unless I produced the contract. As my trainer, Jerome kept all the paperwork, and he'd left them here in Chicago. There vas no way I could produce it at that time, and J.D. refused to pay me. Now, Jerome is gone to God only knows where, J.D. is dead, and I vill never get that money."

She took a sip of the coffee sitting in front of her. "Looking back, I realize that he demanded the contract to buy time before paying me. With the embezzlement and the robbery, I doubt he could scrape up the money."

That made more sense than many things Cade had heard since being assigned this case.

Elsa took another sip of her coffee. "I must tell you that I vas surprised Dora allowed me to compete in this race, but as she said, I am still a considerable draw. She is a businesswoman, and my trouble vas vith her husband, not her."

"That's very magnanimous of her."

The corners of Elsa's mouth lifted in a dry smile. "I'm not sure I would go so far as to call Dora Ames magnanimous," she said. "I believe Leo had a hand in changing her attitude. There are many advantages in not making any unnecessary enemies in any business."

Cade laughed. "You're right. I've heard he's a very clever promotor."

"Indeed, he is, but perhaps now you see why his involvement with Dora makes me hesitant to ask him for help. I cannot chance anything untoward happening during this competition. I need no hint of scandal or gossip. This must be a clean race."

It seemed everyone wanted a clean race, but Elsa was unusually adamant about it. He wondered why. "I understand," he said. "You do know that Lady Jocelyn has arranged to do much the same thing here that she did in San Francisco?"

"What!"

He nodded. "I know for a fact that she told Leo she would not walk at the same time as you, and Dora let him know that she expected him to work something out. According to Rose, Jocelyn made a deal with Leo to walk the opposite direction as the rest of you, or she wouldn't walk at all. He agreed because they need her to pull in the spectators, just as they need you."

Cade felt like a gossiping old biddy, but that was fine. He needed information and alliances wherever he could find them, and he would do whatever it took to lead him to the truth about J.D. Ames's death.

"Vell, if that doesn't beat the Dutch," Elsa said, clearly disgusted. "I vonder what she had to do to get him to go along vith that."

Cade gave her a conspiratorial half-smile. "I couldn't say, ma'am."

He left his meeting with mixed feelings. He knew she was one of the prime suspects in J.D.'s death, and, though he hated to admit it, for good reason. He'd made up his mind to dislike the German pedestrian, but instead, he found himself weighing her actions and comments against the things he'd heard about her previous actions and behavior. He admitted that he was torn.

"Well, what do you think?" Lilly asked the moment he stepped inside the tent.

"I'm not sure what I think." He scraped a hand through his dark hair. "But I told Elsa that Rose and I would be happy to help her with her medical needs as long as they don't conflict with yours."

"Good. Did she say anything that might help us?"

"Not in so many words, but she made it quite clear that she loathes Lady Jocelyn as much as Lady J. does her. Surprisingly, she has a great deal of respect for Rosalie Bertolini, even though they are, in her words, fierce competitors."

"Any notion why?" Rose pressed.

"No. She did tell me what was behind her dropping out of the race in San Francisco. Her story makes more sense now that I have the particulars."

"Enlighten us, please," Lilly said, clasping her hands together.

"It seems Lady Jocelyn made a side deal with J.D. Ames that she could change directions walking anytime she chose, as long as she'd completed a full mile before doing so."

"Very much like the deal she's made with Leo," Lilly said, amazed at Jocelyn's ability to manipulate things to her advantage.

"Exactly. Elsa wasn't thrilled when I told her, and I'm wondering if she'll pull out of this race as well."

"Oh, no!" Lilly was emphatic. "There's no way she'll withdraw this time."

"Why do you say that?"

"First, she doesn't have a contract stating she'll be paid even if she doesn't participate, as she did in San Francisco, and frankly, I'm certain she needs the money."

* * *

Rose was adding some parsnips to a mutton stew when she heard her new friend's voice outside the tent. When she called for her to enter, Ginny stepped through the flap accompanied by a young man who looked as if he were still in his teens.

"Hello," she said, smiling at them both.

"Hello, Rose. I wanted you to meet Elsa's son, Penn."

"Nice to meet you, Penn," Rose said, chunking the parsnips up into the stew. "I'm Rose Wainwright."

"Ma'am."

"Elsa told me that you and Mr. McShane offered to help them out since she has no proper trainer," Ginny said. "She said that Penn should check with the both of you if he needed anything."

"Of course!" Rose dropped the last chunk of parsnip into the bubbling broth and wiped her damp hands on her apron. There was nothing fair in this old world it sometimes seemed, but whatever she could do to help she would. "What do you need?"

"Can you come and help me make an inventory of her foodstuffs and medicines?" Ginny asked. "Maybe the two of us can explain what he's to use for various problems his ma might be struck with during the race."

"Of course!"

"Many thanks to you, ma'am," the boy said with a shy smile.

Rose returned the smile and turned the gas beneath the cast-iron kettle down as low as it would go. "That should be all right until I get back, I think. If not, we'll be having burnt mutton stew for supper."

As she followed Ginny and Penn out of the tent and around the perimeter of the infield, Rose saw Lady Jocelyn headed toward them, walking the opposite direction as the others, even though it was just a practice session. The former actress was wearing a tailored white shirt, a long, plaid skirt, and was carrying a riding crop, as several men and women were accustomed to doing.

She strode around the track with a confident, loose-legged gait that seemed to eat up the distance and seemed focused on something inside her head, almost as if she were walking toward a destination that only she could see. Perhaps she was. The finish line.

The trio was almost to the Dengler tent when Lady Jocelyn came out of her wool-gathering and noticed them for the first time. Her dismissive gaze moved from Rose to Ginny, unimpressed. Then her arrogant inspection moved to Penn. For the span of a heartbeat, Rose would have sworn Jocelyn hesitated, midstride. She looked as if she'd seen a ghost. When her foot finally touched the track, she'd lost her rhythm, and it took a few steps to regain it. The incident, which lasted no more than a handful of seconds, was interesting. Neither Penn nor Ginny noticed the misstep or the expression in Lady Jocelyn's eyes, but it was something Rose wanted to find out more about.

* * *

Thirty minutes later, Rose and Ginny finished their inventory of Elsa's medical supplies and cooking provisions. They made a list, divvied it up, and told Penn they would be back with enough from their own stores to get him through a few days.

Rose was quiet on the walk back, thinking about the Denglers. The handsome boy with the dark-blond hair and blue eyes didn't look a day over sixteen and seemed quite uneasy in the unfamiliar surroundings. As she had watched him awkwardly trying to help, a long-suppressed pain filled her heart. The ache of losing three babies of her own, and the strange mixture of joy and sorrow when Pierce had brought Lilly to her to raise. Rose wasn't certain who was the most in need, herself or eleven-year-old Lilly. She wasn't certain she could do what Pierce asked of her, wasn't sure she wanted the daughter of a woman Rose knew still held a portion of her husband's heart.

She pushed the troubling memories aside. In the end, it worked out perfectly, and Penn Dengler and his situation had nothing to do with the past, but Rose sensed his uncertainty at being thrust into this situation to help his mother.

Poor Elsa! She was a suspect in J.D. Ames's death, had been cheated of her money in California. With her trainer run off to God knows where, a green stripling of a boy was the only person to help keep her in the race she needed so badly to win.

"He's a handsome lad, isn't he?" Ginny said, disrupting Rose's thoughts.

"He certainly is." Rose turned to look at her new friend. "Is he all she has, then?"

"Yes. Elsa dotes on him."

"I saw the daguerreotype of a man sitting on the chest by her cot. It's amazing how much he looks like his father."

"Isn't it? Wolfgang, her husband, died about three years back. It's said Elsa loved him dearly, and it's been hard on her, providing for herself and the boy, especially since the Ameses cheated her of the money she was promised."

"You believe she did have a contract, then, even though she's never produced it?"

Ginny's shoulders lifting in an offhand shrug. "I've no way of knowing for certain and probably never will, but it's a common enough addition to a contract."

"I see." Afraid she might seem too interested in Elsa's past, Rose asked, "How do you like working for Lady Jocelyn?"

"I can't say it's the best job I've ever had, but since she's mostly gone once the races start, I can handle what she dishes out when she is around. What about you? How are the McShanes to work for?"

Tit for tat, Rose reasoned. "Well, McShane is a tad gruff and wants things done the way he wants them, but he's fair, and he cares for his sister and that's the most important thing, isn't it?" She turned to look at Ginny. "I've been wondering about something ever since you mentioned that Lady Jocelyn married well."

"Yes?"

"If she married well, why on earth did she leave Germany and come to America to compete in pedestrian races?"

Ginny grimaced. "Her reasons are anyone's guess. She isn't the type to take those she considers beneath her into her confidence, but thankfully for me, I hear that she's been far more successful at endurance racing than she ever was while treading the boards."

Sunday

Since the race was scheduled to begin at midnight, Lilly had the day off so that she would be fresh starting out. Accustomed to being kept busy with her training, she felt at loose ends. How did the other walkers spend the hours before the race? Were they comfortable waiting for things to get underway? Nervous? What? After finishing her breakfast, she carried her coffee and a chair outside the tent and watched the community of contestants wake up and begin their day.

Dora Ames was already out and about, laughing at something one of the band members said, conferring with the officials, pointing to things she approved of or those that did not meet her standards. Final arrangements. In every instance, she appeared sharp, confident, and in complete control, and even though Dora wasn't particularly likeable, those were traits Lilly aspired to.

She was surprised when Dora saw her, waved, smiled, and started in her direction. What on earth could she want? Whatever it was, she needed to be ready in her 'walker' persona.

"Are you getting nervous?" Dora asked.

"I suppose so. Andrew says I should be resting, but my mind won't shut down."

"I can only imagine."

"I want to thank you for all your hard work," Lilly said. "I have tremendous admiration for the way you've continued on after the death of your husband."

Lilly saw that her praise came as something of a shock to Dora. "I know it must be hard for a woman tryin' to make her way in a man's world."

"Thank you, Lil," Dora said. "And you're right. It is."

"I don't mean to be presumptuous, but would you be so kind as to answer some questions about owning a company?" She smiled, winningly, she hoped. "That's my dream. I want to open a shop that sells Irish lace and knitted clothing back in Ennis one day. My brother thinks it's a terrible idea, but..."

To Lilly's surprise, Dora laughed. "Oh, I don't doubt it! For some reason, men cannot tolerate women invading territory that they perceive as theirs. Just like these races. The fact that women are making names for themselves and that some have bested men at their game is intolerable." She looped her arm through Lilly's, and they began to stroll around the infield. "What is it you'd like to know?"

Evidently, Lilly had struck the right note. "Thank you, Mrs. Ames. I understand that you helped your husband with this endeavor before his... death."

66

"That's true. I took on any and every job he asked of me, even the accounting. Of course, you know that women are notoriously witless when it comes to the sciences and mathematics."

They shared a laugh.

"And Mr. Bertolini? Has he been helpful as well? I mean, I guess I'm asking if there is a place for a man in a company if the woman is the boss? Like Andrew."

"Oh, certainly! Andrew seems very clever and hardworking, and I'm sure he has much to offer, but he must be willing to cede control to you, or what would be the purpose? And yes, Leo has been a tremendous help, especially since he is so familiar with all areas of endurance walking."

"We heard that he tried to buy out you and your husband before his death." Lilly threw out the comment hoping Dora would rise to the bait and offer a piece of information she didn't have.

Instead, Dora pinned Lilly with a severe look. "There must be a lot of gossip among the walkers."

Lilly gave a helpless shrug. "It's a relatively small group, ma'am, and we're stuck with each other for long periods of time. There's bound to be talk about all and sundry."

"I suppose that's true, but I despise blabbermouths! It's hard to believe that even after all this time, we are still a favorite topic of conversation." She turned to Lilly. "Did you also hear that our accountant was caught embezzling money from the business and that he is responsible for the break-in we had a few weeks before J.D.'s death?"

Taken aback by the brutal honesty, Lilly sidestepped the question. "No! Was he ever brought to trial?"

"No one has been able to locate him. We've heard rumors that he went back east, but no one has any idea where he is." She turned to Lilly once more. "Since the gossipmongers are so busy, you've probably also heard that I don't believe in the police theory that J.D. committed suicide."

"What?" Though she and McShane had heard a shortened version of what happened in San Francisco from William, Lilly wanted to hear Dora's account. She summoned a puzzled expression. "So, are you thinkin' this accountant could be responsible for your husband's death, as well?"

"It's something I've seriously considered. Are you aware that Elsa threatened J.D. and that her trainer and the accountant are brothers?"

Lilly raised her eyebrows, as if the information Rose had already given them intrigued her.

"Oh, yes. Something along the lines that J.D. would pay one way or the other. Even more interesting is the fact that her trainer disappeared just hours after my husband's death, and no one has seen or heard from him since," Dora added.

Lilly didn't reply for long moments, hoping to give the impression that she was trying to come to grips with everything she'd heard.

"This trainer of Elsa's," she said at last, "I can see why you might think he had something to do with your husband's death, but you must believe Elsa is innocent, or you wouldn't have allowed her to enter this race."

Dora's smile was downright cynical. "On the contrary, dear, I think there is every possibility that she could be involved, and there are three very important reasons behind my accepting her presence."

She ticked off the reasons as she spoke. "One, she had the entry fee. Two, the fans are quite in love with her story, and three, I need this race to be the achievement of the year."

Her brief laughter was laced with bitterness. "I'd deal with the devil himself if it would guarantee me a success. And you know what they say…keep your friends close and your enemies closer."

Then, as if she realized she had revealed too much of what was going on, both in her mind and in her life, she laughed again, a gay sound that belied the seriousness of their conversation.

"Besides, contrary to my fanciful imaginings, the police are quite convinced it was a suicide, so it would be strange if I forbade her to participate. It makes more business sense to let bygones be bygones."

"Is that why you decided to partner with Mr. Bertolini?"

Dora gave her a sharp look. Her tone was even sharper. "I beg your pardon?"

Lilly's heart missed a beat. Had she gone too far? In her eagerness to find our more, had she crossed the line from innocent curiosity to impropriety?

"I'm just having a hard time understanding," she said, using her most troubled tone and praying her acting skills would hold her in good stead. Did she sound enough like a confused young woman who knew little of life and nothing of the business world?

"Understanding what, exactly?" Dora's tone had lost its friendliness.

"Why you would partner with him if you thought he was taking advantage of your misfortune."

The widow seemed to ponder that, and as she did, Lilly saw her relax visibly.

"As we've discussed, a woman running a venture as large as this meets unexpected obstacles now and again. Though I helped J.D. in many areas, I had no experience in others.

"Leo knows his way around pedestrianism. He's been able to open several doors for me that might not have opened otherwise. He has experience and a wife with the talent to pack the house. He also has available cash." Her smile was unapologetic. "You might say I had little choice."

Chapter Seven

Sunday

When Lilly and Cade walked out of the tent at five minutes before midnight, she could hardly believe what she was seeing. All the walkers and trainers, along with the judges and scorekeepers were gathered on or near the track, waiting for the rules to be announced and the race to get underway.

The closer it drew to starting time, the louder the arena became. Helping to generate a festive spirit, the band had started playing a good half hour earlier, and the hum of voices grew louder as hundreds of conversations melded with the music into one unified murmur.

Lilly's first choice of costume, provided by the intrepid Harris, was vivid purple tights and a thigh-length dress with lace ruffles at the bottom and wrists. A wide belt of black cowhide with a paste jeweled buckle and her dreadful boots completed the ensemble. The get-up was positively hideous and clashed with her hair but, as Harris had argued, its very conspicuousness guaranteed visibility, and that was something she needed if she were to establish any sort of following as a new walker.

Her nerves were wound as tightly as a guitar string. The closer it grew to midnight, the jumpier and more irritable she became. Afraid that seeing all the spectators, many who had come hours before the race was scheduled to begin, would cause even more anxiety, she had stayed inside the tent and tried to sleep, but with the increasing drone of noise, it was an effort in futility.

Now, as she took in the spectacle of it all, she realized she'd had no real idea what the event would be like. It was one thing to hear that the dais could hold three thousand or more people, but seeing them crowded together, elbowing their way toward the tables near the railing as they vied for the best locations, was altogether different than anything she had envisioned.

The spectators were a mix of young and old, rich and not-so-rich. Anyone who could afford the fifty-cent gate fee—which some claimed was too much considering the venue—was welcome to attend. A few ragged-looking individuals leaned against the railing, looking as if they couldn't afford their next meal much less the price to enter the doors. There were ladies wearing the latest fashions showcased in *Godey's* and men wearing suits from Messrs. Brooks, Brothers.

Dora had explained that when the first arrivals grew weary of watching and trundled off to bed at some time in the wee hours, the laborers would begin arriving, lunch boxes in hand, hoping to catch a bit of the action before heading off to work.

Later in the morning, the more affluent ladies would arise, dress for a day of doing little to nothing, and come watch until that, too, began to bore them. Afternoons and early evenings were the most popular times for families, a rare and special treat for the missus and youngsters before returning home to their unpretentious dwellings and the daily grind of their lives.

Already, a thin haze of smoke floated up toward the arched supports, and the scents of dozens of tobacco roll-ups drifted through the air. What would it be like in six days? Would the crowd be able to draw a decent breath?

Since Palmers was smaller than many of the more prestigious venues, most of the additional attractions designed to encourage more spending were set up in tents out back of the rink near the boxing, portable bar, and church tents McShane had shown her earlier. There was now a place for card games, an apothecary, and a minstrel show. Food vendors were scattered about, providing a variety of treats including peanuts, ice cream, fruits, and candy. There was even a small area set up near one of the grog shops where bookmakers took bets on everything from who would win the race to who would drop out and what day. Sometimes why. It baffled the mind.

In their desire to make this a spectacular debut, Dora and Leo had decided to make things 'fair' by having each of the twelve pedestrians draw for their starting place on the track. The lineup would matter little once they began to accumulate laps and miles, but after the abject failure in San Francisco and the questions that still surrounded her husband's death, Dora was insistent that this competition be seen as above reproach in every way.

Finally, after what seemed an hour of waiting, one of the judges announced the lineup and the rules to both spectators and contestants. The race would be walked counterclockwise with the exception of Lady Jocelyn Baldwin who had somehow convinced Leo to allow her to walk in the opposite direction. The judges had concurred. Now the lady waved enthusiastically at the crowd and they responded with roars of approval or boos, depending on who was rooting for her.

Contrary to some races, where "go as you please" was allowed, these contestants would not be allowed to jog, run, skip or sprint as was popular in Britain. Only "fair heel to toe" walking was allowed, meaning one foot must be on the ground at all times. Judges would be watching to ensure that the contestants conformed. Other officials kept track of how many rounds each walker made until they completed a mile. Only then would that mile be posted so the audience could keep track of their progress.

With the rules established, each contestant was introduced to the crowd. Once again, much was made over Lady Jocelyn as well as Elsa Dengler and La Bella Rosa. Lilly was introduced as Lil McShane, an up-and-coming Irish lass with three very competitive races in Dublin and County Clare, Ireland, to her credit.

Even though her stomach churned, Lilly concentrated on using the acting skills she had come to depend on whenever she had no idea what to do. Smiling widely, she waved both arms above her head, bounced up and down a couple of times, and performed a handspring, something she'd learned from Monstery. Then, turning in a circle, she blew kisses to the audience with both hands.

The cheers were loud and plentiful, reminding her of the times she had bowed with her fellow actors to a standing ovation after performing on stage. The adulation went to her head like a glass of the finest champagne. Perhaps she *would* garner herself a few fans along the way!

Smiling broadly, she glanced at McShane who was regarding her with a puzzled expression. "What exactly was that little sister?" he said, leaning nearer.

She turned to look at him. He was far too close. "That, dear brother, was the birth of Lil McShane, pedestrienne. She is trying to get her share of fans from this motley group. Surely there are some who have no favorite as yet."

"Am I to expect more of the same throughout the race?"

"Indeed, you are."

He smiled then, one of those rare smiles that did extraordinary things to his usually somber face, especially his eyes. During these infrequent times, there was no wariness there, no guarded expression, no evasiveness, nothing that said he was weighing a dozen different options and considering which was the best to enact. There was nothing but indulgence and a hint of humor in those blue depths. Suddenly unable to breathe, Lilly looked away.

In a matter of moments, the trainers and non-racers were asked to step away from the track, the judges took their positions, and the walkers found their places. As Lilly took her spot, she looked to see who was on either side. To her left was a tall, lanky girl of about sixteen, with hair so blonde it was almost white. Lilly thought her name was Marta. Lilly smiled at the girl and wished her luck. Shel frowned and looked away without speaking.

To Lilly's right was an older woman as stocky as Marta was angular. Arlene was from a small town in Arkansas. She smiled and held out her hand. The two women shook hands and wished each other well, and then they were instructed to get ready, get set…

"Go!"

Marta broke in tandem with some others in the lineup, getting an early lead, while Lilly, Arlene, and Elsa started a bit more slowly, amid groans from the crowd. Still, six days was a very long time. You would think the spectators would give them a bit of sympathy.

For the first fifteen minutes, Lilly was acutely aware of everything going on around her. Fans leaned over the railing, hoping to reach out and touch their favorite star or at least speak to them...the band drowned out everything but the voices nearest her. The sick feeling had passed, but the nervousness still gnawed like acid in her stomach. Six days. How could she do it?

She couldn't.

Thoughts raced willy-nilly through her head, one after the other. Random. Fragmented. Tumbling through her mind like a circus performer, but not at all funny. She would make a mess of things and would probably have to withdraw before making any kind of a showing. McShane, and more importantly, William, would be disappointed in her, and she was still on probation at the agency, and she would have failed all the women out there she longed to help, and she had realized that she loved the work as much as it troubled her and there was no way she could go back to live with Pierce and Rose with her tail tucked between her legs.... Crazy, random thoughts.

Her mind wandered back to her first assignment and how she had managed to solve a twenty-year-old crime with no real knowledge about how to go about it. And again, in Louisiana and Texas. Of course, she'd had McShane to fall back on then. Still, she had done some improbable things, faced some impossible odds for a woman who had been brought up in a relatively cloistered environment and had little interaction with the world beyond a traveling theater troupe. How had she managed?

One day at a time. The little voice inside her whispered the answer. One clue at a time. One step at a time. Often there had been nothing to keep her going but her insatiable curiosity and her stubborn determination.

She'd done it before, and she could do it again. Somehow, she would dredge up every bit of acting skill she possessed, every move and trick that McShane and Monstery had taught her. She would give this assignment all that she had and find it in her heart to give more.

Feeling somewhat better about things, she looked up at the scoring and saw that she had already walked two miles. Not only that, but she had found her rhythm, a nice brisk pace, much like the one she had found while walking with Cade.

One step at a time.

74

Chapter Eight

Monday

A look at the huge clock on the wall above the band said it was approaching six a.m. As Dora predicted, the crowd had thinned out as the spectators grew weary and went home to their comfortable beds, but still there were hundreds leaning against the railing, calling out to their favorites as they passed and jeering those they had bet against.

Lilly realized she was starving and needed to find a chamber pot. She hadn't had anything of substance to eat since supper the evening before and had kept up her energy by drinking mugs of cold milk and beef tea that Rose prepared and McShane handed her as she passed, drinking it on the run. Or walk. She had only stopped for brief intervals since the race started at midnight.

Too excited to rest before the competition began, sleepiness, the bane of pedestrians everywhere, had begun to creep in. She couldn't feel her legs anymore, and her feet were like bricks mortared to the ends of them.

A glance at the status board showed that she was in the top five. It was no surprise that La Bella Rosa was in the lead and that Elsa and Lady Jocelyn held the second and third spots. Marta was in fourth place, and Lilly was trailing the unfriendly Swede by two miles. Still, fifth place was not so terrible for someone who hadn't the slightest idea of what was going on.

"Out of the way!"

The words were hissed into her ear and she was bumped hard by someone

75

passing. Staggering forward in an effort to maintain her balance, Lilly sprawled face-first onto the track. Overcome with humiliation, she looked up and saw that the culprit was young Marta, who smiled maliciously over her shoulder.

The crowd reacted with boos, curses, and all sorts of name-calling. Many were shouting, "C'mon, Lil!" "Get up, lass!" and "Don't let her do that to you!"

Why on earth *had* she done it? Lilly wondered as she pushed to her feet to the roaring of the crowd. She felt something on her chin, gave it a swipe with her fingers, and saw that her lip was bleeding. She'd torn a hole in her tights, so no doubt her knee was scraped as well. A group of walkers skirted her in passing, and she wanted nothing more than to go to her tent and cry for an hour or so. Instead, knowing there were fans rooting for her, she gathered new determination. She couldn't let them down. Not over something so trivial. Drawing a deep breath, she smiled, waved, and blew kisses.

Amid a storm of cheers, the piano player began to play a better-than-fair rendition of "I'll Take You Home Again, Kathleen," an Irish favorite that had been written some few years earlier. Making a show of dusting off her costume, she was soon back in her natural rhythm. With a bit of luck, she had a few more rounds in her before she stopped for a rest.

With her focus disrupted, she became aware of deep, masculine laughter that caught not only her attention but that of several spectators who had turned toward the sound. It came from a handsome man sitting at the rail, talking to an older, just as attractive, gentleman. Both looked tall and elegantly slender.

The younger man wore a stylish, gray-striped ascot tied loosely at the throat of a blindingly white shirt of finest lawn. His charcoal-gray trousers and silvery gray silk vest were worn with casual self-possession. It was easy to see that he was unconcerned that being hatless and coatless defied convention. Mesmerized by his appearance, Lilly forgot her hunger and her need for the necessary. She was no longer aware of the aches and pains that had begun to plague her. Or that her steps had slowed.

The unknown man's tawny blond hair was worn a bit too long to be in style and looked free of pomade. It begged for a woman's fingers to be threaded through it she thought, and immediately chastised herself for the improper, errant thought. He was clean-shaven but for a trimmed mustache slightly darker than his hair. Deep grooves scored his lean cheeks. His nose was strong and straight, his chin rounded and tilted in unmistakable confidence.

She had often heard the term "to the manor born," but until this moment, she'd had no idea what it meant. With a burst of annoyance, she acknowledged that he was a handsome devil and no doubt knew it. She picked up her pace once more.

Just then, he lifted his right hand and took a puff from his cigar. The ring he wore flashed in the light. Her breath caught. She stopped where she was. Her mother's killer had worn a ring of gold and onyx and diamonds. Lilly, who had been hiding beneath the bed during the whole of Kate's lover's visit, had seen it as her assailant groped beneath the bed in search of his boot.

She needed to get a closer look at that ring. Without a thought to the race, she quickened her pace and was soon no more than five feet from him. He was every bit as fine-looking up close as he was from afar. As she drew nearer, his gaze shifted from his companion to her. Were it not too ridiculous to consider, she would swear she saw recognition in his golden-brown eyes. To her astonishment, he switched his cigar to the other hand and crooked a finger at her, urging her closer still.

Of all the nerve! Surely, he could tell that she was not some unsophisticated young thing to be flattered by his attention. But she *was* flattered. Breathless. And very much aware that she was a woman and not just a Pinkerton operative.

Not since meeting Tim Warner had she been so mindful of her mother's blood running hotly in her veins. Well, perhaps now and again with McShane, but he had no interest in her as a woman and besides, they were partners, so whatever rare feelings she sometimes experienced did not mean a thing.

Instead of obeying the stranger's cavalier command as she was inclined to do, she passed his table with her head held high. He laughed again. On her third round, he called, "Hey, Lil! Don't I know you from somewhere?"

That got her attention.

His tone was teasing, but the earnestness in his eyes was real and hard to ignore. She *hadn't* imagined the recognition she'd seen earlier! When she passed him again, he pulled a bill from his wallet and handed it to his friend. Lilly seethed. They had actually bet on whether or not she would stop and talk to him! She fumed as she made another two trips around the ring, never once giving him the satisfaction of a glance. Instead, she thought about his comment.

Did he really think he knew her or was that a ploy to get her to approach him? Where would they have met? Or even seen each other? They certainly did not mingle in the same social circles. Had it been when she and McShane were in Louisiana? Or as they travelled down the Mississippi on the riverboat?

No. She had not the slightest recollection of running into the stranger at either of those places, and he was not the kind of man easily forgotten. It could have been here in the city. Wealthy young men flocked to Monstery's *salle de arms,* which was the closest she'd ever come to rubbing elbows with the *crème de la crème* of Chicago society. No, she was positive she'd never seen him.

On her fourth-round since spotting the stranger, he called out to her again. The spectators around him were looking from her to him, their curiosity piqued by their back-and-forth banter. At that moment, she and the stranger held more interest than the race to those nearest him.

A man standing behind the stranger pulled a bill from his wallet, waved it at Lilly, and gestured for her to approach the table, indicating that he would give her the money if she did. This time, she took her courage in hand and angled across the track toward the group. Stopping at the railing, she stood staring at the stranger in silent insolence while his gaze moved over her face in a thorough assessment.

Untried though she might be in ways of the world, she was sophisticated enough to know that he liked what he saw. She liked that he did.

"Hello, Miss McShane."

His voice was smooth, deep, and easy on the ear, much like Pierce's. His

78

tawny eyes were surrounded by thick, gold-tipped eyelashes and there were fine crow's feet at the corners, as if he spent a lot of time outside, squinting in the sun or a lot of time laughing. He didn't look the type for either.

"Hullo." Just in time, she remembered her Irish accent. It was imperative that she stay in character.

He propped his elbow on the table and rested his chin in his hand. The smoke from his cigar spiraled upward. "Have we met?"

She mustered the audacity to smile at him. "Not unless you've been to Ennis, County Clare, Ireland."

She risked a glance at his hand, hoping to get a better look at the ring. Without doubt, it was a signet ring in a square setting, but it was hard to make out the design. Without closer examination, it was impossible to tell if the fancy scrollwork was a 'T' or an intricate 'F'.

"I have not," he told her with a rueful shake of his head.

"Then I guess we haven't."

It didn't escape her notice that the people surrounding the table were more than curious about their conversation.

"Have dinner with me."

Not a question. A demand. One that shocked her. Flustered her. "I'm sorry, sir," she said, wrinkling her nose at him flirtatiously. "In case you haven't noticed, I'm a trifle busy at the moment."

"Later then?" The query was accompanied by a questioning lift of his brows.

It was all she could do to draw her next breath. "I can't think about later until later."

"What in bloody hell are you doing, Lil?"

The angry question was yelled over the roar of the crowd. McShane stood across from the stranger's table inside the track's infield. His hands rested on his hips, and his face wore a disgusted expression. Her return to reality was instant and painful.

What *was* she doing? Giving the unknown man a slight smile, she reached between him and his older friend and snatched the bill from the hand of the man who'd lured her over with its promise. For a moment he looked shocked, and then everyone started laughing, including Lilly, who waved it at him and stuffed it into her pocket. Then she was back on the track. She made another three rounds, finishing another mile, and then left the track for a much-needed break.

Lilly entered the tent, told Rose and McShane to leave for a moment, and heeded Mother Nature's call. Then she bathed her face with cold water, collapsed on the cot, and called her friends back inside. Immediately, McShane dropped to his knees, pulled off her boots and socks, and turned her feet this way and that, looking for blisters.

"Nothing yet," he told her with a touch of pride. "The two pair of socks are giving you some protection, I guess. How are you feeling?"

"Sleepy. Hungry."

He got her some fresh socks and changed her shoes to the leather ones similar to those worn by Ella Hattan, whose picture Lilly had seen at Monstery's.

"Here you go," Rose said, handing her a plate with two fried eggs, a thick slice of brown bread toasted in the cast-iron skillet, a few orange slices, and beef tea made from the Liebigs extract that would be a mainstay of her diet until the end.

"Do you hurt anywhere?" McShane asked.

"Other than all over?" she countered, taking a small forkful of eggs and pronouncing them delicious.

"I'm serious. Is anything specific bothering ya?"

"Not yet."

"Good. Ya haven't time to be dilly-dallying with your food, lass. There's no time for manners. Get it down as fast as you can so you can get back out on the track. You're doin' well but watch that Marta girl. She's up to no good."

"I know. Why do you think she made me fall?" Lilly asked, taking a huge bite of toast and chewing as fast as she could.

"Other than meanness, I couldn't say, but I've noticed her hanging around La Bella Rosa ever since we got here," McShane offered.

"So?"

He shrugged. "So, I have no idea, except that Rosalie isn't a fan of yours, and if they're friends maybe Marta is willing to do things for Rosalie that she can't bring herself to do."

"Andrew has a point, Lil," Rose offered. "You're pretty, and from that conversation you overheard, it sounds like La Bella Rosa thinks her rotten husband is trying to add you to his list of conquests. He has been showing you a lot of…oh! Your poor lip! Is it hurting?"

Lilly snorted in disgust. "Only when I take huge bites. Ouch, that's too tight!" she complained, forcing McShane to loosen the laces somewhat.

"Better?"

"Better," she said, talking around a mouthful of food that, had it been any other time, she might have gotten her jaws slapped for doing.

"By the by, who in blazes was that bloke from the audience you stopped to chat with?"

His voice dripped disapproval. "No one special. He called me over."

He glanced up from tying her shoe. "So, do ya plan to stop for every man who speaks to ya?"

"Of course not!"

"Good, because I'll bet my next paycheck that he's got his money on one of the others and was just trying to distract you."

Lilly's heart sank. She had been so caught up in the stranger's looks and the fact that he was convinced that he knew her that she hadn't thought of much else. "I don't think so. He said he thought he knew me from somewhere." Another bite of eggs went in and she yelped at the sting of her lip.

"I'll put some bag balm on it before you go back out," Rose said. "Do you want to change outfits yet?"

"Not yet," Lilly said, her weary mind struggling with keeping up with two totally different conversations.

"And you believed him?" McShane asked. "You've got a lot of learnin' to do about men, Lilly. Hurry and finish those eggs."

"He's right, Lil," Rose chimed in.

Something she was acutely aware of. Her lack of sophistication about the workings of the world was exactly the reason William Pinkerton had stuck her with McShane for the foreseeable future.

Wishful thinking and flattery aside, there had been something about the unknown man that persuaded her he was being truthful. A gut feeling. Women's intuition. Or perhaps she was fooling herself again, just as she'd done with Timothy. Just as McShane feared.

The best course of action was to Listen to McShane, at least until the race was over or she dropped out. If the stranger was still hanging around and she felt like pursuing her interest in his ring—and him—she would be free to do so, with or without her partner's blessing. Right now, her focus had to be on doing her best in the race and getting answers for Dora Ames.

"I really am getting sleepy."

"And I'm sorry about that. Truly." He sounded anything but.

"I've been awake more than twenty-four hours," she reminded him.

"I know, but you have to keep going. Walk faster if you can. You need to make up those miles Marta is ahead of you."

"I think you're trying to kill me, so you won't have to be my partner anymore." She was only partly teasing.

"Nah, lass," he said with one of his audacious winks. He tucked a loose strand of hair behind her ear. "Remember it isn't called a cruel tramp fer no reason."

Blinking back a ridiculous rush of tears, she mopped up the last bit of yolk with the remainder of the bread and dropped it into the cup of broth which she gulped down like a person gone too long without water. Then she scooped up the soggy bread with a spoon, plopped it into her mouth, and stood.

Her legs buckled. If McShane had not been there to catch her, she would have fallen.

"What's the matter?" he asked.

Unable to straighten properly, she said, "I think all my muscles stiffened up while I was sitting."

"Aye. That'll happen. The best thing to do is walk it out."

She glared at him but knew he was right. He gave her a phony smile of encouragement and, throwing an arm around her shoulders guided her out of the tent. "Off ya go, lass. Have a care."

Lilly literally made a growling noise that caused his smile to widen. And then she limped back onto the track.

Chapter Nine

"Go on with you." Rose's simple command was directed at McShane, who, an hour later, was pacing outside the front of the tent. It was what people had done since the beginning of time to while away boredom or help stretches of worry to pass.

"What?"

"You heard me. I'm not thick. You can't stand being idle, so go detect or whatever it is you and Lil do. I'll wait here in case she comes off the track."

Cade took her by the shoulders and planted a kiss on her forehead. "Thank you. Rose. I'll try not to be too long."

She pushed him away, but her cheeks were aflame with embarrassment and delight. "Enough of that nonsense. Go!"

Cade wasn't sure where he was going or who he wanted to talk to, but Rose was right. Sitting around and waiting for something to happen was not his way. He crossed the infield of the rink and the track itself and made his way through the throng on the platform, straight toward Dora's office. A complaint about Marta's conduct was as good a conversation opener as anything, and maybe he could steer the talk around to something more meaningful.

He was about to knock when he heard a man's voice. Pausing outside the office, he leaned against the wall, doing his best to look as if he were waiting for entrance instead of eavesdropping.

"It seems I can do nothing right." The masculine voice sounded irritated. Leo.

"You know that isn't true, but I don't understand why you agreed to let

Lady Jocelyn walk in the opposite direction. You saw how disgruntled it made the spectators, not to mention the other walkers," Dora said. "They feel as if she got special consideration."

"Jocelyn refused to walk on the track at the same time as Elsa. You told me we needed them both to draw in an audience and to fix it, so I did. As far as the spectators being unhappy, has anyone asked for their money back?"

"Of course not."

"And they won't." Silence reigned for a moment, and then in a softer tone, Leo said, "Neither will the walkers. There's too much at stake. When are you going to realize that these petty jealousies only add to the enjoyment of the races? Even the fans love all the drama."

"Perhaps you're right." Dora's voice was softer, too.

"I know I'm right. Now come and let me kiss those worry lines from your forehead."

Cade could only imagine what was happening to turn the lady from an angry termagant to what sounded like a purring feline. Both he and Lilly suspected something going on between the two, but now there was little doubt in his mind that they were right. Fleetingly, he wondered how this new information played into their theory that Leo might have something to do with J.D. Ames's death.

"I do wonder what she did to influence you," Dora said after a lengthy silence.

"You're always saying to keep your friends close and your enemies closer," Leo reminded with a low laugh.

"Not *that* close," Dora grumbled, and then there was silence again. Figuring he had heard all he was going to hear on that subject and unwilling to wait until they finished whatever they were about to do, Cade shifted from the wall and knocked loudly on the door.

It opened a few seconds later. Dora stood there, a pleasant expression of curiosity on her face. Other than her slightly mussed hair, she showed no sign of having been moments away from engaging in an extramarital activity with Bertolini. Leo sat on a worn sofa with his legs crossed, examining a stack of papers, as if he'd been busy doing that all along.

"Is there something I can help you with, Mr. McShane?" Dora asked, stepping aside for him to enter.

Cade adopted an air of embarrassment. "Well, ma'am, usually I'm not one to complain, and I feel like a tattletale for saying anything, but Marta Dolk passed Lil a bit ago and deliberately ran into her. Lil fell and bloodied her lip. P'raps you heard the audience complaining."

"I did hear some commotion," Leo said, "but Dora and I were going over some things and I didn't take time to check it out."

"I know you're a busy man, sir, and that a lot of things go on out there that you have no control over. What concerned me is that she was so obvious about it."

"I'll talk with her people," Leo said. "That kind of behavior is uncalled for and unacceptable."

"Thank you. Lil is relatively new to the sport, and I feel she has some potential, but she's not accustomed to such behavior, being as she walks against her own times for the most part. And, well, all these personal contentions are a bit upsetting to her. For the life of me, I can't understand why the Dolk girl would want to do harm to Lil."

"I have to sound insensitive, Mr. McShane," Dora said, "but endurance walking is a highly competitive sport. The sooner your sister accepts and adjusts to that, the sooner she will find her footing. The older walkers worry about the younger ones coming along and knocking them off their pedestals, and the young ones are trying to carve out a niche for themselves among the established walkers."

She shrugged. "It all works itself out in the end. The weak fall by the wayside and the strong build race by race. If that's Lil's goal, she needs to toughen up."

Cade nodded though he looked unconvinced.

"Have no fear, Mr. McShane," Dora said, placing her hand on his arm and looking up at him with blatant invitation in her eyes. "We will look into it."

"Thank you."

She gave his forearm a squeeze before releasing him. "I want you to be satisfied that everything possible is being done to make our competitors

86

happy. Please let me know if there's any way I can accommodate you."

Good Lord above!

By six p.m., after being on the track for twelve hours, McShane took pity on Lilly and agreed to grant her a few moment's rest.

She staggered into the tent and almost fell into his arms. The sweet scents of dozens of species of flowers assaulted her. Her glazed expression moved around the tent. Vases of multi-colored blooms—so many she couldn't count them—sat on every available surface and even in the corners of the tent. Her frowning gaze moved to McShane. "Have I died?"

He had the audacity to laugh. "Not yet, lass," he said, leading her to her cot. "I think you've got a few more miles in ya yet."

The look she gave him designated him to the hottest regions of hell. Rose stripped her down to her chemise and covered her with a blanket. McShane pulled off her shoes and socks and examined her feet. There were no blisters, but they were swollen twice their size. Depending on what shoes she wanted to change into, it might be time to try the whiskey-in-the-shoes remedy.

Anticipating her muscles seizing again, he gave her bare legs a brisk rubbing with Watkins liniment. When he reached her knees, Rose gave him a slight push, and he moved aside with a wry smile. She had no intention of allowing him to take any kind of liberties with her charge, no matter what the circumstances might be. Lilly, who was already asleep and snoring softly, never moved.

* * *

He awakened her twenty minutes later by lightly slapping her face with a cold cloth. She bolted upright, moaning and cursing. "What coarse language to be coming from such a pretty mouth. What will it be next, I wonder?"

"Drinking?" she shot back, looking him square in the eye. "Or perhaps murder."

"Come, come, lass," he goaded, scooping up a smidgen of bag balm onto the tip of his finger and dabbing it onto her split lip. "Stop feeling sorry for yourself. Get back out there and show Lady Jocelyn and Elsa Dengler what you're made of. Yer fans have been raising the roof calling for you."

Surprise banished the fog of tiredness from her eyes. "They have?"

He sobered suddenly and screwed the lid onto the jar. "They love you, Lil, and that's a fact."

She let that sink in for a few seconds and reached for the mug of coffee Rose held. She quaffed down the lukewarm drink, hoping the strong-enough-to-put-hair-on-your-chest brew would soon give her at least a momentary boost.

Lilly stood with a bowl of mutton stew in her hands, bolting it down as if it might be her last meal while Rose dressed her in another outfit. This one looked as if it had been designed with Cleopatra in mind, only much shorter so as not to impede her walking. Harris was indeed creative when it came to eye-catching costumes.

At McShane's command, she lifted one foot for him to pull on fresh socks, thinner than what she had been wearing. "Do you really think they're pulling for me?" she asked, resting one hand on his shoulder to balance, as he worked her foot into the second sock.

"There's no doubt you have a following, and—where are your shoes? Do you want the canvas again or the boots?"

"The canvas. I emptied the tanbark from them and left them outside the tent."

He went to the flap, stuck out his head, and grabbed the shoes. He tapped her leg, indicating she was to lift it so he could put the shoe on, but before she could comply, the bell rang, and Leo stuck his head inside.

"I hate to interrupt, Mr. McShane, but there's a gentleman in the office demanding to see you. He says it's a matter of grave importance."

Lilly, Cade, and Rose shared a troubled look.

"Did he leave his name?" Cade asked, getting to his feet.

"Simon Linedecker."

A collective gasp filled the tent. Simon had been Lilly's lawyer when she sought a divorce from Timothy. In a move that surprised everyone, he had recently married McShane's sister, Erin.

Intuitively, Lilly knew that the first thing to cross McShane's mind was that something had happened to his sister. Why else would Simon come? She could almost feel the fear radiating from her partner. She reached out to touch his arm. He turned, and she recognized the torment in his eyes. He and Erin had not always seen eye to eye.

"Go," Lilly urged. "Rose and I can manage."

For once, he didn't argue. Without a word, he followed Leo.

When Lilly returned to the tent, Rose was sitting at the table, a dime novel opened before her. McShane was nowhere in sight.

"Where's McShane?" she asked, shuffling toward the table.

"He came back long enough to tell me that he had to go see Seamus," Rose said, indicating the Lilly should sit down in the chair she'd just vacated. "Isn't that his brother, the policeman?

"Yes." Lilly leaned against the table and easing onto the chair.

"He didn't take time to explain everything, but it has to do with Robbie."

Lilly's heart sank. Robbie, the guttersnipe who had saved McShane from the streets when he was at the lowest point of his life was an integral part of her partner's life. And hers.

"McShane was in an all-fired hurry to get gone since he said Seamus live on the other side of the city and it will take a bit to get there by cab."

Unable to look after the boy because of his work, McShane had left Robbie in the care of his brother, a Chicago policeman. He had been living with Seamus, his wife, Megan, and their three children for several months now, and by all appearances, was settling well into a more conventional life than the one he'd lived on the streets. He had even started helping Seamus with his policing in small ways.

"Robbie's all right, isn't he?" Lilly heard the note of panic in her voice.

Rose pulled another chair in front of Lilly, sat, and indicated for her to rest her foot in her lap. "He's gone."

"What do you mean, gone?"

"I don't know the particulars, but there was something about him putting together a race for some children, and—"

"Race? What kind of race?"

Rose made a sweeping gesture with her hand. "This kind of race."

The concept was so Robbie-like that Lilly didn't know whether to laugh or cry. He was sponsoring his own pedestrian race! Well, one had to give him points for being original and clever. She supposed it beat picking pockets.

"And?"

"And I'm not sure. All McShane said was that he got in trouble with the police, ran away, and hasn't been seen since. Simon insisted on coming to get McShane since the boy has been gone more than a day."

"Did he say how long he'd be gone?"

"I suppose it depends on how long it takes to find the boy. He did tell me he cancelled his first boxing match just in case he wasn't back in time. How are your feet?"

"Fine until just a couple of rounds ago," Lilly said. "I must have a sharp piece of bark digging into my foot. It hurts like the dickens."

Rose pulled off a shoe. Lilly's feet were far more swollen than they had been four hours earlier, and the swelling had at last led to blisters. She sighed. She'd suspected as much.

"Cade says I'm to sterilize a needle and drain them," Rose told her.

"Do what you must. I think I can save you the trouble on the other foot. I'm pretty sure that one's already burst."

"Let me have a look." Rose untied the second shoe, drew it off, and gasped.

Lilly, who'd been staring at a spot across the tent and thinking about Robbie, looked down. There was blood inside the canvas shoe. Quite a lot of blood.

"There's too much blood to be from blisters," Rose said. She looked inside the shoe. "There must be something in there."

"I told you I thought I got a piece of tanbark in my shoe," Lilly said.

"Tanbark didn't do this." Rose picked up the shoe, turned it upside down, and tapped it against her palm. Nothing. Then she peeled off the bloodied sock and turned Lilly's bare foot this way and that. "It's here near your little toe," she said at last.

"What is?"

"A piece of glass," she muttered. "It's stuck into the side of your foot."

"Glass! How on earth would I get a piece of glass in my shoe?" The words had no more than left her mouth than she recalled William talking about all manner of sabotage taking place. Someone must have put the glass in her shoe, hoping to eliminate her from the race! Who? And why?

She didn't realize she'd spoken aloud until Rose answered. "I'd say because you've been doing quite well for a newcomer, and someone out there sees you as a real threat."

Lilly rested her elbow on the table and her forehead in her palm. She gave a weak laugh. "If only they knew."

"When do you think they might have done it?" Rose asked. She stood, rested Lilly's foot on the seat of the kitchen chair and went behind the privacy screen. Lilly heard her pouring water from the pitcher into the washbowl.

"When I came in the last time, I dumped the tanbark out of them and left them outside the tent. When Leo came and got McShane, I hurried and put them on to get back onto the track."

"You didn't notice anything? You couldn't feel it?"

"Rose, look at my feet. They're swollen to three times their normal size. They are one enormous pain. My body is one enormous pain. The real question is *who* did it?"

"You have a point," Rose acknowledged. "It could have been anyone who saw the shoes sitting out there. Dozens of folks cross the infield every day, going from one place to another. We'll just have to be more careful from here on out." She set the bowl on the floor and grabbed a clean tea towel. "Soak your foot in the water. I'm going to sterilize my knife."

Lilly absorbed the news with a stoicism she didn't know she possessed. "How bad is it?"

"Bad enough that I'm going to have to dig it out."

Sighing, Lilly watched as Rose held the knife blade in the fire of the gas burner. Satisfied that it was free of harmful bacteria, she handed the hilt to Lilly and went to the wooden box next to the stove. Lilly heard glass clinking together before Rose pulled out a bottle of Irish whiskey, uncapped it, and poured some into a cup. She topped off the spirits off with more of the bitter coffee.

"Drink. The whiskey is for the pain. The coffee is to help you stay awake."

They exchanged knife for mug.

Picking up Lilly's foot, Rose sat down and lifted it toward the light. "Grit your teeth," she said, sticking the point of the knife into the ball of Lilly's foot near her little toe.

Lilly did as she was told and gave a low groan of pain, cringing at the sound of the blade scraping against the sliver of glass as Rose dug deep. If she had thought her pain couldn't get any worse, she was wrong.

"There we go!" Rose said with a hint of satisfaction. "First try. It's bleeding a lot, but I'm pretty sure I got it all."

"Thank God."

"Indeed. Keep your foot in the water a minute and let it bleed. It will help clean the wound."

Five minutes later, the cut had been disinfected with more of the whiskey and wrapped securely with a rolled bandage made from muslin sheeting.

"Get my boots," Lilly said. "And I need to change outfits again."

Rose couldn't hide her surprise. "You aren't going back out, are you?"

"I have to," Lilly said, groaning as she stood.

"McShane will have a tizzy," Rose said.

Lilly gave a grumpy snort. "McShane would carry me to the track and tell me to stop whining. I want you to put out the word about what happened and see what kind of reactions you get."

"But how will you walk on that foot?"

Lilly offered her a wan smile. "Very carefully."

* * *

McShane still hadn't returned. Lilly didn't know whether to be worried about him and Robbie or to put all her physical and mental energy into the blasted race.

Word of the attempt to undermine her chances of finishing the race was making its way through the throng of spectators on the sidelines as well as the walkers battling out for every mile.

Suspicious glances passed between walkers. They knew if someone had done something like that to Lil, they wouldn't hesitate to do it to others. If possible, the vitriol in Lady Jocelyn's eyes seemed worse than before. Lilly tried her best to pass it off as her overly sensitive imagination. All in all, a sense of paranoia claimed the group.

"Do you think it was Marta?" Arlene asked, walking alongside Lilly for a few paces.

"I wouldn't put it past her. In fact, there are a couple I wouldn't be surprised to find out did it."

"Lady Jocelyn seemed particularly pleased when she heard the news."

Lilly looked at her companion. "Who told her?"

"Her cook, I believe."

Hm. Lilly would have to ask Rose if Ginny had heard anything about Lady Jocelyn's reaction.

There was no more flirting with the stranger. When she had returned to the track after the glass incident, he was gone. She didn't expect him to return until sometime the following day. He might never come back. The thought saddened her somewhat.

She pushed thoughts of him from her mind and focused on the time she had gone to watch her friend Nora on stage in Vandalia. Finding a quiet place inside her head and whiling away the miles by thinking about memories from her past kept her thoughts off her weariness and made the time pass much faster.

* * *

Even with her injured foot, Lilly managed to gain on young Marta. For her efforts, she began receiving sly elbow jabs in the ribs from La Bella Rosa and more hateful looks from Lady Jocelyn every round. After one particularly fast mile, Lady Jocelyn went so far as to hiss a warning, "You needn't think you'll win this."

Elsa Dengler passed with no comment. That lady wasted no time with pettiness. She just kept walking.

Suddenly there was a loud roaring from the crowd, and the band broke into a lively ditty. Wondering what the commotion was about, Lilly looked up at the scoreboard. By determination and the grace of God, she had made up the two miles she was behind Marta. She was now in fourth place. Sometimes the simple act of refusing to give up was a good thing.

* * *

"Oh, look, Rose!" Ginny said as she and Rose sat in chairs outside the tent watching the walkers circle the track. "Your Lil just knocked Marta off her high horse!"

"So, she did!" Rose smiled with pride.

"That will make for some hard feelings, don't you know?"

With a sigh, Rose took the opportunity to take the conversation in another direction. "And a new rivalry is born. But what's one more, right? I hear there's a lot of jealousy among Lady Jocelyn, La Bella Rosa, and Elsa."

Ginny laughed. "La Bella Rosa is young, and on her way up. Jocelyn can't stand the notion of being second best—or worse."

"Getting older is for the birds, isn't it? What about her and Elsa?"

"I don't know what's behind it, but there's no love lost between them, that's for sure." Ginny frowned. "I have a feeling there's more to it than who's the best walker."

"Why do you say that?"

Ginny shook her head. "It's just a feeling I have that it goes much deeper than anyone knows."

* * *

Since moving into fourth place, Lilly seemed to have more fans in the audience, more people shouting good wishes and encouragement. Several men handed her bouquets as she passed, and one obviously wealthy man gifted her with a delicate filigree brooch embellished with pearls. It was a lovely piece, and she knew she would enjoy it, but she felt guilty accepting it.

She thanked each of them with a big smacking kiss on the lips before moving on, which brought more cheers from the onlookers. "I'll Take You Home Again, Kathleen" became *her* song, and a few bars were played on the piano for each mile she completed.

She couldn't deny that the admiration was somewhat addictive. She'd had a taste of it while performing on stage. This was different, though. These spectators combined hero-worship with an adoration fueled by support, heartfelt enthusiasm, and even respect that showed itself every time she gained another lap or mile.

Though she knew she didn't have it in her to do what these professionals did race after race, her participation gave her a new insight. She now understood their drive and their passion as well as their need. It was a heady experience.

Chapter Ten

Tuesday

By one p.m., Lilly was starting to worry about Robbie and McShane. While he never entertained the possibility that something might happen to him, she thought about it frequently. Just because he was tough did not mean he was invincible.

Since neither she nor Rose had any idea what they were doing or how to strategize the optimum times she slept, she found herself only sleeping when she positively could not hold her eyes open any longer. She kept reminding herself that every time she stopped, the others were making laps and every seven laps, they logged was another mile.

Two of the women she hardly knew had already dropped out, walking off the track with shoulders that slumped, heavy hearts and tears of disappointment streaking their faces. Their hope of winning the purse and having more money than ever had vanished beneath the harsh conditions of ceaseless walking and its companions, pain and tedium. Dreams were crushed. Money was lost. Even the onlookers seemed infected with sadness. Who would finish of the those who persisted?

Contrarily, their leaving seemed to give the remaining pedestriennes a new energy. Speeds increased, and weariness seemed a thing of the past.

Hoping to boost her spirits as well as those of the spectators, Lilly decided to take a page from the magnificent Ada Anderson's playbook. She limped up the steps to the dais, scooted the piano player aside, and began to pound out a rousing version of "Oh, Them Golden Slippers." She didn't play all that well, but she played with enthusiasm and a winsome, flirty smile. She even sang a verse or two.

The crowd loved it. The crowd loved her. Flowers, Swiss chocolates, and wine kept coming. Somehow, even with her injured foot, she was still in fourth place, ahead of the relentless Marta, who was finally beginning to show signs of fading. Lilly was just four turns of the track ahead of the Swede, but she was still ahead. She couldn't stop. She would not let the little twit take back the fourth-place slot.

* * *

Lilly no longer knew if she was awake or not. Her head ached, and the jubilant noise of the crowd had become nothing but a muted hum. Her world consisted of little beyond putting one foot in front of the other. The tanbark track was her only focus. She was aware of hunger but felt that if she ate anything, it would come right back up. Her back ached, her muscles screamed in agony and her joints were swollen. Her hands felt numb from swinging at her sides.

One more lap. Seven. One more mile. One…

She was slightly aware of a gasp rising from the crowd but had no idea what the problem might be. She didn't care. Then she saw McShane coming toward her, his arms held out, waiting for her to walk into them. Nothing this side of heaven could have stopped her. She felt his arms close around her and she longed to burrow into the safety she knew she would find there. For a moment she did.

She felt the softness of his shirt against her cheek, felt his fingers thread through her hair to cradle the back of her head. Heard the strong beating of his heart and smelled an unusual blend of exotic scents. Sandalwood. Patchouli. Myrrh.

"Are you Kate?" The question was a low rumble in her ear.

"You know who I am, Cade."

"Who?" His voice held a query, and she sensed him pulling away.

"Get off the track, sir!" The voice was hard, harsh, and demanded obedience. She knew it was one of the officials whose job it was to keep the spectators off the track, whether their intention was to help a walker, distract her or slow her down.

The arms supporting her vanished, and Lilly felt as if she might collapse, but she didn't. Somehow, she turned and kept walking. Then, she heard Rose calling and looked toward the sound. She stood just off the track, gesturing for Lilly to come. She managed to make it inside the tent where she fell onto the cot and was out immediately. Her last thought was that Cade had called her by her mother's name. Had he known Kate? No. McShane had never met her mother. Strange.

* * *

"Open your eyes, lass. We have a problem. A couple actually."

She knew who it was by the no-nonsense tone in his voice and the slapdash way he was bathing her face with a cold, wet cloth. McShane. His actions were far different from those when he had held her on the track. "When did you get back?"

"Just a bit ago."

"Robbie?" she croaked, as he helped her into a sitting position. As soon as she was upright, Rose handed her a cup.

"Home safe."

Lilly's weary mind tried to process what she was hearing as she lifted the cup to her mouth. Expecting more of the dratted beef tea, she was surprised to find that it was spirits of some sort and it felt...slimy. She gagged, and the next thing she knew, someone shoved the basin in front of her face.

When her stomach was empty, she fell back onto the cot and gave a cry of pain. She opened one eye and gave her partner a fair rendition of the 'evil eye.'

"What in the name of all that's holy was that vile concoction?"

"A bit o' port with an egg or two beat up in it."

Lilly gagged again.

"Hand me the liniment, Rose," he said. "Her muscles are seizing up again. And mix a little of that arnica into some milk to help the inflammation and ease her stomach. Her joints are a mess."

The next thing she knew, she was partially undressed, and he was rubbing the foul-smelling ointment briskly over her legs, arms, and back. "Tell me about Robbie," she mumbled, turning her face toward him and looking at him with one eye.

"It seems the lad decided to hold his own races to make a bit of dosh."

A rush of maternal-like pride overwhelmed her weariness. It pleased her no end that Robbie was being so clever at ways of earning money. "Better than picking pockets or thieving, I reckon."

One corner of McShane's mouth lifted in a half-smile. "That's what I thought. The little scoundrel had seven other lads signed up to walk, and when Seamus caught him, there were around seventy-five young'uns from all over the area who'd come to watch. He was charging them a nickel apiece to get in. One of the preachers heard what was going on, went to the police, and he got nicked."

Lilly forced one eye open. "They didn't actually put him in jail, did they?"

"No, no. They released him into Seamus's keeping. He took him home, gave him a thrashin', and told him to stay in his room until he was told otherwise. At some time during the night, he crawled out his bedroom window, and they couldn't find hide nor hair of him. Finally, I thought of the cemetery where his folks abandoned him."

Lying on her stomach, Lilly raised her head to look at him. "Why would he go there?"

"I think he felt like he'd been abandoned again in a manner o' speaking."

"But he's back at home, safe and sound."

"Aye."

"Good."

As he talked, McShane kept rubbing her aching muscles. "He keeps telling Seamus he saw a crime committed while he was there, but who knows?"

"Oh, that feels so good. What kind of crime?"

"Someone diggin' up a body, but when the coppers went to check it out, the grave didn't look as if anyone had touched it. We think he's tryin' to get back in everyone's good graces."

"*Hm.* Anything else?"

"Well, after Rose told me about the glass in your shoe, I took time to report it to Dora, who was knocked for six that anyone would do such a thing." As he spoke, he rolled his eyes heavenward. "She also told me that Lady Jocelyn is complaining about you."

"Me? Good lord!" Lilly ranted, "the woman has five or more miles on me. I'm no threat to her."

"Not to her standing in the race, mayhap, but it seems she thinks your interaction with the audience is stealing her thunder. She said, and I quote, 'obviously the Irish twit does not have what it takes to stay the course, so she tries to compensate by stealing fans and ingratiating herself to the press.'"

Lilly sighed. "So much for the camaraderie I hoped to establish."

"I don't think m'lady J. gives one hoot in Hades about establishing a friendship with anyone."

"I warrant you're right."

"I also got a warning for you." He pressed his thumbs into the small of her back and she gave a yelp of pain.

"Stop!" Lilly frowned and sat up. "A warning? About what?"

"The man on the track."

"What man on the track?" Her mind was so fuzzy, she had no recollection of any man being on the track, walking or otherwise.

McShane looked at Rose with a lift of his heavy eyebrows. "Rose."

Rose stepped nearer and handed her a glass of the water she so needed to combat dehydration. "The man you were talking to the other day. He came out onto the track a while ago and the two of you talked a little."

Lilly recalled the man with the signet ring, but she had no recollection of talking to him today. Her gaze shifted from Rose to McShane. The realization that she was beginning to hallucinate from lack of sleep and weariness was more than a bit frightening. "I don't remember," she said in a wary tone.

"It was nothing," Rose assured her. "He certainly meant no harm. He was

100

sitting at his table watching the race, and you looked like you were in a trance or something."

Vaguely, she remembered how heavy her feet felt and what an effort it was to pick one foot up and then the other. She recalled seeing nothing but a colorful blur instead of faces in the crowd. The never-ending oval of the track. The music sounding as if it came from far away, like a memory, or a dream.

"I believe I was," she admitted. "I couldn't see anything but that blasted tanbark in front of me."

Rose smiled. "You'd been shuffling your feet for a while, and then you stumbled. That man had already rushed onto the track by then, and he started running toward you. You collapsed into his arms. He didn't help you with more than a few steps when one of the officials told him to get off the track or he'd be forced to leave."

A fuzzy recollection surfaced. Seeing the man and going willingly into his arms. Clinging to him, holding on to him so tightly. A haven in the hell around her. "But...that was you, wasn't it, Cade?"

"No, lass, it wasn't. What did he want? Did he say anything?"

On the verge of sleep or collapse, Lilly closed her eyes and tried to remember. From the first day he'd spotted her and called her to his table, he seemed to think he knew her from somewhere. As she'd walked, she'd racked her brain, trying to recall where she might have seen him, but nothing came to mind, and he was the kind of man any woman with red blood running through her veins would remember. He was the kind of man she would never forget.

Without warning, she remembered that he'd called her Kate. He'd thought she was her mother. Why? Where would he have seen her? A shiver of anxiety raced down her spine. Was he her mother's killer?

No. This man wasn't that many years older than she was. The person who had made love to her mother and then killed her was a man twelve years ago, not a boy. Did the ring hold the answer? She needed to get a closer look at it to compare it to the memory of the one she'd seen that night. At least then, she would know if there was any connection.

Should she mention it to Cade? No. He knew little of her past, and once this race was over, she could go on her way and not think of this strange incident, except as one of the many memories she would take with her. For better or worse, the stranger would be one of them.

"Lilly?" Rose said, clapping her hands in front of Lilly's face. "Are you asleep? Wake up."

"He thinks he knows me," she said at last, dragging her thoughts back to the present and opening her eyes to look at Rose. "He wanted to know who I am."

"He wants something from you," McShane said.

Did he? Yes. "Dinner. He wants to take me to dinner after the race is over."

"My gut says there's more to it than that. We need to find out what he's really after."

"Why?" she asked, the statement catching her off guard. Why on earth would McShane want to delve into the stranger's life? She didn't like that. He was hers to scrutinize. "It isn't important to the case."

"We don't know that." They stared at each other for long seconds and then Lilly closed her eyes to block out his face. The liniment was burning, reminding her of why she was here. She thought of McShane's impersonal touch and weighed it against the way she'd felt in the stranger's arms.

"I can't think about that right now. Rose, will you get me the bright yellow leggings with the rust vest and olive topcoat, please. I have a few things to prove to Lady Jocelyn."

* * *

He hugged the perimeter of the crowd, taking in the revelry, the laughter, and the hundreds of voices mingling together into one big vibration of sound that fell on the ears like the drone of a giant insect. There were old people, young people, men, women, and children. They all looked happy.

Wasn't that something?

When he'd heard about the people who walked round and round a track for a chance to win money, he'd had no idea what the reality of it would be like. Seeing the spectacle with his own eyes was an amazing thing, and he was glad he had come.

He'd overheard McShane discussing his assignment with Seamus, and it sounded like a right mess. No matter what was going on, Robbie knew he would be able to help. The main thing was to keep to himself and not get caught. If he did, there would be bloody hell to pay.

* * *

Lilly's eyes drifted shut. She would just close them for a few seconds, and then she would open them again to see where she was. Her eyelids felt as heavy as lead, not that she had ever lifted any lead except lead pencils...no lead pipes...but she was certain it was heavy. Everyone said so.

She came to herself for a second and realized she was mentally rambling. Giving her head a hard shake, she forced her eyelids upward and looked to see where she was on the track. She was nearing the spot where La Bella Rosa exited to her tent. Marta was walking just behind and to the side of her, and as Rosalie angled her way off the track, the Swedish girl said something to her. To Lilly's surprise, Rosalie paused for a moment to listen.

Hot color flooded her face, and she turned to look at the pedestriennes who were headed toward her. Her hard gaze found Lilly's. Something inside her recoiled from the venom in that look. Then, in a jerky, angry movement, Rosalie Bertolini whirled and stomped off to her tent. What had Marta said to Rosalie to make the petite Italian so vexed...vexed at her? Lilly sighed. At this point, it really didn't matter.

Feet dragging, she summoned a weary smile, blew her now-famous kisses to the crowd, gathered what last bit of energy she could, and lifted her arms above her head, preparing to do a summersault and praying she wouldn't fall on her face. Just as she was about to push off, she saw a familiar face in the crowd. A pointy chin, freckled face, and a shock of brown hair that seemed forever to be hanging into dark eyes. Before she could do more than gasp, the face had disappeared.

The summersault was forgotten.

* * *

Lilly left the track five minutes later. She entered the tent to find Rose and McShane talking. "Robbie's here," she blurted, interrupting their conversation.

"What?" McShane and Rose said at the same time.

"I saw Robbie in the crowd, over near Rosalie's tent."

"No," McShane said. "I personally delivered him to Seamus's house, read him the riot act about worrying Megan, and told him to stay put."

"Well, he didn't."

"Are you sure?" he pressed, pulling off a boot and carefully looking her feet over. Rose pushed a beefsteak sandwich toward her. The first bite confirmed Lilly's suspicion that it was tougher than the leather of the boots she wore, but she tore into it like a starving longshoreman at the end of a hard day. She had so little time to eat and was so hungry that Rose no longer chastised her for her abominable manners. That was an aggravation she did not need.

"I mean, do ya think you might have been—I don't know—hallucinating again or something?"

"Like when I thought I saw you on the track?" she asked, talking around a cringeworthy mouth full of food.

"Yes."

"No. I saw him, Cade. He looked me straight in the eye and vanished." She chewed a few more times and washed down the bite with a cup of strong black tea laced with plenty of molasses.

"Aye. Vanishin' is something our Robbie's good at, isn't it? All right, then. I'll keep on the lookout for him."

He glanced up at Rose as he gently rewrapped Lilly's injured foot. It was still weeping blood, and no wonder. If she didn't know better, she might think he cared about her and how she felt, but McShane was all business, always.

"Ask Penn to help keep an eye out for him, too," he said now to Rose.

"I wouldn't know the lad if he came up and bit me."

104

"He's about this tall." McShane indicated Robbie's height by raising his hand. "Has a lot of brown hair always in his eyes and a sharp chin."

"What makes you think he'll come around here?"

"He's nosey, and he's run off again because he likes to be in the thick of things. He won't be able to help himself. He'll show up sooner or later."

"It would be so nice to come in for a break and have some good news for a change," Lilly said.

"Is that so?" Rose said, smiling. "Well, as a matter of fact, I have some. Someone who heard about the glass in your shoe left you a 'get well' message, and a bottle of expensive champagne outside the tent." She picked up a clear bottle with a fancy label from the table behind her and presented it to Lilly.

"How do you know it's expensive?" Lilly asked, taking it from her and looking it over.

"Because it's a bottle of Louis Roederer's Cristal," Rose said, a pleased expression on her face.

"And that's good?" Lilly asked, unimpressed.

"It's excellent. Roederer created it for Czar Alexander of Russia. It's very dear."

Lilly couldn't hide her surprise. "How is it that you know this?"

Rose laughed. "Pierce wasn't always a dramaturge," she reminded. "I've always been of the opinion he came from money back in England, though I doubt we'll ever know. He treated us to a bottle on our last anniversary."

The statement reminded Lilly of how little anyone knew of Pierce's background, but now wasn't the time to discuss that. "Do we know who sent it?"

"Probably your special fan," McShane said. "The one who wants to take you to dinner."

"I doubt that," she said with a shake of her head. "I haven't seen him around lately." She held the bottle up to the light. It was beautiful. "Perhaps I should have a sip for energy," she suggested, less concerned about who had sent the expensive champagne than she was about how she was going to make it through the next few hours.

"Not now," McShane said. He took the wine from her and handed it to

Rose, then pulled Lilly to her feet. Taking her shoulders, he pointed her toward the tent opening. "You've already been off the track longer than you shoulda been. Go, woman."

* * *

At precisely that moment, Robbie was wondering if Lilly had seen him, and if she had, was she herself enough to realize it. She looked like she'd been drug through a knothole backwards as his ma used to say. She was thinner than when he'd last seen her, and there were hollows in her cheeks. She'd tried to look happy when she waved to the crowd, but there was no joy in her eyes despite the effort. She looked awful bad, did Lil.

He felt a little pain in the region of his heart. He wasn't a fan of hers, never had been. She had spent more time with McShane than he had these past months.

Admit it, Robbie Jenkins! You're jealous of her. She took McShane away from you.

Admitting it was harder than he imagined, but McShane said a man had to stand up for what was right and admit when he was wrong. Truth was Lilly had been nothing but kind to him. The blame was his, not hers. To give himself credit, it had been all he could do to keep from running out onto the track and helping her when he thought she might fall, but he knew he would get into trouble, and the good Lord knew he'd had more than his share of that, lately.

Who knew you had to get permission to hold a race and such things, even if you were a kid? And it was going so well. A girl had joined the competition at the last minute, and he was certain that Addie Bletchley was a sure bet to beat all the lads who had entered. She was something, was Addie.

He sighed, thinking over the disaster of the past few days. Getting into trouble with the coppers wasn't the worst part. Seamus had given him a licking, which he didn't mind too much, but Megan had piled on the agony by making him give all the money he'd made to the church. Now *that* was a crying shame. You'd a thought they'd be proud of him coming up with something like a pedestrian race for kids. Hadn't he been hearing how good walking was for your health?

Grownups had too many blasted rules. How was a lad to make an honest buck? And it had to be honest since he'd made up his mind to be a copper or a Pinkerton when he grew up. Both Seamus and Cade said the main thing about being a lawman was integrity and honor. As near as he could figure, honor came from keeping your word, doing what was right, and being reliable, which was a lot harder to do than you'd think.

The question now became what should he do? Keep trying to give McShane the slip or let him know he was here, ready to help? The honorable thing would be to let him know he was there, wouldn't it? Besides, if Lilly told McShane she'd seen him, he'd tell Seamus and he and Megan would worry. He hated it when the McShanes worried about him. It made him feel all funny inside. Sort of pleased, but discombobulated, which didn't make much sense at all. But then, he was learning that a lot of things didn't make much sense in the grownup world.

Chapter Eleven

Wednesday

By lunchtime, two officials helped Elsa off the track, complaining of severe back pain. Rose went immediately to help young Penn treat his mother. When she reached the Dengler tent, Ginny was already in attendance, and the officials were pressing Elsa to decide if she was going to leave the race for good or not.

"I'm not quitting!" she shouted, her English sounding harsher in her pain and anger. "I vill be back on the track soon. Now go away and leave me alone!"

Together, Rose and Ginny got Elsa settled and began rubbing her extremities and her back with the same liniment Cade used on Lilly. Rose gave her a cup of tea, liberally laced with cream and molasses. After about thirty minutes, Elsa asked Ginny to see if she was still in second place. She was, but only by a mile.

Lady Jocelyn was circling the track as if the race had just begun instead of nearing the halfway mark. Either the cosmos or the knowledge that Elsa might be forced to leave the competition had given the lady a burst of energy.

"Help me up, Penn," Elsa told her son after hearing the news. "I vill not let that devil's spawn rob me of anything else."

"Ma, please! You aren't fit to be out there yet."

"Penn!" she said. "Help me up." And that was the end of it.

* * *

Lilly was on the track and had no idea what was going on with Elsa, but she saw Rose and Ginny helping the walker onto the track where she was greeted by both cheers and boos. Hobbling a bit, giving in to the pain that still gripped her, Elsa started making her rounds once again.

When Lady Jocelyn passed her in the opposite direction, she smirked and said something meant for her ears alone. Lilly was too far away to read her lips, but she had no problem recognizing the malice on Jocelyn Baldwin's face. Elsa squared her shoulders and kept walking.

So did Lilly. She had *almost* reached a mental plane where she was oblivious to her extreme physical discomfort. Like Lady Jocelyn, she had found an inner strength. Lilly suspected it came from the realization that she *had* gained the backing of a significant portion of the crowd, but it was the grit and determination of Elsa Dengler, who had at least ten years on Lilly that was an even greater influence.

* * *

Lady Jocelyn's burst of energy had run its course. The rugged pace she'd set for herself had shown little to no effect on her stamina, but the past hour or so she had started limping.Lilly was gaining laps on Jocelyn Baldwin for the first time.

Lilly blocked out everything but her thoughts as she walked. It was perhaps an hour later when she approached the place where her secret admirer usually sat and she saw he was there. Looking the height of masculine style in his fashionable, expensive attire, he sat relaxed in his chair, regarding her through eyes half-closed against a haze of smoke. The cherry-scented cloud she recalled from their previous encounter enveloped him and his entourage.

Kate-like, Lilly realized she must look dreadful. The fact that she was concerned about her looks overrode her growing concern about who he was and what he wanted from her. That, and the desire to see that blasted ring up close. As she neared him, he smiled, a slight lift of his lips that hinted that he, too, was a little off-kilter by whatever was happening between them.

Without warning, the crowd erupted. Lilly was caught so off guard that she missed a step.

"Lil! Lil! Lil!"

What in the world? What had she done? Her gaze moved the sign that showed rankings, and she literally stopped in the middle of the track. Jocelyn was nowhere to be seen. Lilly now stood in third place. A sense of accomplishment filled her. She wanted to rush back to the tent and jump up and down in excitement, except that she was so weary, and her body hurt so dreadfully that she wasn't certain she would ever be able to jump up and down again.

As she neared her tent, she saw Cade standing there, holding a glass of champagne aloft. He was wearing his broad, true smile and his blue eyes glittered with undeniable pride.

When she reached him, he handed her the flute and slid an arm around her waist. "Great job, Lil," he told her, guiding her into the tent. "I thought this was a worthy moment to bring out the champagne. If the adulation doesn't give you a boost, maybe the bubbles will."

"You aren't having any?" she said, plopping onto the cot. She raised one foot at the same time she lifted the glass to her lips.

McShane, who was already on one knee untying her shoe, favored her with raised eyebrows and a have-you-forgotten look. Two or so years earlier, he'd been fired for drinking and brawling…actions unbecoming to a Pinkerton. When he reapplied, stating that he had his life in order, Allan wanted him back; William wasn't so sure. They compromised by assigning him as her nanny while she learned the ins and outs of becoming a proper operative. Aware that he might succumb to the temptation once again, he never imbibed.

Lilly had no such constraints. There was nothing remotely refined about the way she downed the glass of effervescence. Wrinkling her nose and giving her head a vigorous shake, she held out the flute for a refill. Rose poured the glass full.

The second glass went by the way of the first. "This stuff may be expensive," she said with a slight shudder, "but cost doesn't guarantee good taste. It's very bitter."

Wearing a grim smile, McShane tied her shoe and cast her a warning look. "You'd best go easy on that stuff, else you're apt to fall on your face when you get back out on the track."

Feeling fuzzy and lightheaded, she responded with a serene smile of her own. She thought she could fly. "Did I ever tell you that when you're down on one knee like that, it looks like you're going to propose?"

She wasn't sure how she thought he might answer, but she didn't expect laughter. "It's not funny, McShane."

"Really?"

"I don't feel well."

"Well, it's no wond—"

Before he could finish whatever he was about to say, she retched all over them both. Cade leaped to his feet and Rose rushed over with the bucket. Lilly heaved some more, then raced behind the screen, screaming for Cade to leave the tent. When she emerged a few moments later, she wore nothing but her shift, which had somehow managed to remain untouched by the vomit. She was as white as the damp cloth Rose handed her.

"Where's McShane?" she asked, mopping at her face.

"You told him to leave."

"So, I did." She sat down on her bed and seemed to lose her starch, falling backward onto the cot and losing consciousness.

* * *

Cade returned after giving Rose time to clean things up. "When was the last time she ate?" he asked, squatting down beside Lilly and laying a palm against her face and neck. She was sweating profusely and had lost consciousness.

"This morning. She's had nothing but beef tea since then."

"Thank God for that."

"What's wrong with her?"

He shook his head and peeled off his shirt as he headed to the trunk that held his clothes. "My first thought was that maybe she drank the champagne too fast on an empty stomach, but with her passing out like this, I don't know. Maybe she's just come to the end of her endurance, or..."

"Or what?"

He disappeared behind the screen to give himself a quick wash-up. "With everything that's happened to her, it's not too farfetched to consider the possibility that someone has done something to take her out of the race."

He shed his pants and pulled on some clean ones, topping them with a fresh shirt.

"What do you mean, *done* something? Not...not poison?"

"I don't think it's anything that drastic," he said, emerging from behind the privacy screen. "From what I've read, I think it would have already done its job if it was poison, but I'm no expert. I'm going to see if there's a doctor among the spectators. In the meantime, keep a close watch on her until I get back. The race is over for her."

* * *

Cade found Dora and Leo in her office. When he explained what had happened, he saw real panic on Dora's face. This was just the sort of thing she'd hoped to avoid. Leo looked stunned as well.

"We'll telegraph the police, too, of course," she said. "And get someone here as quickly as possible."

"Contact Cook County first and get an ambulance here," Cade commanded. "She needs immediate professional medical care that I can't provide."

"Of course," Leo assured him. "I'll take care of it."

* * *

Rose was bathing Lilly's face with a soft cloth and praying. As often happened when she was unburdening herself to the Lord, her mind drifted to things that had nothing to do with prayer and everything to do with her feelings.

She recalled the terrified girl of eleven who had been afraid to sleep in a room alone, after hearing her mother being killed. The girl of fifteen and sixteen who had worked hard at learning everything Pierce had thrown at her, determined to become independent, needing no one but herself.

That one had backfired. Lilly would always need people around her and, like Kate, she seemed to have a knack for choosing the wrong man, yet she needed a man's love so desperately. Ever since Tim Warner, Rose had prayed that Lilly's next choice would be better than her last. Mostly she prayed for Lilly to be all right. Rose wasn't sure how they would go on if something happened to her.

"Is she okay?"

Rose jumped at the sound of the fearful voice. She turned toward the tent's opening and saw a boy of no more than twelve standing there. She knew in an instant who he was. "Robbie?"

"Rose?"

She nodded. "What are you doing here?"

"I needed to be on my own a while," he said, stepping further into the tent. He cocked his head toward Lilly "How is she?"

Rose shook her head. "Until we find out what's happened, we can't say. How did you know something was wrong?"

His narrow shoulders lifted in a shrug. "I saw McShane tearing out of here like a madman. That ain't like him. Figured something was afoot."

He neared the cot, and Rose stood, moving out of his way. She watched as he stared down at Lilly and took a deep, shuddering breath. Reaching out, he touched her hand with a single finger. Then he turned and said, "I'll be back in a wee bit. I'm going to see what I can find out about this."

Rose had heard enough about Robbie to know that there was no stopping him once he'd set himself on a course of his choosing. She would have to trust that he'd be all right. She'd heard how he'd travelled alone all the way from Chicago to New Orleans just to be with Cade, all without mishap. He should be fine sneaking around the Palmer Roller Rink.

* * *

113

As Robbie made his way through the crowd, the chant of "Lil! Lil! Lil!" became a backdrop for his troubled thoughts. He had his own way of finding out things, and there were more than a couple of folks he wanted to check out. The cooks and medical people who cared for the walkers. The boy, Penn, and another one or two who might be up to something. Like that Italian woman's husband. Robbie had seen him toadying up to both Dora and Mrs. Hoity Toit, Lady Jocelyn, but he hadn't yet figured out the man's game.

The short game was easy, o' course. Cozy up to Dora Ames to get in the middle of her business, make himself indispensable, and get the best of everything for his wife, who was the real moneymaker of the family. The long game was harder to figure beyond the knowledge that Leo was doing his best to keep every road to success open. It was important to keep an eye out for any shenanigans by the toadying promoter.

Right now, he wanted to meet the Ginny lady who cooked for Lady Jocelyn, and the boy, Penn, who seemed so fond of Rose. He had to be wearied of sitting around doing nothing and having just a couple of old ladies to talk to. Robbie wondered what it would take to recruit him as an ally.

* * *

"Hello!" The greeting was accompanied by the tinkling of the small bell outside the tent.

Rose was bathing Lilly's face when she heard the masculine greeting. Rising, she went to the flap and pushed it aside. A gasp of surprise escaped her. Lilly's admirer stood there. He'd donned his suit coat in honor of the impromptu visit. His cravat was impeccably tied, and it looked as if he had run a comb through his golden hair. He was even more handsome up close than from across the track. No wonder he'd tickled Lilly's fancy.

"May I help you, sir?"

He held out a calling card. Rose took it automatically, taking in the information in a single glance. His name was Judah Forrester, and he was a medical doctor practicing right there in Chicago.

114

"You're a doctor?"

"I am," he said. "I heard something happened to Miss McShane. I thought I'd see if there was any truth to it and, if so, offer my services in any way that might be needed. I'm afraid I don't have my bag with me, but I can still have a look at her if you like."

Relief and apprehension warred inside Rose. How did she know he was telling the truth about how he'd found out about Lilly? What if someone had sent him to do even more damage? Should she trust him? "Who told you and what did they say?"

"A boy came to my table. Robbie? He said he was afraid she was going to die."

"How did he know you're a doctor?"

"He didn't. He'd seen Lil and I talking. I think he was just trying to spread the news of what happened to her among the crowd. He was very upset."

Relief took the starch from Rose's backbone. Surely Robbie had sent him. How else could he know what was going on? "We're afraid she's been given something."

"Let him in, Rose."

She looked beyond Forrester's shoulder and saw Cade standing a few feet behind him. Forrester turned and the two men regarded each other with the wariness of a pair of boxers circling each other in the ring…waiting, watching, gauging to see who would throw the first punch.

Forrester moved first, extending his hand. "Judah Forrester, M.D. You must be Lil's brother."

Cade reached out and the two men clasped hands. "Andrew McShane."

"Do you mind if I have a look at her?"

"I would appreciate it."

Forrester moved closer to the cot. Taking a seat on its edge, he placed his fingers on Lilly's wrist and pulled a fancy gold watch from his pocket. "What's she had to eat?"

"Nothing but beef tea since early morning, but she had a glass or two of champagne to celebrate taking third place," Rose told him.

Forrester kept his gaze focused on the watch. "Did the symptoms start after that?"

"Yes. She was exhausted but happy about moving into third place. She downed the drink too fast. It was just a matter of seconds before she was struck with a bout of severe nausea."

"Any diarrhea?"

"Mercy, yes," Rose exclaimed. "After that, she came in and passed out on the cot."

"Has she been sweating like this the whole time?"

Rose nodded, and her forehead creased with worry. "She has."

"Do you have the remainder of the champagne?" When Rose nodded, he said, "Will you get it for me, please?"

Rose did as he asked. Forrester uncorked the bottle, lifted it to his nose, and passed it back and forth a few times. "Smells a bit musty." He lifted the bottle to his mouth.

"Sir!"

Startled, he looked askance at her.

Rose shook her head. "Considering Lil's condition, I don't think I'd do that. Just in case…"

To her surprise, he smiled, which made him even more attractive. "Fine, then." Tapping the cork back into place with his palm, he returned his attention to Cade. "Did she say anything about the champagne?"

"Just that it didn't taste so good for a high-priced wine. Said it was bitter."

"Hm." Forrester lifted Lilly's eyelids and looked into her eyes, watched her breathe for long seconds. Then he tucked the blanket up around her chin and stood.

"Well?" Cade and Rose said in unison.

"I'd like to take the bottle with me and run some tests on it if you don't mind. Her breathing isn't labored or shallow, her pulse is within a normal range, and she seems to just be in a deep sleep, which is to be expected considering her activity the past few days. Based on her symptoms then and now, I'm not inclined to believe whatever made her sick is anything as drastic as poison."

A relieved breath escaped Rose. Cade swallowed hard. "Do you have any idea what it might be?" he asked.

"Again, I can't say with any certainty without testing it, but I'm thinking syrup of ipecac."

"Isn't that what's given to people who *have* taken something harmful? Doesn't it induce vomiting?"

"It does," Forrester said, "and it can be lethal in large enough doses, but judging what I see here, I don't believe she was given enough to cause any long-standing harm."

He turned to leave. "Just so you're aware, the symptoms may continue until it works through her system. As long as she doesn't show any signs of worsening, just give her plenty of fluids and keep her comfortable. If she does worsen, get her to the hospital as soon as possible."

"Thank you, Doctor," Cade said.

"You're very welcome."

Cade followed Forrester out. He longed to ask why he thought he knew Lilly, how he knew her, and what in Hades his interest was in her, but now was not the time. And it was really none of his business.

"Forrester."

He turned, inquiry in his unusual golden eyes.

"Did you send Lil that bottle of champagne?"

Forrester stared at Cade for long moments, almost as if he were trying to figure something out. Finally, he said, "Look around, Mr. McShane. This place is filled with people who adore the walkers, and plenty of them can afford expensive gifts to express their thanks for giving them so much pleasure. She's become quite a favorite. The frontrunners often share with those who don't fare so well." He pulled his watch from his pocket and checked the time. "I'll be here until early evening. Send the boy for me if you need me."

Chapter Twelve

Cade and Rose were sitting at the table, having shepherd's pie when Robbie burst into the tent. Surprised, they both looked up. Rose had forgotten about him, which was no wonder with everything that had happened. McShane pinned him with a look of annoyance.

Robbie cringed. He'd forgotten that they'd not spoken since his arrival.

"Well, hello, Mr. Jenkins," McShane said. "I thought I left you safe and sound at my brother's, contemplating a life free of delinquency."

As if he hadn't a care in the world, Robbie sauntered across the small area and reached for a slice of bread. "Stop with the fancy words, McShane. I've no idea what ya mean."

"I mean, you were being punished. You were supposed to stay in your room and think about the things you'd done, and—"

"Crikey!" Robbie burst out, as annoyed as McShane. He didn't much like being taken to task for his wrongdoings. "It was just a bunch of lads and lasses having a race! What's the harm in that?"

Cade continued as if he hadn't been interrupted. "—the trouble and worry you caused everyone—"

Once again, Robbie interrupted, determined to be heard. "I told Seamus I was sorry, gave my profits to the church, and promised Megan I'd do the dishes fer a fortnight. Ain't that penance enough?"

McShane exhaled sharply. "It's a start."

Robbie mumbled something beneath his breath.

"What was that?" McShane got to his feet.

Robbie took a step back and flung his arms over his head as if to protect himself from a blow.

Stunned, McShane stopped in his tracks. "Stop it, damn ya!" he commanded in a low voice that sounded all the more menacing because he wasn't shouting.

Robbie lowered his arms and stood before the man who'd taken him in when he had no one. He didn't know why he'd reacted as he had. The McShanes had shown him nothing but kindness, but some memories from the past were hard to set aside. Sometimes they came back without warning.

McShane pulled out a chair and pointed to it. "Sit. Rose, get the lad some supper, please." He glared at Robbie, who did as he was told. "Have I ever laid a hand on ya?"

"No, but Seamus—"

"Seamus gave you three stripes on the buttocks with his razor strap. Hardly a *beating*."

Rose set a plate of steaming meat and vegetable pie in front of him. Robbie was so hungry it was all he could do to keep from picking up his fork and attacking the food. Instead, he was still as McShane returned to his seat.

"I'll have Seamus come for you tomorrow."

"I'll just sneak out and come back," Robbie told him, digging into his supper.

McShane regarded him for a moment, and then gave a weary shake of his head. "You would, wouldn't you?"

"Does a bear sleep in the woods?" Robbie pointed his fork at his mentor. "You need me here, McShane. I'm findin' out some interesting stuff."

"Is that right?"

"It is." Robbie glanced over at the cot where Lilly still slept, unmoving. "How is she?"

With another shake of his head, McShane picked up his fork. "The ambulance came from the hospital and checked her over. They think she'll be all right in a day or so. And thank you for sending that doctor over."

Robbie looked astonished. Not by the thanks but by the fact that Lilly's fancy man was a doctor. "Didn't know he was a doctor, did I? I just knew they had something going on and thought I'd let him know what had happened.

What did he say about her?"

Robbie listened while McShane gave him Forrester's opinion, and what he knew about the drug. "How do you spell it?" Robbie asked. When McShane told him, Robbie said, "I'll see what I can find out."

"You'll stay out of the walker's tents," Cade said, pointing his fork at the boy.

Robbie smiled and shoveled in another bite.

* * *

Good Lord, Cade thought, the boy's manners, such as they were, had gone to hell in the proverbial handbasket since he'd come back from staying with the Fontenots in New Orleans. He sighed. "At least be careful, will ya?"

"Always, Andrew." He smirked and reached for another slice of the soda bread.

How did the boy know he was using the name Andrew for this assignment? "So, have you heard anything?"

"Don't I always pick up something or other?"

McShane acknowledged the truth of that with a single nod. "Tell us what you found out."

Robbie leaned his elbows on the table, which were promptly pushed off. "First off, I decided to strike up a friendship with Penn. Were easy enough. He's lonely, is Penn. When I told him what had happened to Lilly, he was as mad as a wet hen."

The boy leaned back in his chair and crossed his arms over his chest. "So, I just went up and told him who I was and asked if he wanted to maybe spend some time together now and again."

"And who did you tell him you are?"

"Why, your and Lil's nephew, Robbie McShane," he offered with a smug smile. "I started to say brother, but I figured the family couldn't scrape up enough money to send three of us over from Ireland."

Riveted by Robbie's tale, Rose scooted her empty plate aside and rested *her* elbows on the table. Robbie knew how to spin one all right.

"And are you good friends?"

"That takes time, don't it, McShane?" he said with a frown. "We're getting there. I told him about my race and getting in trouble with the law and all, and that I'd been sent here until Seamus calmed down a bit, which is almost true. One thing I've already figured out about Penn is that he'd rather listen and watch instead of talk."

"Nothing wrong with that. You should try it sometime," McShane said.

Robbie scowled. "Ha. Ha. Ha. So, Rose tells me you've no idea who gave Lilly the champagne, but Penn told me he saw someone deliverin' it to her."

"My bet is on Forrester," McShane said.

Robbie shook his head. "Penn swore it weren't the fancy man."

McShane gave a short laugh at the name the boys had given Lilly's admirer.

"He said it was a man with long hair and a beard. Said there was something familiar about him."

"Has he seen him around anywhere since he's been here?"

"He said he hadn't," Robbie told them. "He's been sticking pretty close to his place in case his ma needs him. I told him to be on the lookout in case the fella showed up again."

"Good thinking, Robbie."

Cade watched his young charge mop up the juices from the meal with his bread, down the last of the milk Rose had poured for him and belch. Discretely. Perhaps he had come farther than Cade thought, considering he'd been abandoned in a cemetery and roamed the streets for months before the two of them crossed paths. Only the good Lord knew how he'd lived before that.

"He said the fella didn't look like he could afford anything so costly, so I've been thinkin' on the idea that the long-haired man could have just delivered it for someone else."

Robbie smiled at Rose, who was listening with rapt fascination. "By the by, Rose, Penn thinks the world of ya. Said you and Miss Ginny had been very kind and helpful since he came to help his ma."

"We were happy to."

"What else did he say?" McShane asked.

121

"We talked about the race, and I asked him what he thought of the walkers he'd met, that sort of thing. He said he'd overheard Leo and La Bella Rosa arguing about Lilly."

Cade looked at Rose who was transfixed by the boy's storytelling, and then back at Robbie. "When was this?"

"I don't know. A day or so ago."

"Why on earth were they arguing about Lilly?" Rose asked. "She barely knows Leo and has never spoken to Rosalie to my knowledge."

"That Marta girl told La Bella Rosa that she'd seen Leo with Lilly getting' all friendly-like at the market the morning before the race started."

A startled expression entered Rose's eyes.

"I been keepin' an eye on Marta," Robbie said, grabbing another slice of bread. "She's like a spoon, she is. Keeps everyone stirred up with some vile comment or another. Whisperin' stuff as she passes the other girls on the track."

"It wasn't Lilly with Leo." Rose's statement fell into the room, effectively halting Robbie's opinion of the Swede.

Both Cade and Robbie looked at her.

She picked up Robbie's plate and put it in the hot dishwater sitting on the stove. "Marta couldn't have seen Lilly talking to Leo that morning, because Lilly didn't go to the market. She was off with you, training. I went to get some things, if you recall, and I remember seeing Marta *and* Leo."

"Together?"

Rose smirked and shook her head. "No, he was all huddled up with Lady Jocelyn when I saw them."

Cade blew out a harsh breath. He'd seen plenty growing up where and as he had, but he hadn't seen anything until he'd come to the endurance races. There were so many resentments and so many affairs it would take one of the official scorekeepers to keep tally of them all.

"Jocelyn and Lilly are about the same size and they both have red hair," he reasoned. "I can see how someone could mistake one for the other from a distance."

"Holy mother of pearl, McShane!" Robbie said, using one of his hero's favorite expressions. "It weren't no mistake! It were an out and out lie! I'm tellin' ya that girl is mean to the bone."

"To what purpose, Robbie?" McShane pressed. "How does Marta making La Bella Rosa jealous of Lilly help Rosalie?"

Robbie shrugged. "All I know is that Lilly's been put out of the race. That seems pretty important to me."

* * *

"Where are you off to next?" Rose asked after Robbie was gone and Cade watched Lilly sleep for a while.

"I'm not sure." He swore softly. "Sorry, Rose, but I feel like I've been running in circles ever since we got here. None of this is what I expected. Officially, we're here to try to determine if Dora Ames's husband died by his own hand or was murdered by one of four people, she believes had reason to harm him!"

He gave a weary laugh. "I can't seem to get more than an hour or two to work on the case for all the other chaos. And then all this with Robbie! I can't believe he ran off the second time."

"Can't you?" Rose said. "He idolizes you, Mr. McShane."

He shrugged and gave a negative shake of his head, almost as if he were uncomfortable with the notion that anyone think too highly of him.

"He's both a marvel and a menace," Rose noted.

Cade grinned, albeit wryly. "You think I don't know that? He's brilliant with what he does, but he's reckless and pulls crazy stunts, and he's sorely lacking in common civilities."

"I understand he comes from bad circumstances. He'll learn, in time."

"I suppose. He's a wily little creature and just one step away from being feral. I'm just thankful he's working for our side."

"Indeed," Rose said, chuckling. "So, do you suggest that we forget this incident with Lilly and concentrate on the Ames case now that she's out of the race, or stick with trying to find out who set out to harm our girl?"

"Lilly is definitely out of the race," he said. "Hopefully in a day or so, she'll be feeling well enough to get out and about. I've been thinking that maybe with you and Robbie and Lilly to help, we can do both."

* * *

Lilly opened her eyes slowly. The effort took more than she thought she had in her. She stared at the ceiling of the tent and took stock of her condition. Her body was one big, throbbing ache, yet contrarily, she felt drained. Empty. Gutted. The blisters on her feet stung. Her joints ached. Her stomach muscles were sore.

Vaguely, like brief snatches of dreams that flit in and out of your mind so quickly they're hard to hang onto, she recalled being violently sick several times and falling back asleep immediately. Dreaming. Hearing conversations around her, wanting to put in her two cents' worth and then falling into the dark void of nothingness once again. She'd heard Cade telling her she needed to hurry and wake up, that he needed her to help with the case. Is that all he needed her for? Is that all she was to him?

And Robbie. He was here, too. She had seen him in the crowd. Or had she been hallucinating the same way she had when she thought the handsome stranger was Cade?

Her brain felt like a pit of quicksand. She was unable to hold any thought for longer than a few seconds before it sank into the void of forgetfulness. As soon as she had that thought, she was off again, deep asleep.

Thursday

"You're awake."

"Am I?"

He dragged a chair nearer, spun it around on one leg, and sat, resting his forearms on the ladder back.

"You look like bloody hell."

Though the words were insensitive and hurtful, she saw the concern in his eyes. She almost smiled, but it seemed like more of an effort than she could manage.

"And you're still the charmer I remember." Her voice sounded raspy, hoarse.

He did smile then. "I'm glad you're back, lass," he told her.

"Back? From where?"

"The gates of Hell."

Her hands clenched around the fabric of the quilt covering her. "What happened?"

"You don't remember?"

She moved her head back and forth on the pillow. "I remember moving into third place and drinking champagne to celebrate." Her face turned beet red, and her eyes widened in mortification. "I upchucked all over you! Oh, I'm so sorry!"

"Don't worry yourself. You couldn't help it."

"I suppose I drank it too fast on an empty stomach."

He, Robbie, and Rose all agreed that Lilly should be told the truth. She couldn't be on the watch for unusual and harmful things if she didn't know what was going on.

"No, Lilly," he told her. "That's not what happened."

"What do you mean?"

"Someone tampered with the champagne."

Her face, which had been so red seconds before, drained of color. Her eyes widened.

"Someone tried to poison me?"

"No, no, no, lass. We don't think they meant to kill you. We think..." he paused "I might be..." He shook his head. "We have a couple of theories we're exploring."

He told her about Marta telling La Bella Rosa that she'd seen Lilly with Leo and that Rose said it was Lady Jocelyn.

"Do you think Rosalie was trying to take me out of the race to get back at me because she thought I was with her husband?"

Cade shrugged. "Everyone knows Rosalie can't trust Leo, and Robbie is of the opinion that Marta might have tattled, hoping to get Rosalie so riled that she'll do the dirty work Marta can't do without drawing attention to herself."

Lilly's head spun. "That's too convoluted to even begin to understand."

"I know. The whole thing is truly a mess. On the other hand, Dr. Forrester said something that makes me think it could all have been an unfortunate accident."

"I'm not following you."

"He says sometimes the walkers have so much, they'll pass some of their goodies on to others. I'm thinking that maybe one of the walkers sincerely wanted to congratulate you and passed on a bottle they didn't know was contaminated."

Lilly's forehead furrowed in concentration. "But wouldn't that mean that whoever gave the champagne to the first person, intended *them* harm?"

"Yes, it would seem so." He shook his head. "I was telling Rose that this is the most shamefully wicked sport I have ever encountered, and believe me, I've seen a few things among the boxers."

"Who is Dr. Forrester?"

"Your gentleman friend you mistook for me."

Her eyes widened in astonishment. "You know who he is?"

McShane nodded. "When you didn't come back onto the track, the fans knew something was wrong. Robbie was trying to spread the word about what had happened to you, and he stopped by Forrester's table to tell him since he knew the two of you had some sort of rapport."

Rapport. Is that what it is?

"As it turns out he's a medical doctor, and he came to see what he could do for you. That's when he suggested the champagne might have been passed on to you unintentionally. It's something we're looking into. He also took the bottle to see if he could figure out what was in it."

"Has he?"

"Initially, he said syrup of ipecac because of the wine's musty odor." McShane reached into his pocket, pulled out a small slip of lined paper, and handed it to her. "I received this from him this morning, but I haven't had a chance to do any checking. It makes sense."

Lilly took the paper. "Dover's Powder. I know what that is. I remember

Kate and Rose giving it to me for colds and such."

"Yes. It contains not only ipecac but powdered opium, which is what gave the wine the bitter taste you were complaining about. It could also be why you slept more than twenty hours. That and the fact that you're worn to a nub."

The last was added with a slight smile. He tried to gauge her emotions as she struggled to absorb the things that had happened to her. He didn't have much luck.

"You know," she told him in a reflective tone, "I was thinking about our work before we came, and hearing this has brought it all back again. It's ironic, really, but no matter how much we prepare, no matter how good we get with our shooting, or our boxing or any of it..."

Her voice trailed away. "I mean, I was feeling good about my training with Monstery, and then instead of needing physical preparedness, I get taken down by a jealous wife and a cold remedy."

"Or a jealous walker."

"Quite possibly," she acknowledged, exhaling a deep breath. "It's over for me, isn't it? The race?"

"I'm afraid so, but you did really well, lass. Gave them a run for their money. I'm proud of you."

"Thank you." She mustered a small smile. "I'm rather proud of me myself."

"Do you feel like getting dressed and taking a walk in the fresh air? We have a case to solve, and as my ma used to tell us when we hung around too long inside, you need to get out and get the stink blowed off ya."

"Your mother certainly had a way with words," she said with a wry smile. "But you're right, I do." She pushed herself into a sitting position and a wave of dizziness washed over her. "Maybe I should eat something first."

"I can make you some nice poached eggs with brown bread."

"No, I want ham and fried eggs, and I want lots of butter and jam on my bread."

He looked at her with raised eyebrows. "Do ya really think that's wise with your wee stomach being all torn up?"

"You are such a misery, McShane," she said with a slow shake of her head.

"But blast it, you're inevitably right."

"Thank you for recognizing that," he told her in a superior tone. "So, what will it be?"

"Well, it looks like I'm having the poached eggs. Three of them."

He rose and went to the small gas stove.

"McShane?"

"Yes?"

"What about Lady Jocelyn? Do you think she had anything to do with it? I mean, it's clear that she has no regard for me, and from what Rose hears from Ginny, she's a horrible person to work for and goes out of her way to be unkind to Elsa and Penn."

He turned on the gas beneath the cast iron skillet and tossed in a dollop of butter. "It's something to consider. And don't forget the glass in your shoe. That was done on purpose. We have to put our heads together and see if we can think of who had the opportunity to do it."

"I doubt we will ever know," she said. "Hundreds of people cross the infield in a twenty-four-hour period. It could have been anyone who took a dislike to me and my standing."

"Good point, lass. And none of this has anything to do with solving our case."

"I know. And time's running out."

* * *

An hour and a half later, wearing her favorite red cloak against the chill of the sunless day, Lilly clung heavily to Cade's arm as they wandered slowly through the vendors outside the main venue. She had been so tied up with the competition there had been no opportunity to experience the other attractions available.

The race had passed the halfway mark, but an atmosphere of excitement still filled the air, along with the aroma of roasting peanuts and popcorn. She felt like a child at a circus. There had seldom been opportunities to attend fairs, festivals and such when she was growing up. The Pierced Rose troupe was always moving or making costumes or studying lines.

She was surprised and pleased when several people recognized her. Without fail, they gave her big smiles and a thumbs up, or hollered "Next time, Lil!" or "Rotten luck, Irish!"

In true Lil McShane fashion, she smiled back and blew kisses. Their encouragement went a long way toward filling the emptiness created by the knowledge that she might have died. Well, not really, but if the dose had been larger, who knew? She was alive, and she would soon be strong again, and she had performed better than she ever imagined she could.

"You're a luminary," McShane said, the compliment intruding on her troubled thoughts.

Instead of feigning awkwardness or embarrassment, she grinned up at him. "I am, aren't I?"

He laughed and the hand covering hers on his arm tightened. "Just promise you won't become another Lady Jocelyn."

"If I do, you have my permission to shoot me."

"Andrew! Lil!"

They turned and saw Robbie pushing through the crowd. Lilly couldn't hold back a smile at seeing the troublesome rascal again. Genuine pleasure shone in his eyes as well and, for a fraction of a second, she thought he might give her a hug, but then he seemed to recover from the momentary weakness, planted his hands on his skinny hips and looked her up and down.

"Well, you're looking a sight better. I thought you were a goner there for a bit."

Lilly pressed her lips together to keep from laughing. He had learned many things from McShane, but tact wasn't one of them. Possibly because his mentor was in short supply himself. "Thank you, Robbie. What are you doing here?"

"I've come to help you and McShane with the case, haven't I?"

"Well, we were just discussing how time is getting away from us, so the more the merrier."

He beamed back at her. It was amazing how much he craved being noticed, feeling important. Amazing how much he needed Cade's approval.

"So," she said, as he fell into step with them. "have you learned anything new?"

He jerked his head toward the rink. "I just talked to Penn. He says his ma's almost done for. Says she can hardly stand, much less walk, but she won't give up until she can't go anymore. I've a feeling this race is very important to them."

"So, do I," Lilly said.

"Do you have any idea why, Robbie?" McShane asked. "I mean, they need the money, of course, but has Penn mentioned any reason in particular?"

Robbie thought for a moment. "Not really. Just that money has been tight ever since his ma's trainer took off."

"Yes. We heard about him leaving San Francisco under suspicious circumstances."

"It's no secret," Robbie agreed. "Penn says they were supposed to get some money from a man his ma knew a long time ago, but there's a kink in the deal, and they aren't certain when it might come about, or even if it will.

He shook his head. "I know they were countin' on the money from this race to tide them over, and now it looks like she'll have to pull out soon. He says she's all possessed with Lady Jocelyn. Mad as a March hare she is. Ravin' and rantin.'"

"That's something we need to look into," Cade said. "We've been hearing rumblings about hard feelings between those two ever since we got here, and it would be a sin to Moses if we don't try to find out what it's all about." He gestured toward an empty table in the sun. "Let's sit and talk about what we do know and see if any of us can add anything."

"Yes, please," Lilly said. "I'm getting really tired, but I need to catch up. I've been so consumed with the race that everything else has passed me by. It feels like time wasted."

"This whole assignment has been a strange one," Cade added, pulling out a chair for Lilly and helping her get settled.

Robbie plopped down across from her, folded his arms on the tabletop and regarded McShane with a hangdog expression. "I don't suppose you'd treat me to some roasted peanuts and a sarsaparilla while we're yammering would ya, McShane? I seem to be without means being as I donated all my cash to the church."

McShane struggled to keep a straight face. "Since you've shared your valuable insights with us, I believe that can be arranged," he said, pulling some money from his pocket. "Keep the change. A man needs some walking around money."

Robbie returned a few moments later. To Lilly's surprise, he dumped some of the peanuts in front of her and McShane.

He reached for one and started filling Robbie in on various aspects of the case, explaining in detail about what had happened in California and J.D. Ames's death, ending with, "Mrs. Ames doesn't believe it was suicide, because her husband had made a few enemies."

"Who does she suspect?" he asked, getting straight to the heart of the matter.

Cade ticked off the suspects on his fingers, "There's Leo, who basically wanted to steal the business from J.D.; Elsa, who claims J.D. cheated her and who threatened to make him pay. Tad Connelly, the accountant the Ameses fired and they both identified as being part of the robbery. And last, Jerome Connelly, who was refused a vendor spot for the race out there. We've just learned that he was Elsa's former trainer. He' s also Tad's brother. It might be any one of them or any combination of them."

"Crikey!"

McShane shook his head. "I've never worked a case like this one, and I confess that I feel like we haven't made much progress."

"That ain't true, McShane," Robbie said, cracking a peanut. "Everything that's happened during the race is showing us in some way if the people who were involved in San Francisco have the makings of a killer. But pay no attention to me. I'm not the operative here."

Lilly glanced at McShane, who appeared as stunned as she was by the boy's ability to see beyond the surface. Even so, for once in his short life, even he looked at a loss. Staring off into space and trying to sort out what he'd heard, he reached for his sarsaparilla and took a healthy slug.

"I've got an idea," he said at last. "We've got a lot of things to check out, so why don't you two concentrate on the Ames fella's death, and I'll try to see what I can find out about what's going on with these barmy pedestriennes and if there's any link there."

He cracked another peanut and tossed it into his mouth. "Take Penn's ma. For all that she has a terrible temper, I'd be hard pressed to think she could kill anyone." He gave an offhand shrug. "I mean to find out why she and Lady Jocelyn hate each other so much, and I intend to find out who gave that bad champagne to Lilly. I'll not sleep well until I know who intended her harm."

And that was as close to a declaration of affection as Lilly was apt to get from Robert Jenkins. She felt tears sting her eyes and wished she could grab him up and hug him, but that would never do.

"That's brilliant, Robbie," McShane said. "You and Penn work together on that, and Lilly and I will see what we can find out where Elsa's trainer went when he left California."

"Why don't we send both Connelly names to William and have him see what the agency can dig up," Lilly suggested. "I think it's interesting that the trainer and the accountant are brothers and that they've both disappeared."

"I couldn't agree more," McShane said. "I'm even considering the notion that even though the Ameses pointed the finger at Tad, the brothers might have been in cahoots in the robbery and could even be behind J.D.'s death."

Robbie stood, grabbed up his drink and the bag of peanuts.

"Where are you going, lad?"

"You two can sit here and jaw all afternoon if ya like, but I have things to find out."

* * *

Later that night, Lilly lay in her cot and thought about the time she had spent with Cade and Robbie. Being outside had done her a world of good. It seemed like forever since she'd breathed anything but the foul, smoky air of the rink and done anything but walk in circles she barely remembered walking. Sitting in the September sunshine, warm in her cape, eating peanuts

132

and discussing the case with her associates had felt good. Right.

She smiled in the darkness. To consider Robbie a workfellow might be stretching things a bit, but there was no doubt that during his hanging about he saw and heard things people had no idea he was hearing and seeing. And his comment about the work they'd done so far being helpful had been spot-on and eased her guilt somewhat. They were forming a baseline of the walkers' personalities that could be used as a measuring rod for future information and incidents.

She heard him shuffling in the darkness, no doubt trying to get comfortable on his makeshift pallet. He'd arrived back from his snooping in time to wolf down the meal Rose cooked and promptly took off again, telling them he had another lead to check out. He'd returned just moments ago, long after the lantern had been turned out.

He was back. She could rest easy. She breathed a sigh of contentment and was asleep in seconds.

Chapter Thirteen

Thursday

When Lilly awakened, Rose was bustling around fixing breakfast. McShane was behind the screen mumbling a naughty Irish ditty while he shaved and dressed. She glanced at the place where Robbie had slept. He was already gone. The blankets he'd used were folded somewhat haphazardly and stacked by her cot. At least he had made the effort.

McShane stepped from behind the privacy screen, looking just the way she liked him. He was wearing the clothes she had dubbed his Irishman's working garb: tan twill trousers, a pale-blue, collarless chambray shirt with the sleeves rolled to the elbows, and workingman's boots. She loved the way he looked in his suits and bowler, all competent and dashing, but in these clothes, he looked more approachable somehow. She stifled a sigh and smiled.

"You sound chipper this morning."

"Well, for the first time since we arrived, I feel like we're actually doing what we came here to do."

"Me, too."

"Yoo-hoo! Is everybody decent?" Ginny called from outside the tent.

"Come on in, Ginny," Rose said. "Coffee?"

"I'd love some, thank you." She came inside, spoke to Lilly and Cade, and took a seat at the table.

"What are you doing out and about so early?" Rose asked, setting a blue and white speckled mug down in front of her.

She rolled her eyes ceilingward. "Well, I have *M'lady's* next meal cooking, and I don't look for her to take a break for another two or three hours, and I wanted to come and check on Lil."

"I'm doing much better, Mrs. Evans, thank you," Lilly assured her. "It's amazing what a few hours of sleep will do for a body."

"No aftereffects from your…sickness?"

"None."

"And you still have no idea who sent the champagne?"

"I'm afraid we may never know."

Ginny looked from Lilly to Cade. "I've been wondering…did anyone think to check with the two men who have the bars out back? One of them might recollect who bought that champagne. I mean, with its cost, they can't have sold too many bottles, can they?"

"That's a good point," Cade said, slanting Lilly a sideways look. "I'll do that this morning."

"Have you heard how Elsa is doing?" Lilly asked.

"Not this morning. I know she was in awful pain yesterday and about done in, but I gave her a good rubdown with some of that liniment Andrew gave us, and it seems to have helped. She's still out there."

McShane smiled. "It always helped the horses."

Everyone laughed.

They chatted a few minutes longer and Ginny left, telling Rose she would see her soon. After she'd gone, Cade shook his head. "Why didn't I think to ask the men out back?"

"Perhaps because you've been busy doctoring walkers, looking for runaway children, and taking care of drugged women?" Lilly said, with a lift of her eyebrows.

"That's no excuse."

"Well, then, excuse me while I go fetch your hair shirt." When he just looked at her, she said, "Finish your breakfast and go talk to those men. Then you can check something off your list."

"Do we have a list, then?" he asked, finally seeing the humor in her statement.

"We don't, but with all the things going on, perhaps we should."

* * *

Cade thought it was time to pay Dora Ames another visit. After all, she was in charge of this event, and he was curious to see what she was doing to find out who wanted Lilly out of the race so badly that they would put her life in danger. He was more than a little miffed that neither she nor Leo had come to check on Lilly. Cade felt like tightening the screws a bit.

He'd seen all manner of women throughout his life, and he'd lost his innocence about their temperaments long go. He suspected the years on the job had made him bitter, or at the very least suspicious, but he sensed a ruthless streak beneath Dora Ames's pleasant exterior.

Ruthless might be too extreme. She might just be a very strong woman, but he had doubts about any female as sweet-tempered as Dora appeared to be could hold an enterprise like this together for long. Society was unkind to women entrepreneurs. Not only would she need backing, but she'd also need plenty of backbone.

Within a couple of seconds of his knocking, Dora called for him to enter. He found her sitting behind her battered desk, going over some figures in a ledger. She looked particularly fetching in a simple blue dress that made the most of her plump prettiness. When she looked up and saw who it was, she smiled.

"Andrew," she said with a pleasant smile. "How is your sister?"

Despite the smile, Cade saw the worry in her eyes and the tension around her mouth. He didn't blame her. Though the incident had been mentioned in the newspapers, it escaped being the news event of the day. To have it plastered all over the front pages would have put an end to Dora's dreams of resurrecting pedestrianism here or anywhere else.

Now he wondered if she and Leo had been avoiding him and Lilly for fear that they might want some sort of monetary compensation for the

136

champagne incident? Or worse, would they press charges?

"She's much improved, thank you."

"Wonderful." Dora indicated the chair across from her. "Please sit. I'm so glad she's all right. I mean, she was doing so well. I can't imagine how something like this could have happened."

Cade had serious doubts about that claim, but instead of challenging her, he said, "I wanted to talk to you about that if you have the time."

Dora regarded him from across the desk for a few seconds, slammed the ledger shut, and stood. "I need some fresh air. Walk with me."

After locking the office, she curled her hand around his biceps and guided him through the throng of people and across the track toward the rear exit.

In moments, they were in the midst of the bustling merchant area. The church was in the middle of a sermon, and the preacher was berating those sitting beneath the canopy of the tent for throwing away their hard-earned money on frivolous bets, card sharps, whiskey, and demon rum.

"Speaking of drinks," Dora said, "how about you buy me one."

"My pleasure," Cade assured her, thinking it was a little early to start drinking even though she looked as if she had already indulged in one or two. "What's your pleasure?"

"Whiskey. Neat."

"A woman after my own heart," he told her with a slight smile. Drinks in hand he secured a table near one of the tents, wondering what she might want to talk to him about. More complaints from Lady Jocelyn about Lilly? If so, he had a few grievances of his own.

Dora downed the two fingers of whiskey in one practiced toss of her head. "Have you ever found yourself in the middle of something you weren't certain how to resolve?"

"A time or two." He cupped the tumbler of liquor in his hands and lifted it, inhaling the intense aroma. Then he set it down and, using his index finger, slid it toward her.

She looked at him, a question in her eyes.

"I think you need it more than I do."

Without another second's hesitation, she pulled the glass closer. "It's been hard keeping my husband's dream going since he died."

"Lil and I heard about that when we first came over," he told her. "You have our sincere condolences. She told me a few days ago that she has tremendous admiration for you, picking up the reins of a business operation such as this."

He tossed out a bit of bait to see if she'd bite. "She appreciates the tips you gave her on opening her own business once we get back home."

"I'm always glad to help any woman who wants to get ahead. Thankfully, I've had some excellent help along the way."

"I'm sure having Leo around to help out has been a good thing."

Dora lifted her gaze from her drink to Cade. "Yes, well, things are often different from what they appear."

Hm. Was there trouble in paradise? "I'm guessing you want to talk about it," he ventured. For an instant, she looked surprised by his bluntness. She hadn't expected that, but he had an idea that she would hold him in higher regard if he didn't let her walk on him. Besides, playing a doormat had never been his style.

"It's obvious that something is on your mind. Why else would you ask me to buy you a drink?" He smiled. "That, or you're trying to sweeten me up, so I won't cause any trouble over Lil's unfortunate incident." He said it jokingly but thought he saw the color drain from her face.

"Are you planning on that?"

The friendliness had vanished. Though she was smiling, her eyes held a wary expression, and he could almost see the wheels turning in her head. What did he have in mind? Blackmail? A lawsuit? What?

"Ah, Dora, lass. Don't fret," he said, reaching out and covering her hand with his. "We came into this race knowing full well that these things happen. Lil is fine, but it might have been far more serious. I *would* like to know what you're doing to find out who did it and how you plan to punish the guilty party once you do."

Magically, her apprehension vanished, and she was all business once more. "For starters, Leo and I are taking the time to question each and every one of the walkers and their people. The police are doing so as well, though you must know I have little faith in their ability to find their posteriors with both hands after the slipshod way they handled things in California."

Cade let the comment pass. "Well, let me ease your mind somewhat. One of the medical people who treated Lil has discovered what was used to taint the champagne." Dora's eyes widened. "It wasn't an actual poison, thank God, though we have it on authority that enough of it could have killed her."

"What was it?"

"Dover's powder."

"I don't think I've heard of it," she said, frowning.

"It's given for colds and such. Comes in a little jar with a blue lid and red print."

"Oh, yes," she said, nodding. "I've seen it. What's in it?"

"Basically, it's powdered ipecac and opium."

Dora heaved a great sigh and took a swallow of the whiskey. "Well, I'll tell the police to be on the lookout for it as they talk to everyone."

"Fair enough," Cade said. "May I ask you something?"

"That depends on what it is." Her smile and good humor were restored now that she felt secure that he didn't plan on pressing charges for any harm that had befallen his sister.

"It's about La Bella Rosa and Lady Jocelyn."

"What about them?" Dora asked looking at her drink.

"Do you have any idea what caused the hostility between them?"

She laughed. "If you had been around a while, you'd know the answer to that. It's common knowledge in the pedestrian community." She took another sip of the whisky. "As you've no doubt heard, not only is Leo ruthlessly ambitious, he has the morals of an alley cat. He and Jocelyn had a brief affair in California. Rosalie found out, and there have been fireworks between them ever since."

Cade shook his head in disbelief. "That must make an awkward situation for anyone in the business of filling races."

"Thorny to say the least," Dora agreed with a wry smile. "To cap the climax, Jocelyn insists on behaving as if she's the wronged woman. On the other hand, if the sport manages to survive, Rosalie Bertolini could be another Exilda La Chapelle. Rosalie has the will and mindset of a champion and were it not for Leo and his indiscretions, she might have already reached her pinnacle."

Cade absorbed that bit of news. Dora was repeating the same sentiments about Rosalie Bertolini that Elsa Dengler had. It seemed that La Bella Rosa not only received sympathy for the way her husband treated her but her abilities were regarded with genuine respect.

"Knowing her husband's penchant for cheating, she views any woman as potential competition and treats them accordingly," Dora added.

"That must be why she's so spiteful toward Lil."

"Oh, most certainly. It's nothing personal." The bartender set another whiskey before Dora and she picked it up and sipped greedily.

"Do you think there's any chance that Lady Jocelyn is behind either of the attacks on Lil? The glass shard in her shoe or the tainted champagne?"

"Oh, heavens no!" Dora said without a second's hesitation. "Jocelyn Baldwin is possibly one of the most selfish, self-serving individuals I have ever met. Everything she says and does is for the betterment of her and her alone, but she is open and above board with her grievances as well as her actions, whatever forms they take. I can't see her doing anything to physically harm someone."

Buying a drink for Dora had been time well spent. Robbie was right. The discussions with various people did help form opinions about those she suspected of being involved with her husband's murder, if indeed it had been murder. Cade hesitated, wondering at the wisdom of pursuing one more question. *In for a penny; in for a pound.*

"Forgive me for being forward, but since we're speaking of Leo and his *weaknesses—*" he emphasized the word "—I was under the impression that the two of you have an, uh, understanding."

Dora sighed heavily and gave a jaded laugh. "You have bollocks, Andrew McShane, I'll give you that."

"I'm an Irishman," he said, as if that explained his forthrightness.

Dora smiled, rather seductively. "Do you have any regrets?"

He smiled at her; the smile Lilly loved. The one that invited camaraderie... and more. "A few."

"Well, I have more than a few, and Leo Bertolini is one of them." She made a little toasting gesture with her glass and took another swallow.

"I suspected as much. Does La Bella Rosa know?"

Dora drew a deep breath and released it slowly. "She has her suspicions, and I've decided that it's time I end things before she finds out for certain. Besides, the race will soon be over."

Cade wondered if Dora realized how much that last comment revealed. She had drawn Leo into her web, and he had done most of the work helping get the race set up. Now that it was winding down, she could handle things herself. Leo Bertolini was no longer needed.

"He's beginning to throw his weight around and act like he's the sole owner of this operation."

Cade crossed his arms over his chest. "In what way?"

"For one thing, he's been making decisions without consulting me."

Knowing her drive and thirst for fame and power, Cade had no problem understanding that comment. As a woman, she would feel threatened by any decisions Leo made without consulting her first. Threatened and angry that her authority had been undermined.

"What kind of decisions?"

She held her glass aloft, toward the bar a few feet away. "Take that liquor establishment. He gave the man running it permission to set up without talking it over with me."

"That doesn't seem too drastic. Is there any reason he shouldn't have?"

"Other than the fact that my husband turned him down in California, I suppose not. It's the principle, Mr. McShane. We're partners."

A piece of the puzzle slipped into place. Cade felt a glimmer of excitement. He recalled seeing Dora and the barman in a heated argument the first day he arrived. Now he knew why.

Could the bartender with the long hair and beard be the same man Penn had seen delivering the bottle of champagne to Lilly...the one who looked familiar? Was it possible that he was Jerome Connelly, Elsa's former trainer who had been denied a spot in California and then disappeared the day after J.D. Ames was found dead? Tamping back a burst of excitement, Cade regarded his companion questioningly, urging her to continue.

"Jerome thought that since he was Elsa's trainer, he had an inside track to all the advantages that came with his close association with the race. When J.D. gave the spot to someone else, Jerome was furious. He packed up and left soon after."

And just that easily, a couple of questions were answered. Cade thought of his and Lilly's speculation that both Tad and Jerome had been in on the Ames robbery and J.D.'s death. "Do you think he had anything to do with your husband's death? It sounds as if he might have a grudge against him."

Dora gave a thoughtful sigh. "I've considered it, yes, but what was I to do? Until he showed up here, I had no idea where he was. And even if he were involved in some way, how could I ever prove it?"

She had a point. "Did you let Leo know how you felt about his decision?"

"I did. He just laughed and told me I was too sensitive. Suffice it to say I no longer feel comfortable with our relationship, which is one reason I wanted to talk to you."

Cade frowned. "Yes?"

"As I mentioned, I think it's time to break away from Leo, and I was wondering if you might be interested in taking over his place."

"Taking over his place?"

She smiled, and her eyes twinkled with mischief. "Oh, come, Mr. McShane! Surely you know what I'm talking about. You're obviously a smart man, and an attractive one. I believe you want to get ahead. With a little training in the ins and outs of this business, I think you'd make an excellent replacement for Leo."

Oh, he knew what she was talking about all right, and he wanted no part of Dora Ames. "You're suggesting that you get rid of Leo Bertolini and bring me in as his replacement."

"That's exactly what I'm suggesting. There are...several areas in this business I believe you would be excellent at filling."

Cade wasn't sure he didn't blush. That was either the most blatant double entendre he had ever heard, or he had been way too long without a woman. He managed a soft laugh and chose to act the unsophisticated fool. "Forgive me madam, but I fear I must pass. I plan on heading back to Ireland as soon as I get my sister better established. Now if you will excuse me, I must go check on her."

Even as he rejected the offer, he wondered what the repercussions of his refusal might be. He left Dora Ames sitting there, her face a study in humiliation and rage. It was a side he had never seen, and it was not pretty.

As he made his way toward the rear entrance of the rink, he wondered how her statements about Leo and Jerome affected the investigation, or even if they did. Maybe it was time to have that talk with Jerome, but first, he needed to send that telegram to William about the Connelly brothers. And while he was at it, he wanted to know everything William could find out about Jocelyn Baldwin. Unlike Dora, who seemed to think the Englishwoman would draw the line at physical harm, Cade wasn't so sure.

Chapter Fourteen

Lilly and Rose were sitting outside the tent when a voice called out. They looked up to see Ginny hurrying toward them, her skirts clutched in both hands. The expression on her face was one of excitement, almost victorious. Clearly, she had something important to tell.

It was no secret that Rose's new friend liked being in the middle of things, and if there was anything newsworthy going on, she would be one of the first to know about it. She thrived on tittle-tattle, and frankly, Lilly was thankful for the woman's outgoing, inquisitive nature.

When Ginny reached them, she dropped her skirts and clasped her hands together at her waist. Exultation filled her eyes, and she was almost bouncing up and down in excitement. "I think I know the problem between Lady Jocelyn and Elsa!"

"Really?" Rose exclaimed.

Ginny nodded. "The picture isn't Wolfgang."

"What picture?" Lilly asked.

"The picture in Elsa's tent. The one of Penn's father, remember? It isn't Elsa's husband, Wolfgang Dengler, as we thought. It's Helmut Baldwin." Lilly leapt to her feet, barely able to control her excitement. Cade had learned from Dora why Lady Jocelyn was so hostile toward La Bella Rosa, and now, perhaps they were about to uncover the source of the enmity between the lady and Elsa. Lilly grabbed Ginny's wrist. "Why do you say that? How do you know?"

"Jocelyn Baldwin was married to Helmut, and until recently, I've been looking at a daguerreotype of him every day for the past three years."

"Why haven't you been seeing it recently?" Rose asked.

"It's an odd thing, really. She's always kept the likeness sitting on a little wooden box next to her cot, but ever since we came back from California, she's kept the picture turned face down, so I just dust around it."

"Why would she turn the photograph face down?" Rose asked.

"I couldn't say, but for some reason, I tipped it upright today to give everything a good dusting, and the truth hit me square between the eyes! Jocelyn's husband…Helmut, is the same man whose picture we saw at Elsa's. The one Penn said was his father!"

Lilly and Rose looked at each other in disbelief.

"I can't believe I never noticed before," Ginny continued, speaking fast in her excitement, "but then, I don't recall ever being in Elsa's tent until we took poor Penn under our wing."

"Are you saying Elsa was not married to Wolfgang Dengler?" Rose asked.

"Oh, no, Rose, not at all," Ginny said, with a shake of her head. "Elsa was married to Wolfgang, but he was not Penn's father. Helmut Baldwin was."

Despite the tumult of the crowd in the stands around them and the sound of the band playing, Lilly felt as if she were thousands of miles away from it all, caught in a bubble of soundlessness with nothing but her and her two companions and the weight of the truth settling heavily on them.

"Come inside," she said, "Let's have some coffee and see if we can sort this all out."

Soon, the three sat around Lilly's small table with mugs of steaming coffee in front of them, Ginny's discovery uppermost on their minds.

"Obviously, at some point, Elsa was involved with Helmut. Considering Penn's age, it was before Helmut and Jocelyn married," Lilly reasoned

Rose nodded in agreement. "And I'd wager there's a big likelihood that Jocelyn came between them."

"Oh, of course, she did, Rose! Don't you remember telling me that you'd heard Jocelyn broke up a wealthy merchant and his fiancé and married him herself?" Lilly reminded.

Rose's mouth dropped open. "Blast it all, I did, didn't I?" She looked as surprised by the revelation as the other two women.

Lilly's eyebrows drew together in a frown. "What I don't understand is why Jocelyn would leave Helmut to come over here and become a pedestrienne. That doesn't make any sense." She looked from Ginny to Rose. "I mean, she'd moved up in the world from third-rate actress to wife of a wealthy merchant. Her life should have been wonderful, so why leave it all behind?"

Ginny had been sitting quietly, thoughtfully, stirring and stirring the spoonful of sugar she'd added to her coffee. She leaned over the table and spoke in a tone not much more than a whisper. "I shouldn't be talking about her private life, but I'll tell you what I know if you promise not to say a word to anyone. I need this job."

"Of course," Rose said as Lilly sketched an "X" over her heart.

Satisfied that her conspirators would keep quiet, Ginny said, "I don't know why she came over here, but I do know Jocelyn has had money problems since Helmut died."

She took a sip of her coffee. "I know for a fact that he sent her a generous monthly allowance before he passed, but the amount was cut considerably after his death. Rumor has it that he left the bulk of his estate to an illegitimate son that Jocelyn knew nothing about until she heard about him from her attorney."

"Penn!" Lilly and Rose said in tandem.

"Do you think she suspects?" Lilly asked.

Ginny shrugged. "All I know is that the terms of the will were very upsetting. I heard her on a tear one day out in San Francisco, ranting and raving to her lawyer that it was a slap in the face, and she couldn't live on the paltry monthly allowance he'd left her. So, she contested the will."

"Of course, she would," Lilly said. "Losing her main source of income puts the burden on her to make her own living. She has to win races or find a man to help support her."

"Enter Leo Bertolini, stage left," Rose quipped. "It's my understanding they had at least a brief fling in California."

"It's true," Ginny said. "They did."

"Do you think she's been using their affair as leverage to force him to give in to her demands? Demands that give her an edge over the other women?"

Rose lifted her mug. "Of course, she is. If he doesn't give in to whatever she wants, she'll tell La Bella Rosa about their affair and Leo loses *his* meal ticket."

"It's all starting to make sense," Lilly said, shaking her head in disbelief. "We may not know why Lady Jocelyn came here, but it stands to reason that she stole Helmut away from Elsa and married him, probably before he knew of Elsa's pregnancy."

"Of course, that's what happened. And it certainly explains why there is no love lost between the two," Rose offered.

"Do you think he and Elsa broke it off after he married Lady Jocelyn?" Ginny asked.

"At this point, it doesn't matter. The important thing is that Helmut and Elsa had a son. When he died, he left the bulk of his estate to Penn and Jocelyn out in the cold."

She looked at Ginny. "You didn't answer before. Do you think Jocelyn knows who Penn is?"

"I couldn't say for certain, but ever since he arrived to help Elsa and I've been trying to help him out, Jocelyn has treated me worse than ever." Her eyes widened at a sudden memory. "One day she told me to spend more time taking care of her needs and not so much with 'that boy,' or I'd be looking for a new position."

Rose's mug thudded on the table, and she looked from Lilly to her new friend. "She knows."

"Why do you say that?"

"Ginny, do you remember the morning after Penn arrived when we went to take an inventory of what he had and would need?"

"Or course."

"As we were going to Elsa's tent, Lady Jocelyn was walking around the track and glanced up as we passed. When she saw Penn, she literally stopped in her tracks for just a second. Think about it. By then, she'd been told by the attorney that Helmut had a son. She knew all about Helmut and Elsa's past. I think she knew who Penn was the minute she set eyes on him."

Ginny's mouth made an 'O' of surprise.

"It seemed a bit strange at the time, and it never made sense until just now."

"I'd almost give a week's salary to know what happened between Lady Jocelyn and Helmut after they married," Lilly said.

Rose gave an unladylike snort. "Well, if she was anything then like she is now, that's easy to imagine."

Ginny laughed. "Good point, Rose. It seems that Bible verse is true."

"Which one?" Rose asked.

"You reap what you sow."

* * *

When Cade returned a bit later, Lilly filled him in on what they'd discovered. He listened intently, waiting until she'd told him everything before commenting.

"Well," he said, "their hatred of each other certainly makes more sense now, and we understand why Elsa was so determined to win this race. Not only did she need the money, but she wanted to best Lady Jocelyn at her own game for once."

"Do you think we can mark Elsa off as the killer?" Rose asked.

"She doesn't seem the type," Lilly said. "I think she's been dealt a bad hand, and she's tried to do the best she can for herself and her son, despite it."

"Isn't it uncanny how they both wound up in the same field?" Rose said.

"In some ways, yes, and some no," Cade said after a moment. "It's the only game around where a woman stands to gain a lot of money, and from what I've seen, they both have the temperament and physical ability for it. What's stranger to me is that they're both so good at it."

He rubbed his thumb over his mustache in a thoughtful gesture. "You know, Elsa kept saying she wanted this to be a clean race, that there couldn't be any notoriety attached to it. I wondered why she seemed so stubborn about it, and now I understand. She doesn't need anything negative attached to her name until Penn's inheritance is settled. She wants to look above reproach for the benefit of the courts."

"That makes perfect sense," Lilly agreed. "I do hope they rule in her favor."

"As we all do."

Cade pulled his pocket watch from his trousers, and then looked from Rose to Lilly. "Has anyone seen Robbie lately?"

* * *

Knowing he couldn't just walk up and question the owner of the outdoor pub about things that had happened in California, Robbie asked the man for a job washing glasses, figuring he could watch and listen and possibly come up with something of value to help solve the murder of Mrs. Ames's husband.

So far, all he had for his efforts were reddened, shriveled hands from the hot water, and a bad case of the sulks. He didn't much like washing dishes, but he had a long stint of it before him when the race was over, and he went back to Seamus and Megan's. He'd promised her, after all, and a promise was something he was learning that a man of honor kept, no matter what.

Which was one reason he tried really hard not to make any.

Still, Megan and Seamus were good to him, and she smelled nice, like garden flowers, so mostly he didn't mind helping her whenever he could with the little ones and such.

He'd been surprised when McShane showed up with Mrs. Dora a bit ago, and he'd watched the exchange between them from his partially hidden spot behind the bar. He couldn't tell what they were saying, but he was rather good at reading expressions and he knew McShane well enough to know he was layin' the blarney on thick to eke out whatever information he could from the widow.

Robbie didn't like her much and liked her business partner even less. He'd been on the streets long enough to recognize a rat when it crossed his path, and Leo Bertolini was a rat if Robbie had ever seen one.

He'd been doing a lot of thinking, and he suspected Leo had something to do with the things that had been done to harm Lilly...not that he had any proof, of course. It was just a feeling.

He was polishing a glass when he saw McShane get up from the table and leave Mrs. Ames sitting there alone. *Hm.* Things had looked all hunky-dory there for a bit, but now Mrs. Ames looked like she could bite a nail in half. Robbie grinned in glee. He wouldn't half mind if she did. Maybe she'd break a tooth.

He was surprised to see her get up and carry her glass to the bar. Not that it was any of his business, but he'd say she'd had enough.

"Any news?" she asked Connelly, the long-haired man.

About what? Robbie took a step back, doing his best to blend into the shadows of the beer barrels.

"Everyone's still talking about it," Connelly said, looking out over the crowd of people milling about. "They can't imagine why anyone would want to harm her. Neither can I for that matter."

"Sometimes things just happen," Dora said, raising the glass.

Jerome poured her a couple more fingers of whiskey, but Robbie saw that he'd switched to the rotgut. Likely as not, she'd never notice.

"At least there's no permanent harm," Connelly said.

"There is that, but the wrong person is out of the running." She gave him a little salute with her glass. "By the way, McShane just told me they'd found out what was used. Too much and it could have been a real mess. God knows I don't need another death within a hundred miles of me."

"Why are you telling me this?" Jerome asked.

Lilly! They were talking about Lilly and the foul drink she'd received that made her sick. He was a little surprised by Connelly's comment.

"Don't play innocent, Jerome. It's a role that hardly fits."

Robbie wanted to jump out of his hiding place and tell them to spit it out, get to the point instead of talking in circles, but that would never do. Patience. Like honor, was a good thing.

Dora had started to slur her words. "I assume you have the medicine in a safe place. I don't need this coming back on me."

"You've had too much to drink, Dora," Jerome said in a disgusted tone. "You're starting to see things that aren't there."

Medicine. Robbie knew instantly what Dora was talking about. As usual, when he had a spare minute, he used the time to check things out. He'd only seen one item that could be considered medicine, and that was a small jar of Dover's Powder. He knew exactly where it was under the counter.

Dora reached out and laid her hand against Jerome's bearded cheek. "I can always count on you, can't I?"

He turned his head and placed a kiss against her palm. "I'll do anything and say anything as long as I know for certain there's a payday at the end."

"Oh, there's a payday," she crooned, scraping her thumb roughly over his lower lip. "And everyone will get everything they deserve."

After Dora left, Robbie thought long and hard about telling McShane what he'd overheard but figured all he'd get for his trouble was a tongue lashin' for putting himself in danger by gettin' too close to someone they suspected of murder.

For the moment, he decided to keep what he'd heard close to his vest, as McShane said when he was playin' cards. Truth be told, he didn't really *know* much. All he heard was a lot of hinting around about this and that.

He was certain that they'd been talking about the bad champagne, though, and almost positive Dora thought Jerome was the one who'd tampered with the drink. Jerome hadn't denied it, but he'd acted like he didn't want to be blamed for it.

To add to the muddle, Robbie had heard enough to suspect it wasn't meant for Lilly at all. If not, who was it intended for, and how had it ended up outside her tent? Even though the answer didn't seem connected to the investigation, neither he nor McShane would be happy until they knew who'd tried to harm Lilly. Which meant Robert Jenkins wanted to check on some things before telling anyone what he'd been up to.

Chapter Fifteen

L illy, Cade, and Rose were sitting around the table drinking coffee when Robbie burst into the tent, tugging off his cap as he entered.

"Whoa, there, lad!" McShane said. "What's the hurry, and where in blazes have you been?"

"Here and there. I got a job washing glasses for one of the bars out back."

"Why on earth would you do that?" Lilly asked.

"A man needs some money in his pocket," he said. "And I figure it'll be a good place to overhear things."

"I can give you money," McShane said.

"Ta, McShane, but I'd rather earn my own if you don't mind. And I'll let you know if I hear anything."

When Robbie left McShane and the others, he headed to the Dengler tent to visit with Penn for a while, eager to hear what his new friend thought about the conversation he'd overheard between Mrs. Ames and Jerome.

"I think the barman out back is the man you saw with the champagne. Have you had a good gander at him?"

"Not really," Penn said.

"Well, you need to. I'm almost certain he's the man you saw, but it's lookin' like it wasn't meant for Lil at all. I've wracked my brain, but I can't think of how we might find out who it was sent to first."

"You're far better than I am at figuring all this out, Robbie. And why does finding out who gave it to her matter? She's fine."

"What if it was your mum what got poisoned? Wouldn't you want whoever did it punished?"

"Punished? Like, go to jail?"

Robbie liked Penn just fine, but some days, he wondered how he got out of bed in the mornings.

"Aye, jail! Mrs. Dora said Lil coulda died, Penn! And if it wasn't meant for her, what about the one it *was* intended for? Don't you think it's important that we find out? I mean, how can we be sure it doesn't happen again if we don't figure out who done it and make them pay?"

"I never thought about it that way."

Robbie sat for a moment, thinking. "What if we sneak into each walker's tent and have a look around?" Robbie suggested.

"My ma would have my hide. Besides, if someone took it from the first person who got it to give to Lil, it wouldn't be there, would it?" Penn pointed out.

Robbie sighed. Good thinking.

"Who do you think might have wanted Lil out of the race?" Penn asked.

"The Swede," Robbie said without a second's hesitation. "She was awful to Lil when she was on the track. Even made her fall."

"Who else?"

"Well, I don't think it were your mum, but I wouldn't put it past Lady Jocelyn. She's another horrid excuse for a human."

"What about La Bella Rosa?" Penn asked. "Didn't Rose say something about her thinking Leo had been with Lil before the race started, but it was really Lady Jocelyn?"

Robbie's eyes brightened. "Yes! And right about that time that piece of glass was put in her shoe. Maybe we should start with those two."

"Robbie, think about this. If we get caught, we could go to jail."

For once in his short life, Robbie heard what Penn was saying and took time to consider the repercussions. He pictured the disappointment on the faces of all the McShanes. Thought about them giving up on him and putting him out on the street. And worse, *not* giving up on him and letting him stay around but no longer allowing him to be part of the family. He didn't like that picture much.

What other option was there? Was it possible for someone to waltz up to the barkeep and just ask about the champagne? Of course. Who, though? Seamus? Oh, he'd stir things up, would Seamus. Bigger than McShane, and with arms as big as tree trunks, they'd think twice about denyin' him anything. But then, Jerome and whoever was in on it with him would know they were under suspicion. They might hightail it again. For now, it seemed best to keep things on the lowdown. They had to find someone to check things out who would be above suspicion.

A face popped into Robbie's mind. He smiled. All right, then. He would see about it, but first, he had to come up with a story the man night swallow, and Robbie didn't think he would be easy to fool.

"What are you thinking, Robbie?" Penn asked. "I'm not sure I like that look on your face."

"Not to worry, Penn," Robbie said. "I may have a better idea. See you tomorrow."

* * *

By eleven p.m., the vendor area behind the roller rink was all but deserted. At this hour, most of the spectators had grown weary and gone home to their soft beds. The nighttime hours were the worst for the walkers. The band and piano players stopped playing, there were few spectators to cheer them on, and the deadly semi-quiet hours dragged, weighing down spirits that were already low and waning step by weary step.

It was a moonless night, and there were no electric lights to illuminate the vacant lot, but a few fires had been lighted here and there, casting brightness for a few feet, but leaving anything beyond shrouded in shadow.

Shadows had been Robbie's friend for as long as he could remember. With a quilt draped over his head so no one would recognize him if he were spotted, he slipped from one spot of darkness to another. When he neared the bar, he crouched and waited, immovable and quiet for long moments. Listening. Straining to see if anything or anyone moved in the blackness beyond the firelight.

He had no idea where Jerome slept and didn't care, but he didn't want to slip behind the bar and stumble across him, either. Finally, satisfied that no one was around, he crept behind the bar and began to search for the jar of Dover's Powder. He had a good idea about where he'd seen it; the problem was to get it without knocking over any of the bottles stored on the shelf and raising a ruckus.

Taking care, he moved his fingers along the shelf, barely touching the bottoms of the bottles with his fingertips, a blind person searching for something. Reaching the spot he thought he might find the container, he grasped a bottle and set it on the ground. Then another. Deliberately, he skimmed his fingers along the wooden shelf, searching for the small jar. Unable to find it, he replaced the bottles, moved more to the right, and went through the whole procedure again.

His hearing was so attuned to the sounds of the night he heard a creature running along the dew-wet ground and the soft suspiration of his own breathing as he drew air in and out of his lungs. It smelled of coming rain and winter.

Finally, finally, his fingers closed around the small jar. Stifling a feeling of exultation, he shoved it into his pocket and replaced the bottles. Standing and adjusting the blanket over his head, he crouched low and ran back the way he'd come, moving from darkness to shadow, never pausing to look behind him. He was almost to the side of the building and safety when someone cried, "You! What are you doing out here?"

Robbie froze where he stood and weighed his options. They were slim. Stay and face the music or go. He ran.

* * *

"I bloody well won't do it!"

"You bloody well will. It's the only way, McShane," Robbie said. "Aren't you the one who's always preachin' that it's all right to ask for help sometimes?"

"Not from him."

Robbie grinned. "Jealous, are ya?"

"Don't be ridiculous!" McShane scoffed. "Why would I be jealous of him?"

155

"Oh, I don't know," Robbie said with a shrug. "P'raps because he's handsome and wealthy and a doctor and he seems to like Lilly an awful lot."

McShane gave him the skunk eye. "Fine. But you set it up. It would never do to have me be seen with him."

"Would it make ya feel any better if I told you I got that item you were wantin'?"

"So that's where you were off to. I suppose it was you everyone is talking about skulking around out back last night."

"I suppose it was."

"What if you'd been caught?"

"Wasn't, was I?"

McShane knew further argument would get him nowhere. "How did you know where to find it?"

"When you're washing glasses at a bar you can see and hear a lot of things. And I like to—what is it you call it? Rekon...rekon—"

"Reconnoiter?"

"Yeah! Reconnoiter."

"It's another word for snooping, Robbie."

"I know that, but it sounds a lot better, don't it? Important. Sort of word an operative would use. Anyway, I have it. What should I do with it?"

"Give it to Rose. She can put it in her knitting bag."

"Right. So, does this mean we can turn it over to the coppers and put this thing with Lilly to rest?"

"We could, lad, but so many things are tied together. I don't want Connelly in the nick until we can see if he has anything to do with Ames's death."

"Makes sense. Where's Lilly?"

"I haven't a clue."

"Well, then, I guess I'll go reconnoiter until lunch is ready. And I'll set up that meeting."

"Not here," Cade said. "Pick a place somewhere down the street where we're less likely to be seen."

Robbie gave a smart salute and was gone.

156

* * *

"Young Master Robbie."

Robbie was glad to see the fancy man sitting at his regular table. He hadn't made an appearance since Lilly was forced to leave the race. He liked Lil. No doubt about it.

"Hullo, sir." Robbie spat on his palm and swiped it against his hair, which was far too long but which he'd taken time to comb. He'd also put on his best everyday clothes, not that they were much, washed his hands and face, and brushed his teeth. The McShanes held with the notion that cleanliness was indeed next to godliness and that first impressions were important.

Lilly's doctor, who was sitting back in his chair with one leg crossed ankle to knee over the other, drew on his sweet-smelling cigarillo and blew the smoke upward, where it drifted ceilingward to co-mingle with the hundreds of other stale scents collecting in the confines of the roller rink.

"What can I do for you, Robbie? Is Lil all right?"

"Right as rain, sir," Robbie said, "but I have something I need to talk to you about."

"Certainly."

Robbie looked at the doctor's companions. "Privately, sir, if you don't mind."

Without a word, Judah Forrester rose and followed Robbie through the crowd toward the front entrance. McShane was unyielding about not meeting the doctor at the rink.

They walked down the street toward a café where they were to meet McShane. The sun was shining, but the late September day was cold. The odor of burning wood from the fires behind the rink that were meant to ward off the chill, drifted through the air along with the leaves of trees that had yet to be sacrificed on the altar of progress.

McShane sat at a table in front of the window, his hands warming on a mug of coffee. Robbie and Forrester went inside, sending the bell attached to the door a-jingling. They stopped at the table. Forrester and McShane regarded each other with wary skepticism. Finally, McShane gestured for them to sit, and Robbie took the seat next to him, where a cup of hot chocolate waited. Forrester remained standing.

McShane spoke first. After all, this was his meeting. "I need your help to find out who tried to harm Lil."

"Don't you think that's something best left to the police?"

"No, I don't, because they aren't privy to the things I've seen since we came over from Ireland. Seldom have I seen a more corrupt bunch gathered under one roof," Cade told him. He was careful to maintain his Pinkerton persona and uncertain why he was sharing his feelings with a man he hardly knew and wasn't certain he could trust. Robbie trusted him, though, and that counted for something.

Forrester regarded Cade without speaking for a few seconds and took a seat across from him. "I agree the personal feuds and politics of the races have become somewhat of a problem."

"It's more than that," Cade said. "Robbie has proof that the champagne that was brought to Lilly's tent was meant for someone else."

Forrester frowned. "What kind of proof?"

"He overheard two people discussing it."

"Who was it?"

Cade shook his head. "I can't tell you that."

"Begging your pardon Mr. McShane, but I don't think overhearing a conversation would be acceptable in a courtroom anywhere in the country," Forrester said, flipping some ash into a nearby spittoon. "I believe they call it 'hearsay.'"

"I'm less concerned about that than I am possibly saving the life of one of those women out there on that track," McShane said. "If the drink was meant for some other walker and was accidentally passed on to Lil, that first recipient is still in danger."

Forrester pondered that for a moment. "And how do you think I can help?"

"You figured out what was used to sully the drink, and we now have the substance that was used in our possession."

"How did you do that?" the doctor asked, frowning.

Cade literally waved the question aside. The less Forrester knew, the better. "I'd like you to talk to both barkeeps and see if they remember who bought the champagne and who it was intended for. As dear as it is, I don't imagine they'll have sold too many bottles, do you?"

"Probably not."

"Will you help?"

"For Lil, anything," he said, standing and heading toward the door.

"Forrester."

He pivoted.

"Time is of the essence. We need some answers before the end of this race tomorrow night."

Forrester nodded. "I understand."

Chapter Sixteen

Thursday

L illy was feeling much more like her old self. With more than twenty-four hours of rest and Rose's good food, she'd come a long way toward restoring her strength and her outlook. They needed some sort of break in the Ames investigation! There were less than forty-eight hours to home in on a suspect or move on to the next race. She wasn't sure she could handle another.

Thankfully, she was alone at the moment, or as alone as a person could be with thousands of people surrounding them, which gave her plenty of time to think about what they did know. Rose had gone to see if Ginny had heard anything new, McShane was taking care of some last-minute thing before his boxing match, and Robbie was off doing whatever it was that Robbie did all day. Once again, he'd disappeared shortly after they ate. When she'd awakened during the night, he was back, fast asleep on his pallet.

Lilly carried a chair and her coffee outside the tent and settled in to watch the race for a while. A few, nearby spectators recognized her, waved, whistled shrilly, and called her name. She smiled, waved back, and blew kisses. It was nice to have the recognition, even if it was just for a short time.

Elsa Dengler had been carried off the track on a stretcher a while ago. There were only six remaining competitors. La Bella Rosa was still in the lead, and Lady Jocelyn was in second place, but looked to be gaining. With Elsa out of the running for good, Lilly didn't see that changing. Marta and

Arlene were battling it out for third place.

It looked as if those four would manage to walk enough miles to get the bonus, which was a good thing, even for the hateful Marta. Lilly only wished Elsa could have finished. She'd come to like Penn very much and wanted only the best for him and his mother. Fearing she might let something slip, she hadn't checked on them since the day they'd learned the truth of Penn's parentage. Maybe this morning would be a good time to remedy that.

* * *

"Have you been here all along?"

The question was asked by Elsa to some unknown visitor and caused Lilly to pause before alerting the now-incapacitated walker to her presence.

"Since before the race started," the man said. "I supposed you knew."

"How would I know? In case it has escaped you, I haven't been outside this building. I've been busy trying to make a living for me and my son."

Her voice rose with every sentence. Thankfully, the sound of the crowd drowned out the declaration, unless you were close, the way Lilly was.

"I cannot believe you have the gall to show up here after the mess you left me to take care of in California."

Lilly moved to the front of the tent, hoping the flap might be tied back and she could see who Elsa was talking to.

"I'm sorry about that. I intended to send you the contract, but I had no address and besides, when I got back here, my landlady had thrown all my belongings into the rubbish bin."

Jerome?

"Are you? I'm sure you're aware that everyone thinks you had something to do with J.D.'s death, including Dora. Especially Dora."

"Why do you think I left?" he replied in a harsh undertone. "I figured I'd be the first person they tried to pin it on when they found out he denied me a place to set up the bar."

Elsa's laughter was brittle glass. "Actually, it vas a tossup between you and Tad. And me, of course." Her German accent grew thicker as her anger

161

mounted. "And you left me in that mess, knowing I vas in a bind for money."

Neither spoke for a long while. Finally, Elsa asked, "Speaking of the bar, vhy did Dora let you set up here?"

"I know how to handle Dora."

"I suppose she agreed if you crawled back into her bed."

"You don't understand."

Elsa laughed again, a sound that held no mirth. "I understand that the joke's on you. She's carrying on vith Leo Bertolini behind your back."

There was another lengthy silence, ostensibly while Jerome tried to come to terms with what his former lover was telling him about his current *paramour*.

"Vhat I understand is that despite you saying you loved me, she lured you into her bed vhile her husband was recovering from the beating someone gave him. You do remember that beating don't you, Jerome?"

Her tone taunted. "She and J.D. both blamed your brother for that, but with everything that's happened since, I've vondered if they rushed to judgment."

Lilly felt as if she were on the verge of hearing something that would break their investigation wide open, but the only thing she was certain of was that Jerome Connelly had wronged Elsa and hurt her terribly.

"So, vhy do you decide to look me up now?" she pressed, "There is nothing for you here."

"I heard you had to withdraw from the race, and I thought I'd come and see how you're faring."

"You haven't been too concerned these past months, so vhy your sudden interest? My lack of proper training is no doubt vhat caused my muscles to seize up, so thank you for robbing me of money for the second time."

Lilly heard someone moving around inside the tent and before she realized what was happening, Elsa had thrown back the flap. There was no place to hide. Lilly stood in plain view, her hands clasped in front of her, looking at Elsa with wide eyes.

"Miss McShane," Elsa said. "How nice of you to drop by." She turned to the man standing a few feet away. "As you can see, Jerome, I'm perfectly fine, and I have a caller, so please leave now."

"Elsa…"

"Now, Jerome!"

Without another word, Jerome Connelly stepped through the opening and walked away. Lilly could almost see Elsa pulling herself together.

"I'm so sorry you had to vitness that," she said at last.

"Oh, I haven't been here long," Lilly lied. "I should have gone the moment I realized something was amiss."

Elsa shrugged. "Don't distress yourself, Miss McShane. Believe me, it is of no consequence. He is just someone from my past. The goot Lord villing, I plan to forget him and the entirety of last year."

The heartache she'd felt when Tim walked out on her was a pain Lilly would never forget. She spoke before thinking. "There was someone in my life who did the same to me. It's very painful."

"It is, but like all hurtful things it vill pass," Elsa said matter-of-factly. "They call these races endurance valking, and since I've been involved in them, I've realized something particularly important. All of life is about enduring something or other." Her ordinary face wore a pensive expression for a moment, then she seemed to give herself a mental shaking and smiled. "Vould you like a cup of tea? I was just making a pot vhen Jerome arrived."

"I would love one," Lilly said.

When they were sitting side by side outside the tent, watching the walkers, Lilly ventured, "It's not an altruistic sport is it?"

Elsa considered that a moment. "Overall, no, but then I don't know of any sport that is. Any nobility exhibited comes from the self-sacrifice each of the pedestriennes make. It is found in their determination and their villingness and capacity to endure mental and physical extremes."

She turned to look at Lilly. "Speaking of extremes, have you found out anything more about who delivered that harmful vine to you?"

"No." She looked apologetically at Elsa. "Are you aware that Penn described the man he saw placing it outside my tent as having long hair and a beard. And that he looked familiar?"

Elsa couldn't hide her surprise. "Are you saying you think Jerome is responsible for trying to harm you?"

"I don't know, Elsa, but I think it's important that we find whoever did it, or every pedestrienne who gets in someone's way may be up against the same thing."

"I understand, but surely there are hundreds of men among the spectators who would fit that description."

Lilly understood Elsa's reaction all too well. Hadn't she made excuses for Tim's behavior until it was impossible to ignore the truth any longer?

"All I know is that Penn said the man he saw leaving it outside the tent reminded him of someone, so I reasoned that he would have perhaps seen Jerome and recognized him on some level."

Elsa's forehead pleated in thought. "Penn vasn't in California. He vas in St. Louis at boarding school. I recently had to take him out but hope he vill be able to return soon."

That caught Lilly off guard. Boarding school was not inexpensive. No wonder Elsa was so worried about money. Had Helmut been paying for the boy's education?

"You're saying Penn has never met Jerome."

"Vell, I can't say that for certain," Elsa said after a moment's consideration. "He vas my trainer for a little more than two years, so it's possible they met in passing somewhere."

"I've been thinking that if Penn saw Jerome before California, before this race, and he's grown the hair and beard as a disguise, that perhaps that's why Penn didn't recognize him, but why Jerome looked familiar."

"That makes sense," Elsa said. "Vhat will you do if you find out it is him?"

"I think you know that the honest thing to do is turn him over to the authorities."

* * *

The powder was gone! Frantically, Jerome pulled the liquor bottles from the shelf beneath the bar. It was supposed to be here, tucked away in the right-hand corner behind the brandy. It wasn't like he'd forget where he'd stashed it. Where in bloody hell was it? More importantly, who had taken it?

Dora? She knew he was the one behind the scheme to put the medicine in the champagne she herself had sent anonymously to La Bella Rosa, but why would she want the powder now?

The answer that came to him left him cold. She'd been upset over the McShane woman getting the wine instead of Bertolini's wife, as was intended, and she was right in stating that the last thing she needed was another body turning up at an event she sponsored. What he didn't understand was why she wanted the Italian woman out of the race, unless she'd placed her money on one of the others and was trying to influence the outcome.

Or…maybe she was just pitting one person against another. Hadn't she done that often in the past? Dora's mind was like a maze. She was always looking out for her best chance and had no qualms about using anyone and everyone to get what she wanted.

She'd said she wanted him and had done everything in her power to assure him of it. He'd suspected there was something between her and Leo, but he hadn't known for sure until Elsa confirmed it.

What if she *was* playing him and Bertolini against one another? What if she had taken the powder and planned to tell the law that she'd found it among his things?

What about Tad? He hadn't seen much of his brother since he arrived, but he knew what was going on. Could he have taken it? After all, no one knew he was here, hiding in plain sight.

Then there was the shadowy figure one of the fellas had seen milling about a few nights ago. No one had claimed anything missing, but why else would someone be skulking around in the dark if they didn't intend some sort of mayhem?

A memory came to him, seemingly out of nowhere…the rich fella who'd been asking all the questions about the champagne. Asking the price, asking if he remembered which walker had been the recipient of one of the bottles, claiming he wanted to send some to Elsa Dengler for hanging on as long as she had and giving it her all, even with the lack of a trainer.

That part had stung, but just a little.

Eager to make a sale, Jerome had told him about everyone he could recall who'd bought a bottle of the expensive Cristal. Of course, he'd neglected to mention the bottle intended for La Bella Rosa.

Not for the first time, Jerome wondered at the wisdom of his actions over the past year or so. He was a good trainer and ran a good bar. The problem was that whenever he saw an easy way to make a buck, he'd take it more often than not. He'd liked Elsa a lot, and she'd been good to him. Their time together had been a pleasant diversion. He could say in all honesty that he'd done his best by her and her training. Until he met Dora.

Dora Ames was not a woman you refused. She was game for almost anything, both inside and outside the bedroom, and it mattered little to her that he was involved with someone else. But once Elsa suspected what was going on, that was the end. It was a shame, really. Elsa used her body to express real emotion; Dora used hers to have her way. There was no comparison, really. All she cared about was getting ahead, getting what Dora wanted.

* * *

Even from where he sat across the lot, Robbie had no trouble identifying the emotions flashing across Jerome Connelly's face. Disbelief. Frustration. Anger. Puzzlement. Robbie smiled. This was better than he expected.

He sat, sipping on a cup of coffee liberally laced with sugar and cream, thinking how nice it was to have a bit o' jingle in his pocket. He coulda stayed around and had coffee with those in the tent, but he liked being out here, watching the vendors, seeing who talked to who and what the general attitudes seemed to be.

At the moment, Jerome's attitude appeared to be one of panic. Who did he think had taken the powder? Would he ever suspect the boy who washed glasses for him in the afternoons? Doubtful. That boy was downright dumb. Did what he was told and gave no reason to be doubted or suspected.

Robbie quite liked role-playing. But he hated washing dishes, even if it was just glasses.

CHAPTER SIXTEEN

* * *

Lilly wasn't certain what drew her to the tent church, but when Cade and Robbie left, she'd felt an urgent need to reach out to God and thank him for saving her from what could have been an agonizing death.

Wrapped in her heavy cloak but shivering nonetheless, she sat beneath the striped awning and listened to a sermon intended to bring tears to the eyes and sinners to their knees. Strangely, she felt closer to her maker walking around beneath the late September sun, looking at the various vendor booths than she did in the improvised house of the Lord.

She was leaving the tent when she spotted Doctor Forrester approaching one of the temporary bars and called out to him.

He turned at the sound of her voice, tipping his bowler and smiling. "Miss McShane."

Now that she had his attention, Lilly had no idea what to say. The circumstances of their meeting were too bizarre, and she was ambivalent about the wisdom of furthering their acquaintance. She paused within a few feet of him.

"You're looking much improved from the last time I saw you."

Her mouth quirked in a quick, tense smile. "Thank you. I'm feeling better every day."

"You shouldn't be out here in the cold."

"I felt the need to spend some time in thought and prayer," she told him truthfully. "I have much to be thankful for."

"Indeed, you do."

"I wanted to thank you for everything you did for me."

"I was only doing what I'm trained to do," he told her with a smile that revealed teeth as perfect as the rest of him.

"Well, it's appreciated."

They regarded each other almost guardedly for a few seconds, and then he said, "Will you and your brother be in the area long?"

For an instant, the question took Lilly aback. She'd forgotten that even though she was finished with the race, her role as Leila McShane was ongoing.

"No," she said. "We'll be moving on. I'm not sure where or when. Why do you ask?"

"I'd still like you to have dinner with me."

"What?"

"When you were walking, I asked you to have dinner with me and you said you were busy. I said we'd do it when the race was over."

The memory of that conversation came rushing back. Had she agreed? She couldn't remember answering. "Did I say yes?"

"You didn't say no."

There was an intenseness in his eyes she hadn't seen since her early days with Tim. Something about dominant male power and primal need. But could she trust him, this man who thought he knew her?

"Why?"

"Because you look like someone I saw only once. The most beautiful woman I think I've ever seen." He laughed. "You can't be her, because that woman would be older now, and, as you said, I haven't been to County Clare, Ireland."

He smiled and his shoulders rose in a negligent shrug. "Don't they say everyone has a double somewhere in the world?"

"I don't know," Lilly replied. "Do they?"

He reached out and took her hands in his. She lowered her gaze. Judah Forrester's hands were warm. Unlike Cade's, that were rough and scarred from work and all the years he'd spent in the boxing ring, Judah's were well cared for.

Ring! She'd forgotten her need to see the ring he wore. Common sense told her that if his name was Forrester, the signet ring would have an 'F' not a 'T.' Still she would like to see for herself, just to make sure. As it was, she couldn't tell since her hands were on top, resting in his palms.

"Let me take you to dinner tomorrow night before you go off to your next race."

Should she? As long as Cade knew where she was, there should be no harm in it, should there? And surely, they could trust this man since he'd come to her aid when she was sick from the Dover's Powder.

168

"All right," she said, lifting her gaze to his. "But nowhere fancy. I don't have the right kind of clothes."

"Agreed. I'll come by the tent to pick you up at seven-thirty tomorrow evening. We should be back in plenty of time to see the end of the race."

The race would end Friday at midnight, and unless something untoward happened—which it could—it looked as if La Bella Rose would emerge the victor.

"That sounds ideal," Lilly agreed.

He gave her hands a squeeze and smiled. "I'll see you then."

With a sigh, she watched him go.

Chapter Seventeen

Rose was peeling potatoes for potato soup, and McShane was lying on his cot with his hands behind his head when she returned to the tent. "Where have you been?"

"Church."

Rose looked up, surprised, and McShane asked, "What on earth for?"

"Because I was feeling grateful to be alive and I wanted to thank God for it."

"Oh." He looked properly rebuked.

"I saw Dr. Forrester as I was coming back."

"Really? What was he doing?"

"I'm not sure. I think he was headed to one of the pubs. Probably wanted a pint."

"Hm."

"He wants to take me to dinner tomorrow night. I said I would go as long as it wasn't anyplace too fancy."

McShane bolted upright. "Do you think that's wise?"

"Why wouldn't it be?"

"You hardly know the man, and I think there's something fishy about him."

"You're the one who had him come check on me." *And you're the one who buys drinks for Dora Ames.*

"Actually, that was Robbie," McShane clarified. "He seems to like the man for some reason."

"And you don't?"

Rose looked over her shoulder at him, her eyebrows raised in question.

"I don't *dislike* him, I just think that until we get this case solved, we need to be careful who we associate with." He got to his feet. "I mean, we shouldn't get too close to anyone. We have no proof that he didn't send you the champagne."

"He came to help me, McShane," Lilly reminded. "And he took the champagne to have it tested. Would he do that if he were guilty?"

"Guilty people do a lot of crazy things to cover their tracks."

He had a point, she thought, recalling all the peculiar things they'd run into on their previous cases.

"Touché," she said. "It's just dinner, and Judah has assured me that we will be back to see the end of the race."

"Judah?" McShane echoed. "You're calling him by his proper name?"

Lilly counted to ten. It didn't help.

"Holy mother of pearl, McShane!" she cried, losing all patience and any semblance of social refinement. "What on earth is the matter with you? You are my partner, not my father. You do not have the right to approve or disapprove of my private life. I am over twenty-one, have been married…" her voice trailed away as she thought of her brief, bogus marriage "…sort of, and I am perfectly able to choose a suitable dinner companion, so please just shut your pie hole!"

Silence reigned in the small, enclosed area. Now that she had stopped yelling, she realized how out of control she sounded. Was. McShane's face was a portrait of astonishment.

She clenched her hands together at her sides, squared her shoulders, and took a few deep breaths to regain her calm. "If you're worried about me, I'd considered the possibility that perhaps you could follow at a distance."

At that, he laughed. "Oh, no! I'd never dream of sneaking around watching ya while yer out with the handsome doctor. Perhaps you've forgotten that we're working a case. I haven't."

"I can question him while we're eating."

He made a noise that sounded like a snort of disbelief.

Her anger fled.

"I want to go, Cade." Her voice was low and earnest, beseeching him to understand. "You're right. There is something about him that's worrisome. For some reason, he thinks he knows me. He said today that the woman I reminded him of would be older now and that she was the most beautiful woman he'd ever seen. He called me Kate, so I think it's all tied to my mother in some way.

"Where did he see her? When? She's been dead for twelve years." Her eyes filled with tears. "I need to know what he knows. Can you understand that?"

Cade stared at her for long seconds. "Aye," he said at last. "I can."

"Thank you."

"But I don't like it one little bit."

"What don't you like?" Robbie asked, bursting into the tent and pulling off his cap as he did.

Lilly sniffed. "Nothing important."

Robbie looked from her to McShane and nodded. "Had to do with Dr. Forrester, didn't it?"

No one spoke until Rose offered, "Lilly is going to dinner with him tomorrow night."

"Oh, well, that's nice, isn't it?" Robbie said with a smile. "Seems like a decent bloke. Speaking o' the doctor, he just waved me down. Had a bit of information for us."

"Did he give it to you?"

"Nothing on paper, but he said that he was right in what he said before. All the gifts that are given to the girls are often passed on to others. He couldn't give any specifics as to which walker got what. Too many of them."

"Are you saying they re-give the gifts others have given to them?" Lilly asked, appalled by the very notion.

"Well, yes. Maybe there's a wine they don't care for or their tent is startin' to smell like a funeral parlor from all the flowers, or they've got too many gold bracelets."

He paused and grinned. "Though I don't suppose you can have too many o' those, can ya? Anyhow, sometimes their trainers or whoever pass those gifts on to the less popular walkers anonymously."

"So, you're telling us that it's not only possible Lilly was given some champagne that was initially meant for someone else, but likely?" McShane said,

"That's exactly what I'm sayin'."

One more theory proved. But who had passed it on, and why?

Thursday night

Lilly lay on her cot, wondering how they would manage to find the person responsible for J.D. Ames's death. There were so many threads to follow, and so many things going on besides the investigation that she wasn't certain they would manage it, at least, not by the end of this race. Thinking of entering another caused her to sigh. She wasn't sure she could hold up to another, though she had to admit that she'd exceeded her own expectations.

Instead of allowing her thoughts to go down that worrisome path, she got up, put on her wrapper, and went to stand outside the tent. The lights had been turned off except for those illuminating the track where the pedestriennes still moved around the oval, their feet making no sound on the tanbark. Occasionally, there was a murmur from someone as they passed, or a cough or mumble. But other than that, it was quiet.

By this time tomorrow, the race would be over, and a winner announced. As hard as it had been both physically and mentally, she realized that she'd learned a lot about the world and even more about herself this past week.

For too many years, she had been Kate Long's bastard daughter, the motherless orphan who lived with Rose and Pierce. An insecure young woman defined by her past, with limited experience in the world.

While all that still applied, her days on the track had proved she was much more than that. There were depths to Lilly Long that had never before been plumbed. Strengths she had no idea existed. Intelligence that had yet to be tested, and growing wisdom.

She'd matured in many ways these past seven months of being a Pinkerton, and somehow, she knew that despite her worries and fears, she was where she needed to be. When her strength faltered, she would just endure, as Elsa said. Whatever happened, the things she needed were there waiting for her if she just took advantage of them.

"Can't sleep?"

She turned at the sound of McShane's voice. "My mind won't be still."

He laughed softly in the semi-darkness.

"I keep trying to think of how we'll figure all this out before tomorrow night."

"We may not."

"That's what I'm afraid of. I've been trying to focus on the things we've discovered, think about what we've learned and how far we've come to know where we should go next."

"I'm a bit that way, myself," McShane confessed. "Let's talk about it."

"Do you mind?"

"Of course not. Let's start with what we know."

Lilly nodded.

"According to William and Dora, who is quite the talker with a few shots of whiskey in her, there are four people who had sufficient motive to harm J.D. Leo is near the top of the list even though, if rumors are to be believed, he is sharing her bed."

"Didn't she all but admit that to you when she wanted you to take his place?"

"She did."

"Any regrets?" She couldn't help teasing him just a little.

"Nary a one."

"Your good sense never ceases to amaze me."

He grinned in the semi-darkness. "Now and again, I wonder what I might be missing."

She gave a short burst of laughter. "A lot of aggravation, I should imagine."

"I would agree."

She turned to stare out across the room. "According to William, Leo's motive could be something as simple as believing that if he got rid of Ames, Dora, being a woman, would be more likely to settle for less than he'd offered J.D."

"He doesn't know the Widow Ames the way we do," McShane said. "I'm wonderin' what he paid her for the dubious honor of being her partner."

174

"And I'm wondering why Dora, with all her suspicions, would enter such an agreement, much less take him into her bed," Lilly said. "What kind of woman would do that?"

"That's an easy one. A woman with her eye on the prize. She was more than candid about needing his money and his connections."

"That's coldhearted." Lilly actually shivered. "Remember how I told you I admired her in the beginning?"

"I do."

"Well, that feeling has changed over this past week or so."

"How so?"

"I'm not sure," Lilly said, drawing her wrapper closer. "I don't know if it has to do with her business dealings, or because she came right out and asked you to take Leo's place. Thank God, you had enough sense to turn her down."

"Would it have bothered you if I hadn't?"

"Of course! You'd have just been a means to an end and easily replaced whenever she'd finished with you. You're far too nice a man to be mixed up with someone like Dora."

He sighed. "I must be losing my edge."

"What do you mean?" she asked.

"There was a time in my life when 'nice' would never be heard in the same sentence as my name."

Lilly gave him an elbow to the ribs. "Be serious, McShane! You know how much I'm for women being recognized for their accomplishments. I support any woman with goals and those who work for the betterment of women everywhere, but I draw the line at some things. I'm too old-fashioned to go along willy-nilly with any and every means to get what you want."

"There's nothing wrong with being old-fashioned, and I agree with your assessment of our widow. Dora's goal is to transform herself into the premiere female manager and promoter in the sport of women's pedestrianism. If she can resurrect it here and keep it going, she will have carved out a place for herself in the history of the sport, and she'll do anything to reach that pinnacle, even if it means sleeping with the devil himself."

175

Lilly laughed softly.

"What's so funny?"

"She reminds me of a black widow spider who uses the male for her own needs and, after mating, kills and eats him."

"A scary observation, but apt."

"I almost feel sorry for Leo," Lilly said.

McShane made a scoffing noise. "Don't waste yer pity on the likes of him. If ever two people deserved each other, it's those two."

"And what about poor Rosalie?"

"I'm thinking poor Rosalie will handle him just fine in the end."

"What are your thoughts about his involvement in J.D.'s death? Do you think he had anything to do with it?"

"I haven't seen much to convince me that he has the guts for it. Lie, cheat, steal, yes. Murder, I'm thinking not."

They stood in silence. Lilly wasn't convinced that Leo had done the deed either, but she was becoming more and more convinced that the Bertolinis, or at least Rosalie, had something to do with her own mishaps on the track. A jealous wife and a husband who dallied with anything in a skirt was a combination that required retaliation, and Lilly thought the fiery Rosalie was just that person. She said as much to Cade.

"La Bella Rosa? Really?"

"It makes sense, McShane. We already know that she's jealous, and rightly so, and we know for a fact that she doesn't like Leo's interest in me. If you recall, the glass incident happened right after Marta said something to her about seeing me with Leo at the market."

"But that was Lady Jocelyn, not you."

"Rosalie didn't know that until later."

"When would she have put the glass in your shoe?"

"Hundreds of people cross the infield, going from one side to the other every day," Lilly pointed out. "She could have had anyone do it. Or maybe not. I do think it would be worth the effort to find out if she sent the champagne, and if so, did she know it had been tampered with?"

"You will be pleased to know that I thought of that, and I'm actually working on it."

"You are?"

"I am. Your friend, Dr. Forrester, suggested that the champagne could have been sent to La Bella Rosa and passed to you by mistake. If that's the case, we need to find out who would want Rosalie out of the picture, and do we have another potential murderer in the house?"

"Leo?" Lilly suggested. "Do you think he's considering something more permanent with Dora, unaware that she'd asked you to take his place?"

"Dear sweet heaven!" McShane exclaimed. "All this almost makes me want to consider celibacy."

Lilly burst out laughing.

"I said *almost*," he said with a slight smile.

"So, you did," Inwardly, she was thinking that if he chose celibacy, it would be a terrible waste.

He yawned. "Sorry, Lil. Rosalie doesn't feel right, but I agree that it would be easy for anyone to do those things to you without looking the least bit suspicious."

"Well, it's all water under the bridge, isn't it?"

"It is." They stood in silence for a few moments. Finally, he asked, "What about Elsa Dengler? There's no doubt she had motive, considering the to-do about her contract in San Francisco."

"She does," Lilly agreed, "but after hearing her side about the contract and having parts of it corroborated, she isn't high on my list of suspects. She's been incredibly open about her past. I believe she wants nothing more than what she feels is owed to her and her son."

Cade cocked his head to the side. "Okay. What about Lady J.?"

"Well, we've found out a lot about her, but we still have no idea why she'd left her husband and came to America. Like Dora, I'm certain Jocelyn has her own agenda," Lilly said.

"And we know she came between Elsa and Penn's father and got him to the altar before he knew Elsa was expecting his child. Now that Helmut is dead and has left the lion's share of his fortune to his illegitimate son, Jocelyn's sole goal seems to be to keep him from getting it."

"So, she's malicious but not a killer," McShane said.

"I don't think so, and we haven't heard of any reason she might have wanted J.D. dead."

He was quiet for a few seconds. "That leaves the Connelly brothers. Right now, I'm less interested in Tad than Jerome. What do we know about him?"

"Not much beyond the fact that he and Elsa were lovers, and that his inattentiveness to business is what kept her from getting the money she was owed," Lilly stated. "I don't think there's much love lost there on Elsa's part."

"Good for her," Cade said. "We know he left San Francisco the day after J.D. was found, and no one heard from him until he applied for a spot here to set up his bar, which Leo granted. Why? And why was Dora so upset with Leo about it? If the gossipmongers are to be believed, she was sleeping with both of them. Still is."

She turned to Cade in the semi-darkness. "I have no idea, but I suspect her anger at Leo over allowing Jerome to set up here is more because he acted without her approval than anything else."

"I agree. She said as much the last time we talked," Cade told her. "I've been giving a lot of thought to whether Jerome left town so fast because he was guilty of the crime, or because he was afraid it would be pinned on him."

"It's hard to say," Lilly told him, "but I have a hard time believing anyone would commit murder over something as insignificant as not getting a spot to sell liquor. Like Jocelyn and Elsa, Jerome is low on my list. His absent brother is a different matter." Of all the people Dora listed as suspects, Tad was the one Lilly liked the most for the crime. The problem was, no one knew where he was.

"The accountant? Tad?"

"Yes."

"There is a lot of evidence against him. Fired for embezzlement. Named by both Ameses as the person who robbed and beat them. Dora's prime suspect."

"And the fact that no one has seen him since the break-in adds to his appearance of guilt," she added.

"It does." Cade covered another yawn. "I'm for bed. Coming?"

She sighed. "I suppose, though I'm still not sure I can sleep."

McShane held the tent flap open for her, and as she passed him, she caught the scent that was uniquely his: tobacco, a woodsy soap, and parsley that he chewed to keep his breath fresh.

"Goodnight."

"Goodnight." Lilly went to her cot and stretched out, listening as McShane did the same. She pulled the covers up to her chin and squeezed her eyes shut as if doing so would stop her mind from going over and over the things she knew and those she didn't.

She recalled Rose saying that worry was like a rocking chair. You could do it all day and never get anywhere. She sighed and forced her body to relax and her mind to go blank.

Finally, she slept.

Chapter Eighteen

Friday

Lilly was awakened by Robbie shaking her shoulder and telling her to get up, he was hungry.

"Where's McShane?" she asked in a raspy voice. "Where's Rose?"

Robbie shrugged. "I think she said something last night about going to fix breakfast for the Denglers. I expect McShane is doing whatever it is he does before getting into the ring."

Remembering her own training, Lilly could only imagine.

"It's nice outside," Robbie told her. "Sunny and a lot warmer than usual. You ought to be plenty warm watching his match."

"Well, that's nice," Lilly said, pushing herself into a sitting position. "Not freezing will make it less of an ordeal." She pinned Robbie with a questioning look. "Why did I ever agree to attend?"

"Better not let McShane hear you calling it an ordeal," Robbie warned with a grin.

"I'm sorry, Robbie," she told him, "but watching two grown men beat each other with their bare fists is not my idea of entertainment."

"Got no stomach for blood, do ya?"

"Not a bit."

* * *

The first thing Lilly did when she and Robbie finished their eggs was take a proper bath and wash her hair. After all, she was going to dinner, and with a doctor, no less. It would be the first time she'd been out with a man who was interested in her as a woman in a very long time.

She sat outside the tent, rubbing her hair dry and watching Marta, Arlene, La Bella Rosa, and Lady Jocelyn circle round and round the track, trying to gain laps and miles, trying to put more distance between themselves and their nearest competitor.

What was going through their minds as the final hours passed? If she were a newspaper reporter, she would ask them all that question. Unfortunately, all the local papers seemed to want was the dirt on the walkers, or to denigrate the sport and belabor its harsh conditions. Ah, well, it was nothing to do with her anymore, though she did wonder at how she and McShane would go about finding out the answers Mrs. Ames was searching for when they left here.

As she sat rubbing her hair, she was surprised to see Jerome leave Elsa's tent. Lilly recalled the look of regret she thought she'd seen in his eyes the day he and Elsa had argued. Is that why he'd come? To try and persuade her to give him another chance?

He was neatly dressed in denim trousers and a plaid shirt that looked to be made of warm flannel. His hair was pulled back with a leather thong at the base of his skull, and his beard looked freshly trimmed, as if he were determined to put his best foot forward. Had it worked? Had he sweet-talked Elsa into changing her mind about leaving him in her past? Had he spent the night there?

Stop it! It's none of your business, Lilly Long!

She watched him walk away and, with her hair almost dry, she went back inside to dress for the day. Even the inanimate things in the tent seemed to sense the end was nearing. The drooping heads of the flowers in the bouquets she'd received looked almost sorrowful; fallen petals were tears of regret.

She was both glad and a little melancholy that her time here was nearing an end, but she knew she would be forever grateful to the women who'd come from all over the world to prove their worth, to show the naysayers that they had what it took to overcome insurmountable odds. That they had grit. Strength. Tenacity. They would not be held back. They would not be stopped. They were lovers, mothers, fighters for their families. Despite their flaws, personalities, and pettiness, they were the summation of woman.

Dressed for the day and with time on her hands, Lilly wandered through the crowd inside the rink, stopping to talk with those who had been so supportive of her and thanking them for that support.

"Hey, Lil!"

She stopped. "Robbie! What are you doing?"

He shrugged. "What I always do. Walk around and listen."

"Well, why don't we take a break from anything connected with pedestrianism and go down the street to that little bakery and find ourselves a sweet of some sort."

"That's the best offer I've had all morning." He fell into step with her, and they headed to the front entrance. They'd just reached the foyer when her attention was caught by a man nearing Dora's office. Neither young nor old, he was dressed in a stylish sack suit and wore nicely polished shoes. His freshly cut hair was parted in the center and his mustache and goatee were both trimmed and neat. Whoever he was, he was clearly someone of standing.

"Why are ya stopping?"

She tipped her head in the general direction of the office. "Just wondering who that man is."

Robbie heaved a great sigh and pushed his unruly hair from his eyes. "I suppose we need to find out."

"I suppose we do. Have you any ideas?"

"Not at the moment, but if you'll go ahead and get the sweets—something chocolate fer me, please—I'll think on it and come up with something."

Lilly smiled broadly. "Robert Jenkins, did anyone ever tell you that you are an angel?"

He colored to the roots of his dark hair. "Now, don't go getting' all squidgy on me, Lil. I'm just doin' my job."

182

"Fine," she said, sobering. Perhaps one day the boy would accept real affection from his adopted family. "One chocolate something or other coming up."

She took her time walking the few blocks to the bakery and selecting an assortment of confections to enjoy. When she returned, Robbie waited outside the roller rink, pacing back and forth, his forehead wrinkled in thought, or maybe worry.

"Well? Did you get anything?"

"Don't I always?" he countered, reaching for the bag with the sweet treats inside.

"And?"

"He's an insurance man."

"Insurance? Are you sure?"

"Positive. Name's Arthur Abercrombie. He's with Illinois Life Insurance."

"How did you find that out?"

"I can read now, you know." He pulled a card from his jacket pocket, handed it to her, and peered into the bag. Reaching in, he pulled out a round roll-type thing smeared with chocolate frosting.

"It has a creamy filling," Lilly explained, but Robbie had already taken a bite and was moaning in ecstasy. "How did you get this card?"

He swallowed and licked a bit of chocolate from his lip. "I just sort of bumped into him, didn't I?"

She looked at him with raised eyebrows. "I supposed it just fell from his pocket."

"No," he said in a serious tone. "Nothing like that. I know I swore not to nick anything anymore, but it was only a card, and I don't mind telling ya, Lil, it's nice to know I haven't lost my touch."

"You little imp!"

He grinned. "Just a while ago, I was an angel. Imagine. Did I tell you the gent was so worked up he hardly noticed when I bumped into him? I have a notion that he and Dora were into it about something."

"What do you mean he was worked up? I don't suppose you overheard anything?"

Robbie crammed the last of the sweet into his mouth and shook his head. "Smaller bites, please."

"I couldn't hear a thing. Sorry," he said after dispatching the last of the confection. "Have a look at the card. It says they specialize in life insurance *investigations*."

She checked. It said just that, which indicated that Dora might have enlisted someone besides the Pinkertons to look into J.D.'s death. Did that mean she doubted the agency's ability to deliver?

What would McShane think about this latest development? She knew nothing about insurance, except that she thought it had something to do with regular installments paid to sort of "hedge your bets" against something dire happening, and if that catastrophe did happen, the company would pay a lump sum in the amount agreed to at signing.

"Have you seen McShane?"

Robbie pulled his second treat from the bag. "No, but you might check the tent or out back. He can't be too far."

"I'm going to see if I can find him."

Robbie clicked his heels together and gave a smart salute. "If I see him, I'll tell him yer lookin' for him."

"Thank you."

She'd just bade her protégé farewell and watched him disappear into the crowd congregated on the dais when the door to Dora's office burst open and the widow stormed through. Fury radiated off her in waves. Whatever her meeting with the agent had been about, it was not to the widow's liking. Lilly watched her retreat down a hall, calling for Leo at the top of her lungs. Hardly ladylike comportment.

Desperate to find McShane, Lilly headed to the back lot. If she expected to see anyone breaking down their stands, she was disappointed. It looked as if everyone intended to stay until the end of the race, in hopes of adding even more money to their gross receipts.

She gave Jerome's bar a quick glance. He looked angry and untidy, far different from the man she'd seen leaving Elsa's tent early that morning. He'd rolled up his shirt sleeves and was up to his elbows in sudsy water, forced to do Robbie's chore, since he had literally thrown in the towel the morning after his late-night excursion to get the Dover's Powder.

Connelly had questioned him at length, but Robbie had steadfastly denied being anywhere near the place and told his boss he didn't have to work for people who didn't trust him. The child was amazing at spinning a yarn. Of course, he'd had to be to survive.

She supposed he should be taken to task for lying, but since it was what she and McShane did for a living, she couldn't bring herself to upbraid him for it...unless he was lying to her or another family member, of course. He'd done it to survive, and she and McShane did it for the greater good. She wondered if that made it acceptable and doubted it did.

"The end justifies the means." Allan Pinkerton's motto flashed through her mind. But did it, really? She supposed that in their line of work, all they could do was try to instill in Robbie that there were times it was okay and times it was not. Which still didn't make it right. She heaved a heavy sigh. Parenting was not an easy task. It might be the hardest thing she had ever done.

Lilly headed toward the boxing ring, hoping to find someone who could point her to McShane's whereabouts. Luckily, she saw him coming around the side of the ring, wearing his usual attire of twill pants and boiled shirt. Today, it was topped with a denim coat lined with blue flannel.

He smiled when he saw her, which caused her to pause. He was usually so serious.

"Why are you looking like the cat who just licked up spilt cream?" she asked.

"I have it on good authority that my opponent isn't at his best today, so that's a wee bit o' good news. And in case no one has told you, you're looking exceptionally fetching this morning. I've never seen your hair down and shinin' like a red cloud in the sun."

Like the smile, the compliment was unexpected and startling. She'd never known him to wax poetic. The only thing she could think to reply was an absurd "I washed it."

"Oh, aye," he said with a nod. "For your rendezvous with the doctor."

A rush of irritation banished her momentary awkwardness. He had to be the most irritating man she had ever had the misfortune to meet! "Having dinner in a public place hardly counts as a rendezvous, McShane."

"You're right. I beg your pardon."

And just that quickly, he reverted to the usual, no-nonsense person to whom she'd become accustomed. It was a transition she'd seen many times during their assignments, usually when he was acting his most charming self to learn something new. Was this an act, or was he sincere? It was hard to tell with McShane.

"Did you need something?"

"I wanted to talk to you about a couple of things."

He gestured toward an empty table in the sun.

"I don't know if there is any importance to it, but as I was drying my hair this morning, I saw Jerome leaving Elsa's. I wondered if he might be trying to get back into her good graces after everything that happened between them in California. Do you think their being together so much of late is personal or that it has any bearing on the case?"

McShane shook his head. "At this point, I've no idea. What else is on your mind?"

"Oh! Here." She reached into her pocket for the card Robbie had lifted from the insurance agent, explaining how getting it had come about.

He studied it with care, and then turned it over to make certain nothing was written on the back. Thorough, as always. "It says they do investigations."

"I know. Do you think Dora has them working on J.D.'s case, too?"

"I couldn't say, but I doubt it. I believe it's pretty standard for insurance companies to look into suspicious deaths if there is a large sum of money involved."

She gave a slow, thoughtful nod. "I see. Robbie said he was agitated when he left, and before I came looking for you, Dora left the office positively gnashing her teeth and yelling for Leo. What do you think is up?"

"Well, I'm not a clairvoyant, but I'm fairly accomplished at reading between the lines." He sat in silence for a moment, thinking things through. "If they were both upset, I'd bet my winnings from the match this afternoon that it

186

has something to do with Dora's claim to J.D.'s life insurance money."

"I don't understand."

"There's no way to know for sure, but it doesn't sound as if they plan to pay it."

Lilly's eyes widened in shock. "Why wouldn't they?"

"Think about it. She's maintained from the beginning that it wasn't suicide, and we were hired to prove it, but we haven't. Neither, it seems, has the insurance company. After so many months of trying to prove her theory, I'd say Mr. Abercrombie's firm is satisfied with the police findings that J.D.'s death was self-inflicted."

"I still don't understand why they won't pay."

"For Dora to collect, it would have to have been accidental or murder. Death benefits aren't generally paid on suicides."

Lilly stared into her partner's eyes, trying to absorb the information and reconcile it to everything they'd seen and heard since arriving.

"Are you saying that Dora's suspicions may not be valid at all?"

"I'm saying for her to get the money, she needs it to be murder. There's a possibility that she pointed the finger at everyone in their little sphere who might have held a grudge against J.D. for any and sundry reason and hired us in hopes we could find enough evidence to prove one of them did it."

"That's terrible!" Lilly cried in disbelief.

McShane shrugged. I believe we've already established the fact that Dora isn't a candidate for sainthood."

"There are a lot of suspects," Lilly said.

"Indeed, there are, but you and I have discredited most of the theories for one reason or another."

"You're inclined to agree with the insurance company, then?"

"I'm not saying that. As we've said before, we have speculations of our own, but no proof. Have you given any thought as to why the gun had two bullets missing and Dora claims it was never shot?"

Her lips curved in a wry smile. "You are no clairvoyant, and I am no novel writer. Fiction is out of my realm."

He nodded. "Are we still in agreement that unless he missed the first time, there is no way J.D. could have fired the revolver twice?"

"We are."

"Good. There are only two or three scenarios remaining, then. First, maybe he shot at someone trying to protect himself, missed, was overcome by them, and was shot after they wrestled the gun away."

It was a scenario Lilly hadn't considered, but viable. J.D. had recently been confined to a wheelchair, and even if he wasn't using it when he was killed, he'd certainly not been at his optimal strength, weakened by his injuries and easy prey for someone with more physical ability.

"Or," she said, "playing Devil's Advocate, he could have accidentally been shot during that same struggle for the gun."

"Excellent point. The third scenario is that someone had the gun, fired off a shot as a warning to try to get J.D. to—" McShane shrugged and gave a shake of his head "I don't know— give in to a demand of some sort, perhaps. Then, when he couldn't be budged, whoever had the gun shot him. What do you think?"

"I think that last situation fits nicely with William's theory that Leo did it so that he could buy into the business cheaper if Dora was in charge."

"Possible. How would he get the gun in this situation?"

"He could have stolen it," Lilly suggested. "Or Dora could have given it to him since it's an accepted fact that they've been close for some time."

"Dora as an accomplice, huh?" McShane said, with a cynical twist of his lips. "I'd not put it past her. She and Leo are both money and fame-hungry. They'd be a good pair to concoct something like that."

"The only problem with that idea is that, according to you, Dora is trying to get rid of Leo now," Lilly reminded. "I think it's possible, even likely, that she always planned to get him to do her dirty work and then rid herself of him once she got her hands on the insurance money."

McShane nodded in agreement. "And if he's arrested, it will be her word against his, and we all know that Mrs. Ames can be very persuasive."

"You would know better than I."

"Tut-tut Miss Long. I turned her down, remember? Do you think we can prove it?"

"Proof." She laughed. "If only it were as easy to come by as assumptions. As much as I like the Leo and Dora idea, I'm still not convinced that Jerome isn't mixed up in it somehow."

McShane frowned. "Why do you say that?"

She gave him a direct look. "There's just something 'off' about him. Why did Leo let him set up here after he took off in California? Why has he visited Elsa not just once, but twice in the past couple of days?"

"Twice?"

"Yes. I saw him leaving her tent bright and early this morning. I have no idea if he was there all night or just paid an early morning call."

McShane shook his head in denial. "I can't see Elsa letting him sleep there. Not with Penn present. She's been too adamant that everything be open and aboveboard. She doesn't want anything coming back on her for fear it will harm Penn's chances at getting his inheritance."

"You're right. Maybe he was trying to get her to give him another chance. He looked..." she paused "...all neat, slicked up, nothing the way he looked when I saw him a while ago."

As she talked, McShane's gaze roamed to Connelly's bar. "He's not looking so fine just now, is he? Conversing with a woman will sometimes do that to ya."

Lilly ignored his barb and studied the man across the way. As she'd noted earlier, he looked far different than he had just a short time before. What had happened? He hardly looked like the same man.

Suddenly, she drew in a sharp breath and grabbed McShane's wrist.

"What's wrong?"

She inclined her head toward Connelly and cut her gaze toward McShane. "That isn't the same man I saw at Elsa's."

Chapter Nineteen

"What do you mean it isn't the same man?"

"That is not the man I saw coming out of Elsa's tent this morning."

"What? Have you lost your mind?"

"Perhaps I have," she snapped, "but there is nothing wrong with my eyesight." She gestured toward Connelly. "It looks like him, exactly like him, but the man I saw was wearing what looked like an off-the-rack shirt of blue plaid."

"C'mon, Lilly," McShane scoffed. "He got cleaned up for his meeting with Elsa and changed into a white shirt for work. Most of the grog shop owners wear white shirts and aprons. It's just a thing they do."

"It's more than that. Look at how untidy his hair is, hanging around his shoulders. The man I saw had his hair tied back with a leather thong." McShane started to speak but she stopped him with a raised hand. "I know. It's easy enough to tie hair back with a thong, but it's a little harder to change a neatly trimmed beard into a week's worth of growth in a matter of hours."

McShane was still regarding her as if she'd lost her mind, but she saw a trace of curiosity in his eyes.

"The man I saw was neat and clean, and his beard was trimmed close." She gave a vague wave toward Connelly. "You can't grow a beard like his in a few hours," she said again.

McShane's eyes narrowed and his forehead furrowed in concentration. "Holy mother of pearl!" he exclaimed. "They aren't just brothers, they're twins!"

"That would be my guess," Lilly said. "The question is, which one is Tad, and which one is Jerome?"

"Which one came to see Elsa this morning?" McShane added. "And what sort of game are they playing?"

* * *

Later that afternoon, Lilly, warm in her red cloak, was on her way to the boxing ring to watch McShane as promised. She was almost there when someone grabbed her upper arm. Sudden fear paralyzed her for an instant. Then, wrenching free, she turned and found herself facing a contrite Leo Bertolini.

"Miss McShane," he said. "Please forgive me. I never meant to startle you."

Lilly forced herself to breathe in and out, willing her racing heart to slow. She thought she'd gotten over the jumpiness that had been her companion ever since she and McShane had returned from Ft. Worth, but clearly, it was a demon that had yet to be fully exorcised.

She forced a smile. "Mr. Bertolini! What a surprise! I haven't seen much of you around of late."

Leo smiled the smile that was as oily as his slicked-back hair. "I was going to say the same about you. I expected to see more of you since you had to withdraw from the race. I'd hoped to buy you a cup of coffee or a glass of wine."

"Yes, well," she said with forced cheer, "I fear it took more out of me than I expected, and then, with the champagne issue..." She let her voice trail away.

His eyes filled with regret at her mention of the tainted wine. Strangely, he looked sincere. "I'm truly sorry, Miss McShane. Normally, Cristal is quite lovely. It was created just a few short years ago for Czar Alexander II, you know."

"Actually, I didn't," she said, though Rose had told her.

"Did the police ever find out who sent it to you?"

"Not to date. My brother has tried to track down all the bottles sold, but there must be more monied people attending the races than one would imagine."

"Either that or they're spending money they can't afford to. Someone sent my wife a bottle of that same label," Leo said. "I haven't seen it around, so I assume she enjoyed it on her breaks." He rolled his eyes. "She says it gives her a boost." The smile accompanying the statement was meant to remove its sting.

Was he insinuating his wife had a drinking problem? No. Many walkers used spirits, believing it enhanced their performance, and champagne was a favorite of many pedestrians. She wondered if McShane had accounted for the bottle given to La Bella Rosa. Maybe it was time to do a little more probing.

Lilly laughed and wagged a finger at him. "If it's as good as you say, maybe you drank it yourself. Or perhaps your wife passed the bottle she was given on to another competitor."

To her surprise, Bertolini looked offended. "I would never touch Rosalie's gifts. She would have my hide."

Oh, dear! Was Leo a bit frightened of his petite wife, then?

"Well, she deserves everything she gets. Your wife is a very talented pedestrienne," Lilly said. "I know you're proud of her accomplishments."

"She is, Miss McShane. She is."

She looked around at the still substantial crowd. "Of course, I have nothing to use as a measurement, but this looks to have been a successful first venture for you and Mrs. Ames."

"Indeed. Other than your mishaps, I've nothing to complain about, but Dora is rather a perfectionist." His eyes held a faraway look as if he were envisioning a scene that had taken place or dreading one about to. He dragged his attention back to Lilly and forced another taut smile. "There are always a few things to iron out after an event such as this if we hope to make the next collaboration even better."

Yes, Lilly thought. Things like whether you'll still be around. "I'm sure it will all work out, especially since this seems like such a success." She smiled apologetically. "Now, if you'll excuse me, I need to find my nephew."

"Certainly. I saw him earlier with the Dengler boy."

"Thank you." Lilly smiled a goodbye and started toward the rear entrance of the rink. She needed to see if Robbie could use his skills to find out anything from Penn about his mother's early morning visitor and if those skills extended to checking to see if La Bella Rosa's Cristal was still in her tent.

Her mind wandered back to her conversation with Bertolini. She'd made several mistakes in character assessment since becoming a Pinkerton, but she didn't think she'd misread the remorse in his eyes when he apologized for the champagne incident. Would Cade think her feelings were enough to eliminate Leo from their list of those who might want to harm her, or would he see it differently? One never knew about McShane.

* * *

Robbie had grown tired of playing poker with his friend who, as a novice, was far too easy to beat. He was only too happy to see Lilly and report what he'd learned.

"Well, don't you look like a little ray of sunshine?" she said, as he joined her, and they headed toward their tent.

"Did I ever tell you I hate it when you get all funny talking?" Robbie said, looking up at her with a frown.

"It's called irony, Robbie, and it can be very helpful in certain situations. So, what's happened to give you that pleased look?

"Good news for the Denglers, is what," he said. "Mrs. Elsa had a visit from her lawyer, and they've finally made a decision about Penn's father's will."

"Since you're so chipper, I can only assume that the courts decided for Penn and against Lady Jocelyn."

"Yep! Penn gets everything, but his mother has control until he reaches the age of twenty-one."

Lovely, Lilly thought, especially since Elsa had been unable to finish the race. Justice had been served, and Lady Jocelyn would just have to be satisfied with the 'pittance' she claimed she could not live on.

Lilly's gaze sought and found the former actress as she made her rounds on the track. That she'd already heard the news was obvious. Her pretty face was contorted with anger. Her lips were compressed into a straight line, her auburn eyebrows were drawn together in a frown, and she slapped her riding crop against the tall boots she wore with every step she took. It would be interesting to witness the first meeting between her and Elsa when the race was finished. It promised to be quite a dustup.

"What did you need, Lil?" Robbie asked as they entered their tent.

"Do you know if Doctor Forrester traced a bottle of the Cristal to La Bella Rosa and if so, did he find out who sent it? It's important, Robbie."

"I'll get right to work on it. Anything else?"

"Thank you," Lilly said with a smile. "There is one other thing. One of the Connelly brothers has visited Elsa twice. The first time, it was Jerome. I heard her call him by name. This morning, she was visited by him again, I think."

"Whadda ya mean, you think?" Robbie asked, unwrapping the tea towel from the remains of the bread they'd had for breakfast.

"He looked the same, but he didn't." Lilly explained the differences she'd noticed and summed it up. "McShane and I believe they are twins, not just brothers. We need you to find out which is which."

"Crikey! What next?" Robbie said, slathering some apple butter on his bread. He took a huge bite and spoke around it. "I'll do my best."

Lilly tapped her closed lips as a reminder not to talk with food in his mouth. He cast a disgruntled gaze ceilingward.

"I know you will."

* * *

Confident that Robbie was busy with his newest tasks and that the dress she planned to wear for her evening with Judah Forrester was ready to slip on at the last moment, Lilly wandered back outside and found a seat near the boxing ring. She would people watch until time for the match to begin.

She and McShane had agreed to wait until his bout was over before setting out to find clarity to the twin possibility they'd discovered earlier. She was anxious to get to work identifying the Connelly brothers. Even though Robbie was working on it, it wouldn't hurt having more than one person checking things out.

As she waited, she sat and listened to a couple of old-timers arguing about the merits of each pugilist. To her horror, she learned that almost everything was acceptable in bare-knuckle boxing, from eye-gouging to hair pulling, throws, kicks, and pummeling an opponent when he was down. There was no set time for a round, and rest periods were limited to thirty seconds.

McShane had requested an Irish Stand Down, which eliminated moving about the ring and required the challengers to stand toe to toe and take and receive blows. His opponent had rejected that notion vehemently.

It all sounded appalling to Lilly, who could not see how anyone received pleasure from such an event. McShane would say the pleasure came from the satisfaction of knowing you'd bested the other fellow and from betting. From the many things she'd witnessed people gambling on since arriving at Palmer's, she thought he might be right.

She was worrying about the possibility of him receiving some heinous injury when she cast another glance at the bar. To her surprise, Jerome, or Tad, or whoever he was, was nowhere to be seen. Where had he got off to in such a short time? Turning this way and that in her seat, she scanned the crowd, hoping to catch a glimpse of his unkempt head.

There was no sign of him, but she caught a glimpse of Dora slipping around behind the vendor tents. Was she meeting Jerome? Or Tad? Lilly needed to find out, but she'd promised McShane, and she knew she was in for at least an hour's delay.

What should she do? And where was Robbie when you needed him?

Finally, McShane and his opponent entered the ring. He was introduced, and when he spotted her in the crowd, she saw the recognition in his eyes. Deciding she couldn't wait until the match was over, she worked her way through the throng to where he'd sat down on a three-legged stool.

"McShane!"

"You need to back away, ma'am," the man who was attending him said.

"Just a moment!" she said in a sharp tone, clutching the ropes forming the ring.

He turned to look at her. "What are you doing here, Lilly?"

"I had an interesting conversation with Bertolini a bit ago, and I've sent Robbie to check on some things. More importantly, Connelly isn't at his bar, and I saw Dora sneaking around behind the tents. I need to see if I can figure out what's going on."

"No! Blast it all, Lilly! You need to wait for me," he said in a low, harsh voice.

"You know as well as I do that I can't," she murmured, staring into his angry eyes. "God knows where they'll have gotten off to by then."

He blew out a harsh breath of frustration. "There's no talking to you when you get in one of these moods," he said. "Go, then, but be careful."

"I will. Same to you."

"I'm always careful, lass." He chucked her under the chin, and she turned and made her way out of the tent. Standing in the middle of the people mingling around the outdoor booths, she looked around, trying to decide where they might be headed and wondering if they even planned to meet up. Knowing them as she'd come to, heaven only knew what they were up to.

When she'd seen Dora, she was behind the tents. Both she and Jerome had been headed to Lilly's left, so it made sense that at least one of them had gone toward the storage tents near the canvas church across the alley. Lilly headed in that direction, making her way toward an area where several crates, barrels, and tarpaulins were stored, things that would be recovered and used when the vendors started taking down their stands.

Neither Leo nor Dora was anywhere to be seen, and a quick look told Lilly that no one was around. Uncertain of her next move, she stood wondering where else they might have gone, when she heard sounds nearby. Fearful of discovery, she froze. Then, with her back to the tarp, she eased along the exterior toward a gap where the lashing between two pieces of canvas hadn't been pulled tight enough.

Just as she turned to have a look, her mind registered what the sounds she was hearing were, but it was too late to reconsider. Right there in plain view, she saw Leo Bertolini and Dora, involved in an almost violent coupling.

Lilly gasped, praying the noises coming from inside hid the sound. A vision of bare breasts, legs, bums, and skirts thrown upward, was accompanied by the sounds of throaty moaning.

Scandalized, Lilly closed her eyes and took a step back. She'd never seen anything like what she'd just witnessed. She was mortified, yet several thoughts flashed through her mind. What did this mean for Dora's statement to McShane that it was time to break free of Bertolini? Why would she implicate Leo in her husband's death along with the others and still carry on an affair with him? And, what about her alleged liaison with Jerome?

She took a step back, anxious to return to the tent, and backed into something rock solid. A muscular arm slid around her midriff, and a rough hand clamped over her mouth, stifling her cry of surprise and fear. She was half-carried, half-dragged away.

When her captor reached what appeared to be the rear of a nearby building, he whirled her around to face him. Keeping one hand over her mouth, he slammed her against the building so hard it almost knocked the breath from her.

Jerome!

Trying to breathe and struggling to free herself, Lilly looked up at the face so near hers. He was so close she could see the shattered-glass pattern in the iris of his brown eyes. The expression she saw there was meant to intimidate, and it was working very well.

"I'm going to let you go, but if you make a sound, it will be the last one you ever make."

The same terror she'd experienced in Ft. Worth made it difficult to breathe and harder still to think. Fear was an invisible cord that prevented any movement. This was the sort of moment she'd dreaded, the one she'd been uncertain she could face again. Yet, despite her panic, she realized this was the very thing she'd trained for so long and rigorously with Monstery. Taking some small comfort from the reminder, she nodded. He released her instantly. As her breathing became easier, her sense of preservation returned.

Whichever brother he was, he took her by the shoulders and gave her a rough shake. "Who are you?"

"Lil McShane."

"Why the bloody hell are you following Dora and Bertolini?"

Lilly forced a breathy laugh. She couldn't tell him she was following him and Dora. That would only make matters worse. Hoping to buy some time, she straightened the clothing he had mussed by his rough handling and reached into her pocket for her revolver. Nothing! She fought the dual urges to curse or cry. Would she ever learn to take the little derringer with her no matter where she was going?

With few options at her disposal, she decided it was a good time for a lie. Stifling a sigh, she lifted her chin and faced her captor with a look of insolence. "I was trying to see what Leo was up to."

"And why is that?"

"He's been showing me a lot of attention since I had to drop out of the race, and he's insinuated he would like there to be more between us." She shrugged. "Of course, his reputation with women is well known, and…" she let the starch go from her spine in a gesture of resignation "…I suppose I wanted to see if he was sincere. Obviously, he was not."

Connelly laughed. "Jealous, are you?"

"Aren't you?" she snapped. "You seem to spend a lot of time with Dora yourself."

"Whatever is between me and Dora is none of your business."

"So, it doesn't bother you that she's carrying on with him behind your back?"

A muscle in his jaw tightened. "I never said that."

"At least you aren't completely besotted," she noted. "I don't know what you think the two of you have, but I've only been here a short while, and I can see that she's using you, just as she uses all men. Leo included."

"And Leo?" Connelly shot back.

Feigning confidence she was far from feeling, Lilly said, "Obviously, they're two of a kind. May I go now that you know what I'm 'up to'?"

"Go!"

Doing her best to hold her anxiety at bay, she turned to leave. She'd taken no more than a half dozen steps when she had an idea and turned back. "You'd be much better off with Elsa, you know."

"Elsa and me?" He laughed and turned away, but not before she thought she saw a hint of regret in his eyes.

* * *

Needing to steady her nerves but hesitant about returning to the empty tent, Lilly bought herself a cup of coffee and took a seat at one of the outdoor tables. She felt safer in the midst of a crowd of people than she would have in the privacy of her own living quarters, and after a time, her breathing became a little easier. Connelly still hadn't returned to his bar, which was being manned by one of the men she'd seen helping him now and again.

When her coffee had grown cold, she made her way slowly back to the tent, wondering if Rose and Ginny were still at the market and praying that they'd returned. Wearily, she pushed aside the flap and stepped into a nightmare.

Her mind seemed to take in the entire scene at once, like a daguerreotype that captured its image forever as the photographer saw it. All three cots had been overturned and stripped of their bedding. The dress she'd planned on wearing to dinner with Judah Forrester lay in a pile near the corner of the tent. Every wooden box holding their necessities had been dumped out. Cutlery, pans, and bottles littered the canvas flooring. Multicolored balls of Rose's knitting yarn lay scattered about. Personal items had been strewn around the space and the screen that defined their washing up space lay flat on the tent floor.

And in the middle of it all, next to an overturned chair, lay Robbie. Still. White. Unmoving. He must have walked in on whoever had wrecked the place and they had done their best to eliminate him. For the span of a heartbeat, she stood wondering how she would deal with this new crisis after just escaping one of her own.

Then an inherent maternal instinct pushed all thoughts of her own narrow escape aside. Concern propelled her across the space to his side.

"Robbie!" she cried, dropping to her knees beside him. Up close, she saw

199

that his head lay in a pool of blood. There was little color in his face. In a tender gesture, she brushed back his unruly hair and found him warm to the touch. Taking his wrist in her hand, she checked his pulse. It was strong, just like the boy. Even so, there was so much blood....

Rising, she went to the pitcher, poured some water into the basin, and grabbed a clean cloth. She needed to find help but was concerned about leaving him alone in case whoever had done this terrible thing decided to come back. Going out and screaming for help wasn't what a Pinkerton agent would do so, for the moment, she would just make Robbie as comfortable as possible until McShane returned, which should be any time now.

As she gently washed away the blood, her mind raced between frantic prayers and jumbled questions to which there were no answers. Who could have done this terrible thing? Who would attack a child? And why?

She was not unaware of the fact that the same thing, or worse, could have happened to her. Shivering in reaction, she shoved the thought from her mind and concentrated on Robbie's injury.

When the worst of the gore was washed clean, Lilly examined the gash, which had been made by something readily handy in the small enclosure. It needed stitching up.

In the meantime, she got her feather pillow and folded a clean towel over it for protection. She tore another into strips and folded a piece for padding, pressing it against the wound and tying it tightly. The pressure should stop the bleeding, which seemed to have slowed already. She covered him with a quilt and sat down to wait.

"What in blazes happened here?"

McShane! She turned to look at him and saw the confusion and disbelief on his face as he took in the desecrated surroundings. Trembling with the aftereffects of her ordeal with Jerome and the shock of finding Robbie, Lilly pushed to her feet, stumbled across the room, and fell into his arms. They closed around her in a reaction as natural as breathing. She felt truly safe for the first time since walking away from Connelly.

"Someone's hurt Robbie. When I went to look for Dora, Jerome grabbed me, and when I came back I..."

He placed his big hands on either side of her face. "Slowly, lass. Slowly."

She shook her head. "Later. I'll tell you later. Robbie needs a doctor."

"Where's Rose?"

"She and Ginny were going to some shops this afternoon. She's not back yet."

"She's fine, then." He squatted, scooped Robbie into his arms, and stood. "Leave her a note. Tell her we've gone to Cook County with Robbie and we'll be back as soon as possible."

Lilly nodded and watched him duck through the door flap. She heard the difference in the mood of the crowd as he made his way across the infield and track toward the front entrance. Gasps of amazement. Calls of "what's happened?" A sudden barrage of hundreds of conversations wondering what was going on.

It was only then that she realized that McShane didn't look the best himself. He had a rapidly blackening eye, a nasty cut on his cheek, and a split lip.

* * *

An hour later, Robbie was in a ward with several others, tucked into a pristine white hospital bed with five stitches in his scalp. Lilly thought he was showing signs of coming around. They'd been assured that he would be fine when he woke and that he could leave as soon as he was fully conscious.

She went to a window and looked out at the darkening day. Streetlights glowed, illumination for those making their way home. Normally, the night didn't bother her, but this gloaming seemed somehow representative of the bewildering air of ruthlessness that pervaded this case. On the outside, all appeared well enough. It was only when you ventured deeper into the various deceptions that you began to see the premeditated malice.

Now that things had settled down, she was feeling guilty for not returning to the tent sooner. If she hadn't been so afraid, if she hadn't stopped for coffee, this wouldn't have happened to Robbie.

"Are you all right?"

McShane's voice intruded on her thoughts. Doing her best to summon a smile, she turned to face him. "More or less. It's been quite a day."

"It has at that. You need to stop it."

"Stop what?"

"Blaming yourself for this."

"But I…"

"Ah, ah, ah, Miss Long. None of it was your fault. If you'd been there, Robbie might have been the one finding you, or it might have been both of you lying in a hospital bed."

"But—"

"Do I need to go find that hair shirt? I'm finished with it for the time being."

Common sense told her he was right, and the fact that he remembered the words she'd spoken to him brought a smile. "You should have had a stitch or two on your cheek," she noted.

"I've had worse. I'd rather have a steak."

"Oh. For your eye?"

"No. To eat. My belly's asking if my throat's been cut."

"I could use a bite, too. Did you win? In all the hubbub I forgot to ask."

"I did." He flashed a weary smile. "It should be just enough to cover the cost of Robbie's injuries."

She laughed, but there was no joy in the sound.

"How about you? Are you all right?"

"I was terrified," she said, pushing away from the windowsill and plunging her hands into the pockets of her skirt. "I haven't been that frightened since Texas."

"But you handled it. When it came down to it, you handled it. That's what we do."

"Are you ever afraid?"

It was a question she'd long pondered. No matter the circumstances, her partner dove into whatever situation presented itself and did what he had to do with no apparent concern that anything might happen to him.

"Often. But then my training kicks in, and I do what needs doing, the way you did today."

She drew in a deep breath and released it slowly. "I think Jerome is the one who ransacked our tent."

"Wasn't he with you?"

"I don't know. It was the same brother we saw at the bar, so I think so, but after my run-in with him, I was nervous about coming back here alone, so I stopped for a cup of coffee." She shook her head. "I felt safer being with people. I kept watching, and he didn't go back to his bar, so he had plenty of time to go to our tent and do this."

"Like you, I'm pretty sure that's Jerome," McShane said.

She turned to look out the window again. "If it was Jerome who accosted me and tore up our tent, his brother is somewhere out there. What is he doing besides visiting Elsa?"

"Delivering tainted champagne? Pretending to be his brother whenever they need to be in two places at once? Your guess is as good as mine. Other than him having the opportunity, what makes you think Jerome is the one behind the robbery?"

She whirled around to face him. "Robbery?"

"You don't think he just decided to go in and mess things up because he could?" McShane shook his head. "No. He was looking for something, and I'll bet my winnings that when we go back and check, we'll find that the Dover's is missing."

It made sense, she thought. "But how could he know Robbie had taken it?"

McShane glanced at the child lying in the bed. "Our boy is a clever one, but none of us gets everything right. If you recall, he quit his job washing glasses the morning after he took the powder. I imagine Connelly's been thinking on it for a while and finally put two and two together."

"And Robbie walked in and surprised Connelly, so he took it out on him."

"That would be my guess."

"If Connelly has it, we have nothing to connect him to the bad champagne."

"True."

"Once again, are we any closer to thinking that Jerome has something to do with Ames's murder, or has he just been working for someone else to get me out of the race?"

"I'm still not clear on that," McShane said, "but someone is getting nervous, and when that happens, people panic. When people panic, mistakes are bound to be made."

"I'm hungry."

The comment came from the bed where Robbie lay looking at them with slightly glazed eyes. Lilly and McShane rushed to his side, touching him, smoothing back his tousled hair, asking him how he felt and if he wanted anything. Another blanket? Water?

"I just want to go home."

* * *

It was almost 9:00 p.m. when Lilly, Cade, and Robbie returned to the rink. If the speed in which Leo Bertolini descended on them was any indication, he'd been hovering near the door waiting for their return. No doubt he was anxious to know what they planned to do about the attack and try to keep the incident from tarnishing the race.

"How's the boy?" he asked, as if Robbie wasn't there, walking on his own two feet.

"*The boy* is fine," he said in typical Robbie fashion.

"Doing well as you can see." Cade looked at Lilly. "Do you mind taking him back to the tent? I'll be there to help you straighten up in a bit."

"Certainly. Come along, Robbie."

Cade watched them disappear through the still substantial crowd waiting for the results of the competition. Barring anything untoward happening, La Bella Rosa would be announced the winner, the prizes presented, and another pedestrian race would be recorded in the annals of the sport.

Unraveling the many violations in human decency they'd encountered, not to mention finding out the truth about Ames's death, was a goal still out of reach. Like Robbie, all Cade wanted to do was go back to the tent and rest. Instead, he turned to Bertolini, who wasted no time getting to the point.

"Is the boy going to be all right?"

"The doctors assure us that he will."

"Do you have any idea who would want to hurt him?"

"I don't think anyone set out to hurt him. According to Robbie, he walked in on someone ransacking the place."

Leo's shock appeared genuine. Was he wondering how something like this could have happened when he and Dora had tried their utmost to present a faultless and fair race? Was he wondering why? Maybe, Cade thought, it was time to come clean with the manager…or as clean as Andrew McShane could come without exposing his identity or the reasons behind his and Lilly's presence.

"We believe it had something to do with the champagne that was sent to Lilly." Color leached from Bertolini's face. What did the manager know that he wasn't telling?

"D…did the boy see who it was?"

"Oh, yes." Cade figured there was no harm in fiddling with the facts a bit. "He's certain it was the same person Penn Dengler saw leave the champagne outside the tent. Jerome Connelly. Or perhaps Tad. You are aware they're twins and they're both here."

Chapter Twenty

With Robbie following close behind, Lilly pushed through the tent flap, dreading the mess she knew awaited her. Just inside, she stopped. Everything was as it had been before the attack. Rose was at the stove cooking something that smelled heavenly.

Hearing them, she turned, a happy smile on her face. "Thank God you're back!" She laid down the spoon and rushed over to them. To Lilly's surprise, she pulled Robbie into a close embrace. Even more surprisingly, he let her. Then she held him at arm's length, looked him over from head to toe, and said, "You look sound enough."

"Get on with ya, Rose!" Robbie had had his fill of coddling for one evening. "I'm fine. What's for supper?"

"Just the last of the bacon and biscuits and gravy. I was trying to use up what we had left and didn't want to buy anything more since we'll be leaving tomorrow."

"It sounds wonderful," Lilly assured her as she, too, was drawn into a brief, loving embrace.

"Where's McShane?"

"Talking with Leo. Robbie, why don't you lie down until he gets back? I'll set the table."

"Will someone please tell me what happened while Ginny and I were out shopping? No one seems to know much of anything beyond that we were robbed, and Robbie was hurt."

"That about sums it up," Lilly said. "And by the way, thank you so much for putting things back in order."

Rose gave a dismissive wave of her hand. "Do you know who did it?" She directed the question to Robbie.

"My former boss, Jerome Connelly," Robbie told her. "He must've figured out I took the Dovers and came to get it so we couldn't prove he had anything to do with Lilly's champagne incident. But I *can* prove it was him," Robbie said.

Surprised that he had come up with the same reasoning she and Cade had for the robbery, she asked, "How?"

"Before he conked me on the noggin, I took a plug outta his arm."

Lilly considered that for a moment, and then she and Rose both burst out laughing.

"Did you contact the police?" Rose asked when they'd settled down.

"And tell them what?" Lilly countered. "That someone came and took something we'd stolen from them?"

"Oh," Rose said with a grimace. "That might be a bit awkward, mightn't it?"

"Just a bit."

"You do realize you missed your dinner engagement with Dr. Forrester. He came by looking for you round 7:30."

Wide-eyed, Lilly looked up from the silverware she was placing. After her run-in with Jerome and finding Robbie, she'd thought of nothing else, certainly not a dinner invitation with a man she barely knew. Recalling Judah's genteel manner, his tempting good looks, and the intriguing air of mystery surrounding him, a little regret crept into her heart. She sighed.

"They say things happen for a reason. Leila McShane will probably be heading back to Ireland soon. Besides, she isn't in the same league as our handsome doctor."

"I'd say the doctor wasn't in *your* league," Robbie corrected. Before Lilly could remark on the unexpected comment, he said, "Are those biscuits ready yet?"

Rose had just poured the thick white gravy from the cast iron skillet into a crockery bowl and placed the pan of biscuits on a towel in the center of the table when McShane stepped through the opening. He paused.

"Things look much better than they did when we left. Thank you, Rose," he said, pulling out the chair where he usually sat. "And thank God I didn't miss supper."

"What did Leo have to say about today?" Lilly asked, once their plates were filled.

"Not much. He was more interested in what we planned to do about it. I decided to go with the truth as much as possible, so I told him we thought Jerome was behind the break-in, and how it tied into you getting the bottle of bad Cristal. After a while, he broke down and admitted that he was the one who sent it to you, via Jerome."

"What! Why? What have I done to Leo Bertolini?"

"Calm down, lass. It's really an interesting circumstance. Leo said someone sent it to Rosalie—he swears he has no idea who—and he passed it on to you, just as Dr. Forrester told us sometimes happened. By the way, you do know you missed your dinner date." He looked at her with raised eyebrows.

If the gleam of satisfaction in his eyes was any indication, he was not in the least bit sorry. "I am aware of that, yes," she said in a calm tone. "Why would Leo send me champagne?"

"He said Rosalie had so much she would never miss a bottle, and he wanted you to experience some of the good that comes with racing when you did so well."

"He told me he would never touch any of her gifts," Lilly said,

McShane shrugged. "Are you surprised he lied? Personally, I think he did it because he was trying to add your scalp to his collection. He's been waging a half-hearted campaign to get you to notice him."

Lilly stated with some asperity. "He already has so many women he can't keep them straight."

"Changing the subject, and not that it has any bearing on anything we've been talking about, but Ginny found out why Lady Jocelyn came to America," Rose told them.

"Do tell," Lilly said, pushing her plate aside and leaning her forearms on the tabletop.

"She got up her courage and came straight out and asked Lady J.'s trainer about it. Ginny reckoned Karl would know since he was with Helmut for years."

Lady Jocelyn's trainer was a big blond German who'd made it clear that he had no desire to be part of the community of walkers and their staff. He kept so much to himself that he was seldom seen, and Lilly had even forgotten his existence.

"According to Karl, after Jocelyn and Helmut married, it didn't take him long to realize Jocelyn was seeing other men on the side. After a while, he couldn't bear the whispers and embarrassment anymore. He didn't believe in divorce, so he decided to pay her to stay out of his life. She came here, and when she took up endurance walking, he sent Karl as her trainer and to sort of keep an eye on her."

"Thus, the princely monthly allowance," Lilly said.

Rose nodded.

"And now, she'll have to be content with whatever he's left her in his will."

"Yes. According to Ginny, Lady Jocelyn is still in a state over the whole thing, but since she's already contested the will and things didn't go her way, she hasn't any recourse but to grin and bear it."

"I'm glad things worked out for Elsa and Penn," Lilly said. "Lord knows Jocelyn Baldwin has taken enough from them."

"She did." Rose gave a deep sigh. "And then to have another heartbreak at her age. It's tragic."

"What do you mean?" McShane asked. "She and Penn are Helmut's heirs. It sounds as if they'll be set for life."

"Of course, but heartbreak is still heartbreak."

"What are you talking about, Rose?" he asked.

"Why Jerome, of course." She leaned forward conspiratorially. "Ginny said it was common knowledge that Elsa and her trainer, who we now know was Jerome, were involved. When he left, he not only took her contract, he also took her heart."

"Are you certain it was Jerome?" Lilly asked, recalling the neatly dressed man she'd seen leaving Elsa's tent. "I know we've heard that before, but somehow, I can't see the two of them together. If she was involved with one of them, I think it must be Tad. I'm pretty sure that's who I saw leaving her tent."

"The embezzler?" McShane said. "You can picture her with an embezzler?"

Lilly propped her elbows on the table and rested her head in her hands. "I don't know, McShane," she said to the tabletop.

"All I know is what Karl said. Elsa and Jerome were an item, but when they went to California, Dora stole him away from Elsa."

Knowing Dora's tendency to use and discard men willy-nilly, the notion wasn't that far-fetched. A bit of information she couldn't quite summon teased her memory.

"Tell us what happened with Jerome, Lilly. There hasn't been a chance to hear the whole story," McShane said.

She told them about finding Dora and Leo in a compromising situation and her run-in with Connelly, trying her best to gloss over the incident between Dora and Leo for Robbie's sake. She bumbled it badly.

"Have no fear," he said in the boastful tone Lilly had come to associate with him. "I didn't live on the streets as long as I did and not see what you're talkin' about now and again. I, for one, don't see the appeal. It looks positively disgusting."

Lilly caught McShane's eye. They both fought to suppress a smile. Since she was partly responsible for bringing up the boy, she hoped his attitude didn't change any time soon.

"I'm glad you're all right," Robbie said, almost as an afterthought. "I'd hate to think of Jerome roughing you up like he did me."

"Thank you, Robbie. That's very sweet."

"I'll be glad when this is over," he said. "My brain is tired."

Though he was much better with any of the McShanes than he'd been when he was roaming the streets of Chicago, Robbie's life was still far from what anyone would consider 'normal.' What twelve-year-old was allowed to roam the streets at all hours and was included in risky schemes to bring lawbreakers to justice? Never mind that he often came up with his own agenda. Lilly sighed. It was troubling, but there was really nothing to be done about it since legally, none of them had any hold on him.

All she said was, "So is mine, Robbie."

* * *

At a quarter to midnight, the crowd was no smaller than it had been at the beginning of the six-day event. Though many spectators had spent time at the match every day, and there were those who were almost permanent fixtures, the crowd seemed to multiply with every minute that approached the end. Not only were the numbers increasing, so was the intensity. The band seemed livelier, the piano player more animated. Even the spectators appeared more enthusiastic than they had the past couple of days.

Part of the energy came about when Arlene from Arkansas passed Marta Dolk. The girl had been showing signs of losing steam ever since before Lilly was forced to drop out. She was convinced Marta was powered by the physical strength of a young, healthy woman and the inexplicable power of hostility.

Over the past twenty-four hours, the young Swede had slowed down, and the mother of five from Gurdon, Arkansas, had found an untapped source of strength and energy, narrowing Marta's lead. Arlene had passed Marta about the time Lilly and Cade returned from the hospital and she continued to pull away with each lap around the rink.

Reporters from most of the Chicago newspapers had come out for the finale, including the *Herald*, the *Times,* the *Record, Tribune,* and *Post.* Lilly wondered if they'd come to actually report on the winners and give them the homage and glory they so deserved, or if they'd come to heap on more criticisms, grumble about the 'appalling' conditions, and voice their objections to the matches for reasons the average spectator cared not one whit about.

They left Robbie sleeping, but Rose, Lilly, and McShane had pushed and fought their way to the finish line. They didn't want to miss a thing.

"Miss McShane."

She and the others turned toward the familiar voice. "Hello, Ginny," she said with a smile. "Are you ready to move on to the next match?"

"I'm not certain I will be."

"What do you mean?"

"I mean that I've had about all I can take from *Lady* Baldwin," Ginny said in a tart voice. "She's insufferable on a good day, but ever since she found out she couldn't change the will, she's even worse.

"I may try my hand at something new. But that isn't why I'm here. Elsa asked if I'd try to find you. She has something important to tell you. Your brother, too, if he's a mind to come."

Lilly wondered what the pedestrian needed to say that couldn't wait until morning. She looked at Cade who gave a nod. "We'll be back as soon as we can, Rose," he told her. Looking as perplexed as Lilly felt, Rose nodded, and the trio made their way through the crowded infield toward the Dengler tent. They found Elsa sitting at the table. A blue flame burned beneath a copper tea kettle. Penn was nowhere to be seen.

"Thank you, Ginny," the German woman said. "I'll see you in the morning."

Elsa seemed calm, but as usual when she was upset, tension thickened her accent. Ginny smiled and backed out of the tent. "See you then."

"Please sit," Elsa said, rising and pouring the boiling water into a brown earthenware pot.

Setting the kettle back onto the stovetop, she took her place at the table and clasped her hands on its scarred top. Then she looked from Lilly to Cade and drew in a steadying breath. "I know you're vondering vhy I've brought you here, and in fact, I'm vondering, too, since it may go poorly for me." A laugh that sounded very near a sob escaped her.

"I've thought about this for a long time, almost a year in fact, and I was reluctant to admit to anyone, but all of you have been so kind and helpful to me and my Penn, and...I decided that I couldn't remain silent any longer, no matter vhat the outcome. Now that I know Penn will receive his inheritance and vill be taken care of if things don't go vell for me, I can speak freely."

Lilly and Cade exchanged troubled looks. What on earth could Elsa possibly tell them that would cause this much suffering? What had she done to make her think that her future was in jeopardy?

"Why don't you start at the beginning," Cade suggested. "Wherever and whenever that may be."

"Yes. Goot." She nodded and cleared her throat. "San Francisco vas supposed to be a new beginning for the sport of female pedestriennes, and I believe most of us vent believing it vould be. Jerome vas convinced it would be so since J.D. had convinced Leo Bertolini to join him and his vife to help manage and promote the events."

Her comment confirmed what William had told them, but they had not been told that Leo was actually working for and with the Ameses when he made the offer to buy them out.

"Leo was employed by J.D. and Dora in California?" McShane asked.

"Yes. Leo is very good at vhat he does, and J.D. and Dora knew they needed every advantage they could find. They offered him the position of assistant manager and chief of promotions in exchange for La Bella Rosa's guaranteed participation, the allure of her name, and a hefty fee." She shrugged. "To give the devil his due, Leo had had much success in the east the previous year."

"That gives us a plausible explanation of why he and Rosalie reconciled," Lilly observed.

"That is so. Unfortunately, vhen one moves, our baggage goes vith us." Elsa tried to smile. "Forgive me. My thoughts are vandering. I need to stick to the part that concerns you, Miss McShane."

"All right," Lilly said. For the life of her, she could not see how anything that happened in California could have any bearing on her.

"At that time, Jerome and I were involved in more than a trainer and pedestrian relationship, vhich you no doubt already know."

"We've heard as much," Lilly said.

"There had been no man in my life for a very long time," Elsa explained, "and he vas good to me and made me feel pretty and special."

It was strange to hear such praise about the man who had sent a boy to the hospital.

"He vas an excellent trainer, too," Elsa continued, "but after a vhile, I realized he vas somewhat lazy, always looking for an easier vay to get ahead."

A cynical smile curved her mouth. "I did not believe he vas a bad man, even vhen I realized that he was riding on my coattails..." she shrugged "...or however it is the Americans say it. As long as I vas a successful pedestrienne and he represented me, our association vas beneficial and helped open many doors for us both."

"That's common in any business," McShane said.

"It is," Elsa said, nodding. "Before ve ever left for San Francisco, he'd negotiated a contract with J.D. guaranteeing I vould receive a certain fee and a reasonable veekly vage vhether or not I participated in the race, if I agreed to lend my name and support to them. I later learned that Jocelyn got the same deal, vhich did not make me happy."

Her gaze encompassed both Lilly and Cade. "It is no secret that Jocelyn Baldwin and I despise each other."

"Yes, we've heard the story about how she came between you and Helmut, and how she convinced Leo to let her walk in the opposite direction as the rest of the field," McShane said.

"I felt Jocelyn vas getting special treatment, so I vithdrew."

Elsa rose and set a sugar bowl and three spoons on the table. "I'm sorry, I have no cream," she apologized, pouring them each a mug of the strong black tea. When everyone was served, she picked up her story.

"Vhen I did, J.D. refused to pay me the money I vas promised, saying he couldn't because I couldn't produce my contract. Jerome had left it in Indiana. By this time, Dora had her claws in him, and he could have cared less vhat happened to me. Of course, Lady Jocelyn vas thrilled that I was pulling out. One less competitor to deal vith."

Lilly frowned. She was still wondering how all this had anything to do with her. "What about Leo? I was under the impression that he and Dora had an arrangement," she said.

"Oh, they did. Do. But to my knowledge that didn't come about until after J.D.'s death and Jerome left."

"Tell us about Tad," McShane said. "He and Jerome are twins, aren't they?" Elsa nodded.

"Was that him I saw leaving your tent early this morning?"

"It vas." Elsa leaned forward, an earnest expression on her face. "This is vhat I vanted to talk to you about. Tad heard about you receiving that

214

harmful bottle of champagne and that Penn had given a description that fit him and Jerome. He vanted to tell me that he had nothing to do vith it."

"Why did he risk coming here after all these months? Wasn't he afraid Dora would call the authorities and have him arrested for embezzling the money in San Francisco?"

"He didn't embezzle it."

"What!" Lilly and McShane exclaimed in unison.

"That vas Jerome." Once again, Elsa wore a sorrowful expression. "It vas so simple, really. They vere both clean-shaven at the time. If Jerome happened to go into the office vhen Tad wasn't around, who vas to know it vasn't Tad? It never occurred to him that his brother vould do something like that and let him take the blame.

"Vhen Dora discovered the discrepancies and told J.D., Tad had to go into hiding or go to jail. Jerome had so ingratiated himself vith the Ameses and Leo that they never once considered looking at him."

Lilly listened in astonishment, trying hard to reconcile everything she was hearing with what she and McShane thought they knew.

"Tell us about the robbery and assault," McShane urged. "If Tad had gone by that time, why would both Ameses name him as their attacker?"

"No one knew for certain that he'd left California, but he couldn't be found, so they assumed he had. Everyone in the pedestrian community, as vell as the police, believed that Tad came back for more." She paused and looked from McShane to Lilly. "I know differently, and I can prove it."

"What do you mean?" Lilly asked.

Elsa drew in a deep breath. "Shortly after the embezzlement, I was vith Jerome and Tad. He vas literally gathering his belongings to leave, vhen Jerome came up vith the idea for the two of them to break into the office and steal the money and the belt. He said it vould serve Dora and J.D. right."

"Why was Tad letting his brother hang about, knowing he was the one who put him in the fix he was in?"

"At that point, none of us suspected that Jerome had anything to do vith the embezzlement. J.D. left that part of the business up to Dora, and Tad vas vell aware of her expensive habits. Vhen money got tight, and she allegedly

215

found the discrepancies, he assumed she'd taken the money and fixed the books to hide vhat she'd done and let him take the blame. She's a very clever voman, Miss McShane."

Lilly had already begun to suspect just how clever, and just how manipulative she could be. "Go on."

"Jerome suggested we divide the money from the robbery into thirds, claiming we deserved it. I vould get recompense for J.D. not paying me vhat he owed me, Jerome could have at least part of the money he'd been denied when J.D. refused to let him set up his bar, and Tad, wrongly accused, vould have something to live off of until he got settled somewhere."

"Bloody hell!" McShane scraped a hand through his dark hair. "I've seldom heard of such conniving. Clearly, you turned him down."

"Of course. Both Tad and I did, so Jerome found a couple of flunkies to help him. The last thing he expected vas that Dora and J.D. vould be on the premises, but they vere. J.D. had already lost a goodly sum from the embezzlement, so he put up a fight that Jerome wasn't expecting, but J.D. vas no match for Jerome."

"Is it true that J.D. was in a wheelchair for a while, and that Dora sustained a few injuries as well?"

"Yes. One doctor even questioned if he vould ever valk again, but he surprised everyone and vas almost back to normal in a couple of months."

"And once again, Tad got the blame," McShane said.

"I've always been convinced that J.D. truly believed his attacker vas Tad," Elsa said, "but you must remember that J.D. had no idea Dora vas sleeping with Jerome, so he had no reason to think poorly of him. And since Tad had already been accused of the accounting fraud, it vas easy enough to pin the robbery on him. It even made sense."

There were things Lilly wanted to ask but couldn't without exposing her identity. The frustration on McShane's face told her that he felt the same. "Do you think Dora knew the wrong brother had been implicated?"

Elsa shrugged. "All I know is that she stood by and let Tad take the blame. Dora Ames is an ambitious voman who has no qualms about using whomever she needs to use to get her vay. She and Jerome are a lot alike in that."

"Did Tad have anything else to say about either of those occasions when he came to see you?" McShane pressed.

Elsa ducked her head, and even in the dim light of the tent, it was impossible to miss the color that suffused her face. Finally, she looked up. "He came to tell me he loved me, that he'd loved me from the day I first met him shortly after Jerome became my trainer." She drew in a shuddering breath. "He said he had nothing to do with the champagne you received."

Cade was able to ease part of Elsa's worry. "We know Tad is innocent of that. Leo himself told me that he's the one who sent the bottle of champagne to Lilly and that Jerome delivered it for him."

It was Elsa's turn to looked confused. "Why would he want to harm your sister?"

"It wasn't intentional. The wine he sent was some that had been given to La Bella Rosa. He didn't think she'd miss it."

"Are you saying that someone intentionally tried to take Rosalie out of the race?"

"It would seem so."

Elsa's eyes narrowed in thought for several seconds before she leapt to her feet so quickly that she overturned her chair. "Dear Got in heaven! Is there nothing that spawn of Satan would not sink to?"

"Who?" Cade asked.

Elsa uttered a weary laugh. "Lady Jocelyn Baldwin. Who else?"

* * *

By the time Lilly and Cade left Elsa's tent, the winners had been announced, monies dispersed, and accolades given. The newsmen had gone back to their offices to write up whatever they planned to say about the event for the morning editions. The few women who'd managed to stick it out to the end and provided the entertainment for a huge section of Chicago's population had retired to their individual tents to sleep, to rest, and to heal. The crowds had thinned, but there were still those who lingered, laughing, collecting their bets and congratulating one another.

Without her being aware of it, Lilly's gaze drifted to the table where Judah Forrester had sat. She could not stop another small pang of regret at missing him, or the sigh of melancholy that escaped her.

"I'm sorry you missed your dinner engagement with Forrester."

Was her partner a mind reader now? Lilly looked up at him with a weary smile. "It was only a dinner engagement, McShane," she said. "Nothing of real importance."

"If you say so."

"I do."

They stopped outside the tent. "I understand now why Elsa was so determined to keep her part of the race on the up and up," McShane said. "She didn't want to be involved in anything that smacked of impropriety, because she was trying to secure Penn's future."

"What will happen to her?"

"Nothing as far as I'm concerned. Technically, I suppose she could be charged with withholding evidence about what happened in California, but that was such an unholy mess I think the only thing she's guilty of is falling for the wrong man. I'll not be the one who throws her in jail because she heard something illegal being planned and turned it down."

"And you can live with that decision?"

"My dear Miss Long," he said, looking at her with clear blue eyes, "after Louisiana, I have not one moment's hesitation about this decision."

"Yes, well…" She cleared her throat and shifted in her chair. "I do see your point."

"I'm glad we're in agreement. I believe Elsa has helped solve the mystery of who sent you the bad wine, and we've established that anyone could have put the glass in your shoe."

"I'm still concerned about La Bella Rosa. If the Roederer's champagne I was sent was intended for her, I worry that her life is still in danger. Do you think Elsa is right in thinking Lady Jocelyn sent it to Rosalie? Or that maybe Leo is lying about sending it to me?"

"Good questions. We know he's been involved with both Jocelyn and Dora and Jocelyn has been with Leo and Jerome." He planted his hands on his hips and shook his head. "I'd need a record book to keep it all straight."

Lilly scoffed. She'd seen how women reacted to his presence. Knew how he affected her.

Seeing her skepticism, he said, "Believe it, Miss Long. I am strictly a one-woman man."

"If you say so. So, tell me, Agent McShane, how do we get Jerome Connelly in jail?"

"I've been thinking on that. We have to be out of here by tomorrow afternoon, but I'd like to confront him first thing in the morning and see if he'll admit knowing who sent the wine."

"Won't we expose ourselves by questioning him?"

"I thought I'd send a message to the station and have Seamus come around about 8:30 to ask a few questions. Pedestriennes aren't the only ones who receive things anonymously, and my brother is about to get a tip from an unknown grass."

"I hope we can be there," Lilly said, smiling. "I'd like to see Jerome imprisoned for the robbery and J.D.'s beating, at least. Do you think he had anything to do with his death?"

"I wouldn't be the least bit surprised."

"Nor would I."

Chapter Twenty-One

Saturday

The morning was brisk and cold, even though the sun shone brightly. Lilly and Elsa, who had been brought along to verify the accusations they were about to make against Connelly, trailed behind Cade and Seamus, who looked very authoritative in his dark blue policeman's uniform.

The McShane brothers' features were remarkably similar. The shapes of their chins, noses, and eyes were the same. They both sported a mustache. But Seamus weighed a couple stone more than his younger brother and stood half a head taller. Cade's hair was black, and his eyes were dark blue. In contrast, Seamus's hair was rich auburn, and his eyes were as black as the pits of hell. Still, if one knew to look, they wouldn't miss the resemblance.

When Seamus had first seen Lilly outside the front of the Palmer rink, he'd played his role to the hilt, shaking her hand and acting all professional-like. But the gleam of mischief in his eyes told her that if they were anywhere else, he would pick her up and swing her around, much as he would his girls.

He'd told Lilly and Cade that the California crime did not fall into the purview of the Chicago police department, but that as private contractors, the Pinkertons had the authority to apprehend whomever they found guilty of a crime. He was there to lend authority so that, if possible, Lilly and Cade would not have to reveal their true identities.

Somehow, Lilly didn't see that happening.

Cade insisted they stop by the office to let Dora and Leo know what was about to happen. When no one answered their knock, they assumed the duo was taking care of the one hundred and one things that needed doing to bring the event to a close.

There was plenty of activity out back of the rink, but it was different than it had been the past two weeks. There were conversations, but the area lacked the constant hum of voices Lilly had grown accustomed to hearing. There was no scent of roasting peanuts on the air, no sound of cheering and jeering coming from the boxing ring, or 'Hallelujahs' and 'Amens' emanating from the temporary house of worship.

She wasn't surprised to see that Jerome was already packing up. A wagon had been backed up near the bar, and wooden crates of glassware were being loaded by two lackeys. Jerome himself stood away from the action, talking to Dora. Good. They wouldn't have to go in search of her. Leo was nowhere to be seen.

From the looks of things, the conversation was not a pleasant one. Neither of them noticed the McShane contingent approaching, but the presence of a Chicago copper did not go unnoticed by others in the area. In fact, Lilly saw that they had already collected more than a dozen interested bystanders.

Stopping a few feet away, Seamus straightened to his not inconsiderable height. "Jerome Connelly?"

Connelly and Dora turned. Her eyes narrowed as she regarded the quartet. Lilly could almost see her mind spinning, trying to figure out what was happening. When Connelly saw Elsa among them, his eyes widened in surprise, but he made a swift recovery.

"I'm Jerome Connelly," he said. "What can I do for you?"

"I'd like to ask you a few questions about the robbery and assault of J.D. Ames in May of this year."

That did catch Dora off guard. Lilly suspected that Dora expected to hear that Lil and Andrew McShane were pressing charges against her for the things Lilly had suffered during the race.

"I can assure you that—"

"I'll get to you in a moment, ma'am," Seamus said, interrupting whatever

221

it was Dora planned to say and leaving no doubt as to whom was in control.

Jerome gave a short, harsh laugh. "This is uncalled for. Ridiculous! The San Francisco police have already established that my brother committed the crime, based on the statements of Mr. and Mrs. Ames." He gestured toward Dora.

"That's true," Dora said, glancing around at the gathering crowd. "My husband and I did identify Tad Connelly."

She looked at Seamus in the beseeching way she did all men when she was trying to sway them to her way of thinking. "Officer, may I suggest that we move this conversation to my office? I would rather not have the entire world privy to my business."

Of course, she wouldn't, Lilly thought. Like Elsa, Dora wanted her competition free of controversy, drama, and anything that suggested illegal behavior. It was beginning to look as if she'd missed her mark.

"Certainly, Mrs. Ames," Seamus said, making a polite sweep of his arm toward the rink. He, Connelly, and Dora led the way, and Lilly, Cade, and Elsa followed.

Once they were secluded and seated in Dora's office, Seamus picked up the conversation where they'd left off. "I well understand your confusion about the allegations, Mrs. Ames, but we've received new information that has thrown some doubt about Tad Connelly's guilt."

"What!" Jerome looked positively ill.

"You and your husband were aware that the brothers are twins?"

"Of course, we knew. How could we not? They were both in and out of our offices on a regular basis. As far as any new evidence, I'm sure you're aware that when the robbery took place, Tad had already made off with the money he'd stolen from us while he kept our books."

"The authorities were aware that he couldn't be found, yes."

Dora smiled as if the matter were settled. "That aside, I had no reason to believe Jerome would do such a thing to me and my husband. And still don't," she added with some asperity.

Seamus released a broadside. "It is our understanding that you and Mr. Jerome Connelly were involved in an extramarital relationship during that time."

Jerome looked stunned. Dora lifted her chin, prepared to brazen out the allegation. "We were, but don't forget, Sergeant, that I was assaulted during the robbery, too. It makes no sense that I would protect the man who attacked not only my husband but me."

Seamus pinned Connelly with a hard stare. "You *were* aware that the lady had a husband?"

Lilly was beginning to think all the McShanes could have made a good living on the stage. Seamus's rugged features wore an expression of piety that would have made a saint proud.

"Yes."

He made a *tsking* sound before turning to Elsa. "Mrs. Dengler, would you please tell Mrs. Ames and Mr. Connelly what you confided to Miss McShane last night?"

"I vould be happy to." Elsa squared her shoulders, cleared her throat, and started telling the gathering about Jerome's suggestion to rob the Ameses, concluding with his rationalization for doing so.

"Lies!" Connelly shouted, his face contorting with anger. "She's only saying that because I threw her over for Mrs. Ames. Her accusations are based in spite not truth!"

McShane was taking everything in, and the pride on his face at the way his brother was handling the matter could not be clearer.

Seamus ignored Jerome's outburst. "Mrs. Dengler, how did Mr. Connelly's brother feel about that suggestion?"

"Tad had no interest in the plan. In fact, he vas getting his things together to leave town when Jerome came up with the idea."

"Why was he leaving town if he was innocent of the embezzlement, as you told Miss McShane?" Seamus queried.

"What else vas he to do?" Elsa cried. "He vas innocent, but as Jerome said, the police had already made up their minds after Mrs. Ames discovered the discrepancies. He had access to the books. Assuming it was his handiwork was the easiest and most logical thing for them to believe, even if it isn't true."

"You believe Tad Connelly is innocent?"

"I do." Elsa was preparing to elaborate when the door burst open, and the other Connelly twin rushed through the aperture. "Tad!"

"I can't believe you had the guts to show up!" Jerome muttered in a bitter tone.

"And I can't believe you can stand there and lie to send your own flesh and blood to prison," Tad replied. He looked at Seamus. "It's taken me a while to figure out a way to prove my innocence, sir, but I believe I have found it."

Dora and Jerome exchanged uneasy looks.

"I'm convinced that a closer examination of the accounts will prove that I had nothing to do with the embezzlement."

"Continue," Seamus said.

"It's simple, really. Jerome and I were in and out of the offices all the time. At that time, we were both clean-shaven. With a change of clothing, he could easily pass himself off as me and manipulate the numbers. If anyone saw him going into the office, no one would think a thing of it."

"But how do we know that happened, sir?" Seamus persisted. "How do I know this isn't a clever ruse to throw the law off your scent, so to speak?"

"Because our handwriting is vastly different," Tad said, looking around the group. I make my threes with straight lines on the top half and my fours with a closed point at the top, like a triangle with a leg. Jerome makes his threes round and his fours open. His fives are made with a single stroke and look more like a haphazard 's.' My penmanship is precise, always legible, as accounting should be. What you'll find in the records where he's tried to cover things up is the work of someone who takes little pride in his."

"Do you have the account books, Mrs. Ames?"

"Yes." Dora's voice was little more than a whisper, and she didn't sound nearly as confident as she had just moments earlier.

Seamus held out his hand. Dora opened a desk drawer and pulled out a large ledger. "I'll have those at the precinct take a look at this, and we'll determine who's telling the truth."

He tucked the book under his arm and turned back to Tad. "Now, tell me more about the robbery your brother suggested."

Once again, Tad related his version of the story that Lilly and Cade had already heard twice, including Jerome's intention for him, Elsa, and Tad to split up the money. "Neither Elsa nor I wanted any part of it," Tad said at the end. "All I want is to have my name cleared so that I can live my life in peace."

Lilly glanced at McShane. His expression told her that he had questions of his own he'd like answered, but she'd worked with him long enough to know that out of respect for his brother, he would remain silent.

"Are you suggesting that your brother went ahead with this scheme alone? That he is the one who broke into the Ameses office, robbed them of the cash and the championship belt? That he then beat Mr. Ames within an inch of his life and injured the woman he was involved with?"

"I am. The fact that I was identified by both Ameses, but I can prove I was in Texas at the time, tells me without a doubt that my brother is the guilty party. There can be no other explanation." The sadness in Tad's eyes was tangible as he looked at his twin. "I'm sorry, brother," he said, "but I'm finished taking the blame for everything from your pranks to your sins."

With a cry that sounded more like a mad animal than a human, Jerome launched himself across the room toward his brother. Before Seamus or even McShane could respond, Lilly turned, took a single step to the side, planted her feet apart, and herself directly in Jerome's path. Then, with a single right-hand punch, her fist connected with his jaw, and the guilty Connelly twin fell to the floor. A perfect Irish Stand Down.

She swore and shook her hand. She may have broken every bone in it. She glanced at her partner and saw that he was looking at her with new respect.

Smiling broadly, Seamus punched Lilly in the shoulder, just as he might have his brother. She staggered back a step. "Well done, Lil."

Jerome raised himself to one elbow, rubbing his jaw with his free hand. "Who the devil are you?" he asked, looking from Cade to Lilly.

Cade gave Lilly a single nod and together, they drew out their Pinkerton badges. "Andrew Cadence McShane and my partner Lilly Long with the Pinkerton Detective Agency. We were hired to determine if J.D. Ames's death was suicide or murder, but with all the things we've heard here today,

I believe it's safe to say that we have our murderer in hand."

Dora gave an audible gasp and looked as if she might faint.

"What?" Jerome cried, scrambling to his feet. "Me? The hell you say! Who hired the blasted Pinkertons?"

Since McShane was doing such a bang-up job, and her hand hurt like the very devil, Lilly decided to let him explain things. With an encouraging smile, she reached out with her left hand and clasped Elsa's. The German walker looked as taken aback by what she'd just seen and heard as Jerome.

"Mrs. Dora Ames."

The name fell into the room with the impact of a giant tree falling in the stillness of the forest. No one said a word. Cade and Seamus were focused on Dora and Jerome, alert to any movement. Tad stood near Elsa, apprehensive, but waiting to see his brother's reaction.

To Lilly's surprise, Jerome began to laugh. "*Dora* hired you to find out the truth?" Tipping back his head, he laughed again, a weary, almost defeated sound. "Now, that is truly rich."

"Why would anyone think Mr. Ames's death was murder?" Elsa asked. "The police ruled it suicide."

"Several reasons, actually, Mrs. Dengler," Cade said. "It might interest you to know that you were one of her suspects."

Elsa paled. "What! I knew I'd heard rumors that I was suspected, but she actually named me to the Pinkertons?"

"You, Tad, Leo, and Jerome were all on Mrs. Ames's list. According to her, every one of you had reason to want her husband dead. Miss Long and I were sent here to find out the truth, and I believe we have."

Jerome, who had stood in stony silence as Cade ran through the litany of Dora's suspects, suddenly started laughing again. Then he turned to Dora. "I must give you credit, my love. You are certainly thorough."

Before anyone realized his intentions, he'd thrown himself at her so hard that her chair tipped over. The sound of her head striking the tiled floor sounded like a ripe watermelon being dropped. And then both hands were around her neck...squeezing....

Cade and Seamus were on him instantly, and Seamus soon had him in handcuffs while Cade examined Dora, who lay unmoving on the floor. Lilly watched him take Dora's wrist in his hand and place his fingers on her pulse point. After a moment, he shook his head.

Lilly drew in a sharp breath of shock and dismay, and McShane straightened. "Seamus will you push up his right sleeve, please," he asked.

"What?" Seamus looked at his brother as if he were a couple bricks shy of a load.

"Just unbutton his sleeve and let me have a look at his arm."

Without another word, Seamus did as he was asked. Right there, just as Robbie said, was the perfect imprint of his teeth. And from the looks of it, he'd drawn blood. Cade couldn't hide his smile.

"Jerome Connelly, you're under arrest for the assault of Robert Jenkins and the murder of Dora Ames."

Epilogue

Pinkerton Offices

89 Dearborn

F ive days later, Lilly paused just outside the door of the inner office, mentally preparing herself for the debriefing with McShane and William. She felt at least ten years older and probably looked like the wrath of God. She'd put on a few pounds of the weight she'd lost during the competition, and her energy was returning a bit at a time. The blisters on her feet had all but healed, and the cut on her foot caused her no trouble at all.

Her heart had yet to heal from all the ugliness she'd witnessed.

Humans were supposed to be the most complex and highly developed of God's creatures. Superior. Made in His image. Yet they were the only species that deliberately set out to hurt and destroy one another. The only species to plan, plot, and deceive for their own selfish reasons.

"Waiting for me?"

The sound of her partner's voice brought her back to her surroundings. McShane stood a few feet from her, serious as he so often was. She hadn't heard him approaching. The cuts on his face from his boxing match were healing well. He, too, looked tired.

"Don't, Lilly."

228

"What?"

"Don't do this to yourself again." He reached out and touched a rough finger to the corner of her downturned mouth. "You can't keep asking yourself why, or you'll wind up a nutter."

"I know," she said, nodding. "I do. It's just…"

"D'you know how to ride horseback?"

"Yes, why?"

"Did you ever fall off when you were learnin'?"

She frowned at him, wondering where his questions were leading. "Yes."

"It hurt."

She nodded.

"What did Pierce tell you to do?"

"To get back on and try again."

"Exactly. And you did. And it became a source of fun and satisfaction. That's what you have to do with this job. It'll never be fun, but you can learn to take satisfaction in the good you do."

"I know that," she told him, touched and a little surprised that he saw what she was feeling. "I'm not as melancholy as I was after Ft. Worth."

"Good."

He smiled then, that smile that took her breath away and made her heart flutter. "Blast you, McShane," she said, without thinking.

"What did I do?"

"Nothing," she said, turning and grasping the doorknob. "Let's go give William our report."

"Good to see you both," William said after greetings had been made and everyone was seated around his massive desk. "First, Miss Long, I want to offer my congratulations on your outstanding performance during the race. I couldn't be prouder."

"Thank you, sir," she said. "I believe I owe my stamina to Colonel Monstery."

William laughed. "So, does he. I've already heard from him. He's quite proud of you as well."

Lilly smiled, although a bit self-consciously.

"So, it was Dora Ames all along?" William said, jumping straight to the subject.

"It was."

"Why don't you start by telling me how you determined that it was murder and not suicide?"

"I believe it came down to those two bullets for us both," McShane said. "Neither Lilly nor I could logically explain that away. "First, we looked at it from the suicide standpoint and decided that while it *was* possible that J.D. chickened out at the last minute and had to try a second time, neither of us was convinced by that premise."

William peered at Cade over steepled fingertips.

"Then we remembered that Mr. Ames purchased the weapon after the robbery, which suggested that he was still fearful for his life. Taking that into consideration, we played around with a couple of other workable ideas."

"Go on."

"Lilly thought it was possible that Ames shot the first bullet at someone he believed intended him harm."

"That makes sense. How did they get the gun away from him?"

"It would have been an easy enough task, even for a woman, since he wasn't fully recovered from the attack in his office," Lilly offered.

She was feeling better after McShane's encouragement but was still smarting from the fact that in the beginning, she had admired Dora Ames. Would she ever reach a point where she wasn't fooled?

"Go on," William said again.

"The third likelihood is that someone gained access to the gun prior to his going to the park that morning, with the sole intention of shooting him and making it look like a suicide. Dora Ames had access."

"Hm. Had you ruled out the others at this point?"

"More or less. We were impressed with Elsa Dengler and the way she conducted herself, despite the fact that she'd threatened J.D. in California."

William smiled. "How many of us haven't said things in anger and frustration that we don't mean? And the others? Leo? When we were hired, Mrs. Ames's reasoning was that if he got rid of J.D., he could buy the company from her for a song, since she had no real knowledge of the business."

"Neither Lilly nor I have ever been keen on that idea. Dora Ames was plenty smart, and cunning to boot, as she proved."

Lilly chimed in. "After talking to some of the others who had known the Ameses for a while, we learned that it was common knowledge that she considered her husband weak and ineffective. "She was tired of his failings. When Jerome arrived with Elsa, Dora saw someone as ambitious as she was, someone she thought she could manipulate, and she wasted no time seducing him. Apparently, she was always on the lookout for a man to help her move up in the pedestrian circuit."

"Enter Leo Bertolini," McShane said. "He may be a moral midget, but after questioning him and the Connelly brothers at length, we're convinced that he didn't take up with Dora until after both Connellys were gone, and her husband was dead. Obviously, there's no way we can confirm any of this, but considering that Leo has a weakness for anything in skirts, it makes sense."

"Dora Ames was a master manipulator and a user," Lilly added. "She was always looking for her next victim. She saw a chance to use Leo's knowledge and contacts to help her get ahead and had no qualms about doing so. She never once considered Rosalie." She turned to her partner. "Ask McShane. She'd already confronted him about replacing Leo."

"Really?" William cocked his head in interest.

McShane turned three shades of red. "She did, but I'm thankful to say that I'm smarter than some and not nearly so eager to fall into bed with every woman who flings herself at me."

"Knowing your background, I never thought you were," William said, referencing the past that McShane rarely spoke of. William smiled. "I'm thinking Leo Bertolini should be grateful that you two intervened. Lord only knows what might have befallen him since Agent McShane turned her down." He drummed his fingertips on the desktop. "We come to Tad Connelly."

"Yes. We're convinced Dora added him to the list because he'd already been judged by the law and the press for the embezzlement as well as the robbery and assault. Thanks to her, he was the perfect suspect, but his claims about the bookkeeping have checked out, and he was indeed in Texas at the time of the robbery. He wasn't involved with any of it."

"So, what you're saying is that the evidence points to Dora Ames as the perpetrator for all three crimes, and she came to us to throw the law off track."

"That, and she also needed us to pin the shooting on someone, so it would be recorded as a murder, not a suicide."

William's forehead puckered in a frown. "Why? What was her reasoning?"

"She needed proof that J.D.'s death was murder in order to collect the insurance money from the policy she'd taken out on him the previous year."

"Ah." William sighed and shook his head. "How do you explain the suicide note and assault on her during the robbery?"

McShane laced his fingers across his middle. "In his sworn affidavit, Jerome said he was instructed by Dora herself to rough her up a bit, just to make things look good, and he claims she forced J.D. to write the note before they took him to the park."

"Jerome said it best, sir," Lilly told him. "Dora was thorough. She left little if anything to chance."

"Do we know which one of them actually pulled the trigger?" William asked.

"It was all Dora. Jerome says the first shot was at him. When Dora sent for him after he disappeared after the robbery, he went to see what was up. She told him her plan, and he refused to be part of a killing.

"In his statement, he says that there's a big difference in stealing a few thousand dollars and murder. Taking a shot at him was Dora's way of encouraging him to help her after she accused him of being a coward."

"What happened to him after she shot her husband? How did Connelly wind up here?"

"Once J.D. was dead and Dora had the money from the robbery in hand, she scurried off like a cockroach in the light, leaving Jerome behind," McShane explained. "He had no idea where she'd gone, but he felt like he'd earned a fair share of the loot and the insurance money she hoped to collect. It took him months to figure out that she would stick to what she knew, which was endurance walking."

Once again, Lilly picked up the tale. "When he saw the advertisement for the competition at Palmers, and that Leo was the manager as well as heading up the promotion, he figured Dora was in the middle of it."

"And he was right."

"He came to Chicago, blackmailed Leo into letting him set up his bar, and when Dora objected, he told her that if she made him leave, he'd go to the police with everything he knew."

"And she couldn't let that happen," William said.

"No."

"Well, I must say this is the most convoluted case we've dealt with in a long time," William said, getting to his feet. "More often than not, an offense is more or less straightforward, but Dora Ames was quite skillful at weaving several crimes into a whole."

"Indeed, she was, sir."

William came around the desk and shook hands with them both. "Miss Long, put some weight on."

"I'll do my best, Mr. Pinkerton."

They left William's office and said their goodbyes to Harris. Then McShane helped her into her coat, and they went out into the cold, October morning. A gust of chill wind tugged at Lilly's navy blue felt hat. Laughing, she reached up to hold it in place, fearing her jeweled hatpin would fail. When she looked at McShane, his rugged face wore an unreadable expression.

Frowning, he plunged his hands into the pockets of his trousers. "Any word from Elsa?"

"She stopped by for a few minutes a day or two ago. She and Tad are getting married. Penn approves. Word around the pedestrian circles is that Jocelyn is leaving the walking circuit and going back to England to be with family. Rosalie is divorcing Leo and retiring from racing altogether. She has plenty of money set aside for the future and wants to spend time with her children."

"Good for her. How about you. What's next?"

"Well, until William gives us another assignment, I'm going to my little room and eat. Rest. And eat some more," she said. "And you?"

"I plan to spend some time with Robbie. He wants to learn to skate and shoot."

"That's an excellent idea. He idolizes you, McShane."

"I don't know about that," he said, clearly embarrassed. "Do ya think he's happy with Seamus and Megan? I mean, do ya think he ran away because he's unhappy?"

"No! I think he's very happy there. He talked about the girls a lot, and no, I don't think that's why he ran away. He got in trouble. He needed to find a friendly face."

McShane thought about that.

"He's still trying to figure out the rules of a normal lifestyle and how he fits in with all you McShanes. I'm certain he gets frustrated from time to time, the same way you and Seamus get frustrated with him."

"You're right. He told me he thought the race he organized was a good way to earn money. I tend to agree. Maybe we have a budding entrepreneur on our hands."

Lilly's heart missed a beat at being included in the statement. "Maybe we do."

He drew in a breath. "Do you think he feels no one cares?

"I think he knows you all care for him, but what he needs is stability and love."

"That may be true, but I can't take him to live with me. He needs structure. My life is too unsettled."

"It certainly is. Megan and Seamus are perfect for him right now. Maybe one day when you stop being an agent, you'll find someone and become his real parent."

"Maybe I will," McShane said with a nod.

"Do you have anyone in mind?" Dear Lord! Where had that come from?

"Are you fishing around to see if you're in the running?"

"Of course not, you buffoon!" she sputtered. "Any woman who would want to saddle themselves with the likes of you would have to be daft. You're bossy and impatient, and possibly the most exasperating man I've ever known."

"The feeling is mutual, Miss Long," he said, unsmilingly. He took her gloved hand and hooked it through his arm. "How about some hot cocoa? I think it's my turn to buy."

He smiled down at her. "By the way, that was an impressive uppercut you gave Jerome. I believe your time with Monstery did you a world of good."

Acknowledgements

Pedestrianism: A sport where thousands packed stadiums to watch men and women walk in circles, sometimes for days and even weeks, in hope of winning sums of money they had no chance of earning in any other way.

This book would never have happened without my dear friends LaRee Bryant and Sandy Steen who told me about pedestrianism and bought me a copy of Harry Hall's book *The Pedestriennes* and suggested that the world of women's endurance walking would make a great background for a Lilly Long Mystery. She was right!

Searching for more information, I discovered Matthew Algeo's book, *Pedestrianism*, that helped me paint an even clearer—I hope—picture of some of the inner workings of this little known and amazing sport. Endurance walking was only popular for around seven years and, with the exception of one man, the few I mentioned it to had never heard of it.

The research was fascinating, from the food they ate, how their ailments were treated, and especially the personalities, formidable determination and rivalries among the women pedestriennes. It was just the sort of issue that would interest Lilly, who is all about helping women.

The procedures of the race, foods, living conditions and other actions described in the book are based on fact. The plot of Hasten to Their End is a combination of three or four happenings rolled into one fictitious situation created by an imaginary power-hungry character's thirst for a spot in history.

In thirty-five years of publishing, this was the hardest book I have written. I hope I have done the concept justice and that you get a feel for the mental and physical trials the women faced, as well as the atmosphere and environment of the event. I especially hope that I have shown the grit and determination of the women who gave so much to try to make an impact on a sport, paving the way for women in sports everywhere.

Also, many thanks to Ginny Evans and Jerlyn Stone for reading and giving me pointers and for listening to me whine. You're the best!

About the Author

Penny Richards has been writing and selling books since 1983 with more than 40 books in print. Many have made various best-seller lists and won or been nominated for industry awards. After moving to Arkansas, she decided to take a break and pursue other things on her bucket list, including hosting a B&B and Catering business. She returned to writing in 2012, moving from contemporary romance to historical inspirational romance and historical mystery. Learning to write two new, different genres was not easy, she says, but it was worth it. She loves the research and setting familiar crimes in a different time with different social conditions, mores, and settings, not to mention limited forensics. She lives with her dog Cali and writes from her home in a small rural town in Arkansas.

CPSIA information can be obtained
at www.ICGtesting.com
Printed in the USA
LVHW021423010821
694125LV00006B/832